"Quite a fun premise. . . . Great read!"
—Kings River Life Magazine

"[An] amusing cozy filled with romantic angst and peculiar characters." —*Kirkus Reviews*

"The characters are realistic and relatable, with engaging situations, bright dialogue, and a snappy pace. *A Perfect Bind* continues an entertaining series with a certain panache." —Fresh Fiction

Beloved Bookroom Mysteries
by Dorothy St. James

The Broken Spine
A Perfect Bind
A Book Club to Die For

A
Book Club
to
Die For

Dorothy St. James

BERKLEY PRIME CRIME
New York

BERKLEY PRIME CRIME
Published by Berkley
An imprint of Penguin Random House LLC
penguinrandomhouse.com

ISBN: 9780593098646

Berkley Prime Crime hardcover edition / November 2022
Berkley Prime Crime mass-market edition / November 2023

Printed in the United States of America
1   3   5   7   9   10   8   6   4   2

Book design by Alison Cnockaert

For booklovers and book warriors everywhere.
You are the spark that keeps the world interesting.

Chapter One

———— •• ————

Librarians are keepers of knowledge, caretakers of truth, and sowers of wisdom. Many of us rush out to share the world with our communities with the enthusiasm of a child who has suddenly mastered a new skill. We want people to know, to know . . . well, *everything*.

This is our mission. This is our passion.

We are the bringers.

We are the beacons cutting through the darkest of nights.

I should be thrilled to be able to provide this service to the Arete Society, the town's most influential book club. So why did I have this sudden desire to turn around, march back to my car, and drive home as fast as my old Camry would take me?

I'd been asked to give a presentation. I'd been tasked with sharing my knowledge of books and my experiences working at the library with a group of ladies who love books as much as I do. I lived for moments like this.

Didn't I?

Usually, yes.

But.

Not.

Tonight.

"Trudell Becket, what's got you dragging your feet like this?" Flossie Finnegan-Baker turned her wheelchair toward me. "I do believe a cornucopia of slugs just passed us."

"Cornucopia? Of slugs?" I asked. That couldn't be right. But before she could explain that a group of slugs was indeed called a cornucopia, I said, "Never mind." Flossie was rarely wrong when it came to grammar and etymology. Besides, slugs weren't important. "*This*," I said. "This is a mistake." I felt the truth of it like a stone in my gut. I stood in the middle of the long, winding sidewalk leading up to Hazel Bailey's front porch and scrunched my eyes closed. "I shouldn't be here."

"You're suffering from a case of the jitters." My friend touched my hand. I looked at her, and she smiled encouragingly at me. Flossie had dressed for the book club meeting in muted shades of turquoise and tan. The colors spiraled together on her long, homemade tie-dyed dress, but it was quite a shift from the bright (and often) clashing colors she usually wore. She'd attached a large golden pin in the shape of Edgar Allan Poe's face to the collar of the thick white button-up sweater she'd worn over her dress. "Honey, even I get the jitters every time I do something new. Everyone does. That's why you brought me. To have your back. And I do. I've got your back. And you've got this. Let's go."

Our host lived at the edge of town in the middle of a forest of cypress trees that gave the town its name. The cypresses' silvery trunks stood tall and straight, like the spines of books on a shelf, gleaming in the fading embers of the sunset.

Books were the reason I'd been asked to speak to the

Arete Society. And those same books were the reason I couldn't go through with it.

Sure, I'd been excited at the opportunity to share my experiences working as an assistant librarian. Nearly as excited as Flossie was now. My friend started spinning pirouettes with her wheelchair on the sidewalk in front of me.

This invitation meant that finally the town was taking me and my work at the library seriously. Finally, the townspeople saw me. And most of them even knew my name.

"Tonight! Tonight!" Flossie sang happily. "Tru, you do know what an honor it is to be here tonight, don't you?"

I did.

The Arete Society wasn't simply a book club. It was known throughout the state as the best and most prestigious book club. They rarely invited anyone outside their membership to speak at their meetings. Being asked to make a presentation was like being invited to dine at the governor's mansion. No, this was better. The current governor was rather unpopular.

It wasn't until we were walking up to the house that it had hit me.

"Rebecca invited me to talk about my work with the books at the library," I said, still unwilling to move any closer to Hazel's house.

"Yes, dear." Flossie tilted her head and gave me a searching look. "I know why we're here. That's one reason why it's so exciting."

"Yes, but Rebecca wants me to talk about my work *with the books* at the library." I shivered in the cool January air. Even though Cypress was in the middle of balmy South Carolina, it still experienced occasional winter cold snaps. A sharp northern breeze rattled the branches in the trees above us. "I shouldn't have agreed to come."

"Oh, go on with you. I'm sure you can steer the conversation," Flossie said, now grinning like a teen going out on her first date. This was really a big night for her.

But could I pull it off? Most of my work at the library was a secret. While half of the book club members were in on the secret, the other half had no idea I'd set up an unauthorized bookroom in the library's basement.

"Just talk about *why* you carry around that tote bag of yours and dodge any questions about *where* the books came from," Flossie suggested.

"That's not going to work. I shouldn't have even brought the tote bag. What is wrong with me? I'd been so dazzled by the invitation that I completely ignored the problem with my being here." I held up the tote bag as if it were filled with explosives.

It wasn't.

I'd filled the canvas tote with books I thought the ladies attending tonight would enjoy.

"I don't understand. You're a modern-day book-hauling Robin Hood," Flossie said. "That's something you should be proud of. That's something to be celebrated."

"I can't be here because of Lida Farnsworth." *My boss.* My intimidating boss, who was possibly the cleverest woman in town. Cypress's head librarian had been a member of the Arete Society for longer than anyone could remember. "I'd forgotten that she would be here. Well, I knew she would be here, but I didn't stop to consider what her listening to my talk might mean."

"So? She should be just as proud of you as I am." Flossie still didn't get it.

"When I start to hand out the books from my tote bag, Mrs. Farnsworth will recognize them as library books. You know, the same library books that were supposed to have been removed from the library? If she ever discovers I converted her library's basement into a secret bookroom without her consent, I will be out of a job before you can say, 'Bob's your uncle.'"

"That's a funny phrase, 'Bob's your uncle.' Not awfully common in the United States. It's Irish in origin, so I suppose it shouldn't be too surprising we say it here in Cypress. After all, several of our town's founders arrived here from Ireland. According to my research, the phrase arose in the late 1880s, when British prime minister Robert Cecil appointed his nephew to the post of chief secretary for Ireland. The Irish were quite unhappy with this act of nepotism. And that's how people started saying 'Bob's your uncle' whenever anything was sure to happen. The man had literally been given the post because Bob was his uncle."

I usually enjoyed Flossie's impromptu etymological musings. But right now, I was in full panic mode. I didn't want to lose my job. Working at Cypress's public library was my life. I considered taking the tote bag back to the car. But that wouldn't work. I already had a reputation for carrying that tote bag everywhere. *Not* bringing it to the book club would invite more questions, not fewer. And when I stood up in front of the book club and someone asked me about the books I lent out, what in the world was I going to say?

I needed to get out of there.

My friends and I had started the secret bookroom a year ago, after Cypress's town leaders had hatched what they'd called a "brilliant" idea. It was, in truth, the worst idea ever. They had decided to modernize the library and create a bookless technological center to impress the kind of high-tech industries the town manager had wanted to woo.

Yes, the town desperately needed higher-paying jobs, but the idea of getting rid of our books still rankled. How could anyone want to transform our beautiful library into a place that had no books? None. Zip. Zero. Apparently, the town manager at the time had read articles about libraries that had gone all-electronic. He had fallen in love with the idea.

With the town manager leading the way, the mayor and council members ordered all the hold-in-your-hands printed books removed and replaced with ebooks. It broke my heart to see it happen.

Books provide escape, comfort, and knowledge. Sure, ebooks could do the same thing. But there was something magical about wandering through a library and stumbling upon the perfect book without ever realizing you were looking for it in the first place.

I had no choice but to do something to save the books that had been boxed up as if they were worthless tchotchkes collected by a distant relative who'd recently passed.

Before the boxes and boxes of books could be carted off, my friends and I moved as many as we could handle into the library's basement, where we set up an unofficial (and super-secret) bookroom. Only residents who could be trusted to keep their grandmother's best secret recipes were invited.

Upstairs, the library became a shining example of cutting-edge services.

Down in the basement, we turned back time and started using old-fashioned card catalogs and hand-stamped due dates on paper book slips for checked-out material.

I hated that we couldn't invite everyone into the basement bookroom's stacks. That was why I had started carrying around the tote bag filled with books I thought people needed. My plan had been working out quite well . . . until Rebecca White, former TV soap star *and* current president of the Arete Society, invited me to give a presentation to the book club. Silly me had immediately agreed.

"You've got this, Tru." Flossie patted my arm. "Just keep the facts vague, and everyone will leave happy."

"Keep the facts vague, even when someone asks me a direct question, like where all these books are coming from?" I shivered again. This was not going to work.

"If things get sticky, I'll cause a distraction. I promise."

"Is that why you invited yourself along? To create a scene when someone wants me to talk about our secret bookroom?"

She beamed a wide smile that showed off her straight white teeth. "Friends lend each other courage. That's why girlfriend weekends always turn wild . . . from all that courage being passed around." She patted my arm more forcefully. "Now, let's get in there. I can already smell something savory and wonderful coming from the house. I've heard that the hostesses at these meetings always try to outdo themselves with the dinners they serve." She smacked her lips. "I aim to discover if that's true."

Remember that time Flossie and I broke into the library in the dead of night? My adventurous friend wasn't nearly as excited then as she was now.

Don't get me wrong. I understood why she was bubbling over like a washing machine with too much soap. Flossie had been on the waiting list for membership in the Arete Society for five years now. Three ladies' applications had been accepted ahead of hers. One of them had only moved to town last year, which had hurt Flossie worse than if someone had stabbed her in the heart.

Although she refused to come out and say it, I knew she had wanted to accompany me tonight so she could quiz Rebecca about what she could do to win the group over.

"'Arete' is a term the founders back in the 1930s adopted from the ancient Greeks," Flossie said, speaking as if in a rush to get all the words out at once. "It means 'knowledge is the highest virtue.' I've always thought that was a clever name for a book club. Don't you agree, Tru? Isn't it clever?"

"Um . . . yes, clever." I knew the meaning of the word from an Intro to Latin class in high school, but really, I was more concerned about the tote bag (or should I say albatross) hanging from my arm. Even if arriving without it did cause people to ask questions, I needed to get it back to the car. I couldn't give Mrs. Farnsworth the opportunity to look at those books too closely. "I need to get rid of these library books. I'll be right back."

"Be a dear and grab an umbrella while you're at the car. I think I just felt a raindrop," she called after me.

The Baileys' sprawling ranch home with its oversized stone porch columns was one of Cypress's most talked-about residences. It also had one of the longest twisty sidewalks I had ever encountered. It took forever to jog to where we'd parked at the curb and then to jog back to where Flossie was waiting. Even though the air had a chill, a bead of sweat had trickled down my back by the time I was done with that little footrace of mine.

I fanned myself with my hand and hoped my cheeks weren't as red as they felt. The silvery Spanish moss weighing down the tree limbs above my head seemed to wave back.

"Flossie, I don't know if I can pull this off. Deception isn't something—"

"Pshaw! You've been practicing your speech for days now. And besides, you do these all the time."

Was Flossie serious? "I never—"

"Your programs at the library are super popular!" she practically shouted.

"This isn't the same thing. I'm in charge of children's programming. My audience is rarely older than five. These women"—I pointed toward Hazel's door in the distance—"they scare me."

"They're simply children who grew up. Heck, most of them still act like spoiled tots," Flossie scoffed. "And they asked you to come and speak to them, I might add. They've never asked *me*."

Flossie, who was forty years older than my thirty-eight, explored mountains, pushed her way through exotic jungles, and wrote best-selling novels under a pseudonym she refused to divulge. And she'd done all this while using a wheelchair. Just last week she bought a speedboat with the royalty check she'd received from her publisher. The year before, she'd used her royalty check to purchase and customize a cherry-red Corvette so she could speed around town using hand controls.

No one could deny that Flossie had stories to tell. Plus, she had an electric personality that made whatever she said sound exciting. The more I thought about it, the more I had to agree with her that her exclusion from the Arete Society seemed suspect.

If anyone should be a member of this book club, it was Flossie.

"Don't forget, Tru. Everyone sees you as a real-life heroine now. I know *you* don't feel like one, but you're a star in this community. You deserve this."

"No, Flossie. You deserve this. But I understand what you're saying." And with that in mind, I gathered up all my wavering courage and finally hurried up the long, winding sidewalk toward Hazel's house. Flossie was one of my dearest friends. She deserved the chance to find out why the book club continually denied her. If I could help her get the answer to that question by making this presentation, I needed to do it. That's what friends do.

"They did ask me to be here," I told myself before smoothing away a crease in the black maxi dress that Tori—my best friend since kindergarten—had helped me pick out for tonight before rushing off to meet up with her latest beau. "Besides, tonight will be over in a few hours whether I wow them or not. And tomorrow morning I'll be reading a book about a cranky rabbit to a group of preschoolers."

"That's the spirit!" Flossie rubbed her hands together. "Now, is that tuna I smell? I do love a good tuna steak. Especially when it's served with capers and a white wine cream sauce and potatoes. I do hope she's serving potatoes."

My stomach gurgled happily at the mention of food. "I've never been one to pass up a good meal. Let's go see what Hazel has on the menu."

I helped Flossie maneuver her wheelchair up the few steps onto the porch and then rang the bell.

Our hostess pulled the door open with a violent jerk. She sucked in a sharp breath. "What are you doing here?" she snapped.

Gracious, I knew I should have stayed home. The hair on my arms stood up. I suddenly felt as nervous as a long-tailed cat in a room full of rocking chairs. I shivered. My mimsy used to tell me that she'd feel the wind tickling the back of her neck whenever the air around her was trying to tell her something important. I rubbed the back of my neck and shivered again. Tonight was not going to end well.

Chapter Two

———•———

Hazel Bailey was a petite woman. Just under five feet tall and soft-spoken, she'd never possessed an intimidating personality. But the way she was standing at the door now, with her mouth pulled down in a deep scowl and her arm flung out to block our entrance into her home, so surprised me that I backed up a few steps.

I had thought she liked me.

A few months ago, Hazel had believed a rumor that I was pregnant with her only son's child. She'd been thrilled. Of course, there'd been no truth to the outrageous rumor. And once she understood how ridiculous it all was, Hazel and I had laughed together.

Much to her delight (and grandmotherly aspirations), I had recently started dating her son. A few weeks ago, she'd asked Jace to invite me over for a family Sunday supper. I'd reluctantly declined because my own Mama Eddy had threatened to throw a hissy fit if I even suggested I would miss having Sunday supper with her, since Sunday was one of the few times a week she got to see me, her only daughter. But I had asked Jace to tell his mom that I'd be happy to come on any other night.

Was she upset that I hadn't come to her house for Sunday supper? Had he botched explaining to her why I couldn't?

Or was it something else?

Oh gracious, I bet it was something else. Jace had been acting secretive lately. He'd also been canceling our dates for no good reason. Just last night we were supposed to bundle up and go for a moonlight boat ride on the lake. But he'd called at the last minute to tell me he couldn't make it while offering no other explanation. He often claimed that he'd been working long hours for the police department, but whenever I would ask him about why his work hours had recently been expanded, he'd change the subject.

I hadn't dated enough men to know all the games they played.

But I did know my best friend, Tori. She'd dated more men than I could count and had married (and divorced) four of them. She would claim she was working long hours whenever she started growing bored in a relationship. Only rarely would she actually be at work. Most of the time she'd be at my house watching chick flicks. A few times, she'd even be out on a date with someone new.

Was "working long hours" the lie everyone told when a relationship got stale, and no one had bothered to tell me? Had Jace told his mother that the relationship was over?

Oh. No. Oh. No. Was I the last to know that my relationship with Jace was over? Of course I would be the last to know. I'm always the last to know when it comes to things like this.

I started to hyperventilate . . . just a little bit.

"What's wrong with you?" Hazel demanded, her hands on her hips. "Jace already explained to me why you couldn't come to Sunday supper, if that's what you're huffing and puffing about."

Oh! She was still miffed and feeling like I'd snubbed her invitation. I tried to apologize.

She cut me off with a gruff "No apology necessary. Anyone who's ever met Mama Eddy understands."

Did she just insult my mother? My shoulders tensed. I opened my mouth, prepared to defend Mama Eddy. My mother wasn't as crazy as most in these parts thought. She was just . . . well, just a bit more eccentric than the average Southerner. And I suppose that really *is* saying something considering how colorful Southerners could be, especially those Southerners who called Cypress home.

I took a deep breath and willed my shoulders to drop back down.

"You did ask me to come a half hour early," I gently reminded Hazel. Perhaps she'd forgotten.

"Did I?" She rolled her eyes before adding, "I suppose I must have."

"You remember Flossie Finnegan-Baker. She came along to assist me. You did say it would be okay if she accompanied me when we spoke on the phone," I added, since she was still blocking the doorway and staring at the two of us as if we were trying to sell her an outdated and overpriced set of encyclopedias. "May we come in?"

Warm, spicy aromas that reminded me of my grandmother's house wafted out the front door to tease our senses.

Hazel finally stepped to one side of the door. "I suppose you can set up in the living room. That's where you'll be giving the presentation. I am looking forward to hearing what you have to say."

We followed her inside.

A few steps in and I felt as if I'd been transported onto a page in *House Beautiful* magazine.

Wow, I mouthed. She had completely redone her living room since my last visit.

Well, she did still have her collection of weird dolls. They stared at you from every corner of the room. But she'd arranged them tastefully, having them sit in beautiful crystal bowls, peering down from bookshelves, and peeking out from behind the lamps.

Everyone in town kind of just ignored the dolls, since we already knew they were there and weren't startled by them anymore. Despite the weird doll collection, the room was impressive. Hazel had managed to seamlessly blend a formal Southern style with casual chic. "Who did you hire to decorate your house?" Flossie asked as she looked around the room. "It's brilliant."

"This?" Hazel acted as if she were seeing her home for the first time. She relaxed into a smile. "It's just something I put together. I like to change things up every season. Don't you?"

Flossie made noises indicating her agreement even though the décor in her lake house hadn't changed a jot since her husband's death nearly a decade ago. His winter coats were even still hanging in the front closet.

"Gracious sakes, Hazel, you know I'm allergic to gluten," a woman shrieked from another room. "Are you trying to kill me? I can't eat any of this." A plate clattered as if tossed down in anger.

Hazel flashed a tense smile before murmuring, "Excuse me. I need to take care of that. If you don't mind waiting here." She nodded toward one of the overstuffed sofas in front of a bank of windows that looked out into the fading gray sky. "I'll be back with a few stiff cocktails in a moment."

"Did you recognize that voice?" Flossie whispered after Hazel had disappeared through a swinging door that (if the delicious scents coming from that room were any indication) led to the kitchen.

Although the high-pitched screechy voice sounded familiar, I couldn't put a name to it.

"That's *Rebecca White*," Flossie whispered with trembling reverence. When I didn't faint away from rapturous joy at the mention of the name, she added with a huff, "The woman who invited you here? She once had a starring role on *Desiring Hearts*. You remember that soap opera? It was a-maze-ing. I heard she believed the job was a waste of her acting skills and quit after one season even though her character was on her way to becoming wildly popular. Surprisingly, she never managed to find another acting gig. At least, none that matched her talent, and she decided she'd rather never work again than accept an inferior part. You have to respect her integrity. We're so lucky she moved to Cypress. You do know who she is now, don't you?"

"Yes, yes, I know who she is," I said with a laugh. "I've lived in Cypress all my life."

"She's also president of the Arete Society and arbiter of literature in Cypress." Despite my protests that I'd heard it all before, Flossie continued to rhapsodize about the former starlet. Her voice remained soft with a hushed admiration. "Nothing gets read by the members of this group without her approval. And I mean nothing. A few years ago a member was spotted reading a best-selling novel that didn't meet Rebecca's high standards. And poof. The poor woman was banned from ever attending another meeting. The woman's friends, those who were still club members, stopped talking to her. She ended up moving to Charlotte."

I stared hard at Flossie. "And you want to be a part of this group? Why?"

"Because it's the only book club in the state worth joining," she said, as if that should have been obvious. "It's the Arete Society, for goodness' sake."

I felt a bit hurt. "I think our book club is the best one around."

"We're a casual meeting of friends who share a love of mystery books. The Arete Society is formal and . . . well, it's—it's different."

"You *are* trying to kill me!" we heard Rebecca screech from behind the door Hazel had gone through. Another plate clattered. "There's gluten in this dish too! Did you not read any of the instructions I'd sent over?"

"Please, Rebecca, I did read them. I'm not—!" Hazel cried.

The door to the kitchen swung open. The former soap star, dressed in a wide-legged red pantsuit, marched out carrying a plate of mini lobster tacos. She reminded me of a diva entering from stage left.

"This sauce has gluten in it." Rebecca bit off the words. Her short curly hair bounced, echoing her agitation. "There's nothing on the platter I can eat. It's all contaminated because you put that sauce everywhere."

"I know. I'm sorry." Hazel followed behind Rebecca. She darted a worried glance in our direction and mouthed *I'm sorry* before chasing after Rebecca, who was rushing toward the front door. "In my defense, though, the placard for that appetizer does mention gluten. I thought that since the book we'd read for this month was set in Maine, it would be fun to serve something with lobster in it as an appetizer. Most of the other appetizers are gluten-free. I promise. And I replaced the steak dish I'd planned with a fresh tuna macaroni salad for the entrée because you decided two days ago to give up red meat."

Rebecca stopped her tirade when she seemed to notice she had an audience watching her with mouths gaping open. "How would *you* feel if you were invited for dinner, but you were unable to eat everything served?" she asked us, sounding much less hysterical.

She swung the platter in our direction. I don't know what was in the white sauce that the lobster-taco filling was swimming in, but its tangy, spicy aroma made my mouth water.

"You'd feel terrible," she declared with deep, round tones and then pulled the plate away just as I had started to reach for one of those plump little tacos.

I made a distressed sound that Rebecca mistook as my agreeing with her. In reality, the cry was a knee-jerk reaction to smelling something *that* delicious on an empty stomach and being denied the chance to eat it.

"Please," Hazel pleaded. "Please, don't get so upset. Please, don't run off. I'll remove them. There are plenty of other dishes that are gluten-free. I promise."

"Other dishes?" Rebecca's lips tightened. "You're serving macaroni salad as your main dish."

"The pasta is gluten-free." Hazel twisted her hands in the flowered apron she was wearing. "I can show you the box."

"It's macaroni salad." She looked as if the words somehow tasted sour in her mouth. "This isn't a church picnic, Hazel. It's the Arete Society. We have standards. High standards. I thought you understood that. You certainly had no trouble wolfing down the gourmet meals the other hostesses have prepared."

"But, but I assure you—" Hazel tried to say as she continued twisting her hands in her apron.

"And I forgot to tell you, Emma called about an hour ago. She says she's too sick to come tonight."

"Emma? Is that sweet girl okay?" Hazel asked, sounding genuinely worried. "She was here earlier today. I've been giving her sewing and cooking lessons."

"If you ask me, she backed out because she didn't read the book. Not that it ever matters. She never has anything intelligent to add to the discussion. I swear, if not for that icebox cake she always brings, I'd kick her out too."

"*T-too?*" Hazel's voice quivered.

"I should have kicked her out ages ago, I suppose. Now Hazel, if you can't pull yourself together, this will be your last night in the society," Rebecca warned. "If not for your grand house and reputation for being able to pull off elegant society events, you would have never been invited to join the society in the first place. And don't forget our special guest. We all want to impress her, do we not?"

"Of course we do," Hazel said softly.

I blushed when I realized that *I* was the special guest that Rebecca and Hazel were making such a fuss over. "I'm easy to impress," I assured them.

No one seemed to have heard.

"Tonight will work out. But . . . but . . . Emma isn't coming?" Hazel whispered. She shot Flossie and me a panicked look. "I was counting on her dessert."

"You don't have to stand here and tell me about it. Just go whip something up," Rebecca said, as if it were as easy as that. "And while you're at it, find something more appetizing than macaroni salad to serve as a main dish. I want everything to be perfect. I have an important announcement I want to make this evening."

Hazel muttered nervously under her breath as she headed toward the kitchen door.

"While you're busy in there, I'll help get things ready out here by rearranging your living room. This setup will never do. With my help and a little luck, I think I can keep this meeting from turning into a complete disaster."

"You're going to rearrange my furniture?" Hazel squeaked.

"Ye-e-esss." Rebecca drew out that one word until it had three syllables. "You wouldn't want your guests seeing your place looking like this. It's a pity we don't have time to do anything about the color of those drab gray walls. Blue would have been a bolder choice. Besides, I always look better in front of a blue backdrop." Rebecca pushed Hazel toward the kitchen. "The only thing I like is how you arranged those cute little dolls of yours. But don't worry. I'll take care of everything out here. You have enough to handle in the kitchen. Go on. Go on. Tonight is going to be epic."

Hazel opened and closed her mouth like a fish that had been pulled from the water, but no sound came out. "But I worked so hard on everything," she finally managed to croak.

"I know you did your best, dear." With one last shove, Rebecca managed to get Hazel back into the kitchen. "That woman is in hopelessly over her head. This is her first time hosting the book club. I had expected that she could . . . Well, I should have known she wasn't up to the task." She looked over at me. "Now, stop standing there gaping like an imbecile and help me move the sofa. It really needs to be on the other side of the room. We don't have much time. Our special guest, Joyce Fellows, from *Ideal Life*, will be here in less than a half hour."

"Joyce Fellows?" Flossie asked, her eyebrows shooting up into her hairline.

"Jo-Jo will be producing a segment about the Arete Society for her television show. She says what I've done with the group and how I've made it the best book club in the state should be a model for book clubs all over the country to follow. She insisted she come and film. Of course, it will be quite an honor to be back on national television." She thought about that for a moment. "It's also a huge honor for Jo-Jo's little television show to feature me. I'm sure this episode will set a ratings record."

"The Arete Society has been one of the most respected book clubs in South Carolina and in the Southeast for nearly a hundred years," Flossie murmured. "Long before—"

"What's that?" Rebecca asked, but she didn't wait for Flossie to repeat herself. Instead, she turned to me and clapped her hands. "Get moving. We're running out of time."

I jumped to action and raced across the room toward where Rebecca had already lifted one end of the sofa. That was when I heard a sob coming from the direction of the kitchen. Poor Hazel, no wonder she had been so frazzled when we arrived a few minutes ago. Rebecca was acting simply awful.

I bypassed the sofa and continued toward the kitchen door. The Grind, a restaurant not that far away, sold the best caramel drizzle cake anyone's mouth had ever tasted. If Hazel was agreeable, I could pick up a cake for her and get back before cocktail hour was over.

"This sofa isn't going to move itself," Rebecca barked at me. "And Jo-Jo expects perfection. We all do."

"I . . . The room looks fine," I said.

"Not for a *televised* book club meeting, it doesn't. I should know. I was in television. We don't have much time before the members start arriving. Come help me move this sofa."

"But I was going to—"

"Tru, don't keep Miss White standing there with half a sofa in the air. It's bound to be heavy," Flossie said, sending a pleading look my way.

For Flossie's sake, I supposed I could move one sofa

before rushing off to pick up the cake and still get back in time to have the main course.

"Rebecca White, I'm not sure you remember me." Flossie rolled behind us as Rebecca and I slowly moved the heavy sofa from one end of the room to the other. "I'm Flossie Finnegan-Baker. I have been on the society's waiting list—"

"When there's an opening," Rebecca said without glancing in Flossie's direction, "an invitation goes out to an applicant who we think will elevate our discussions. If we let just anyone join, we wouldn't experience the intelligent conversations that are expected at each meeting."

"I assure you, Rebecca, that with my education, travel, and experience penning books, I would—"

"I'm sure you would. Unfortunately, there are no openings for new members right now."

Flossie tapped her chin as if in deep thought. "People travel from miles around just to buy some of the deep dark chocolate brownies I bake for the church bazaar every year. I buy the chocolate from a shop that makes their own bars from the bean. It's fair trade and delicious."

"Chocolate gives me a migraine," Rebecca grumbled. She set down a small, round side table next to the sofa I'd helped move.

"Oh, well," Flossie pressed on. "I write a fair bit, as you might have heard. And I read a wide range of books, both fiction and nonfiction."

"Don't we all?" Rebecca directed me to move the chairs from one place to another.

"Flossie makes a mean catfish stew," I offered with a grunt as I lifted a heavy armchair. "I don't know what she puts in it, but it's like nothing I've ever tasted. In a good way."

"An old fisherman's wife in Morocco taught me the recipe." Flossie mouthed *thank you* to me when Rebecca's back was turned. "The stew is delicious with almost any kind of fish, really. It's the blend of spices that really makes it work—a mix of coconut sugar, paprika, cumin, cinnamon, ginger, cloves, salt, pepper, and a pinch of cayenne. I serve it over a fragrant basmati rice. I'd be happy to make it for you sometime."

"I don't like spicy food," Rebecca said, still not even bothering to glance in Flossie's direction. "Trudell, not there. Put the chair by the window. We need to hurry." I was working up quite a sweat moving furniture for Rebecca. The maddening woman would have me put something in one place only to decide that it would work better somewhere else.

"The stew is not *hot* spicy," I assured Rebecca.

"Just rich with flavors," Flossie explained, starting to look panicked. "But I have collected dozens of recipes from all around the world. I'm sure I can make something you'd like."

"I doubt it." She finally gave Flossie the courtesy of looking at her when she spoke. "Look. I get what you're trying to do, but I think you'd be happier if you stuck with being a member of that little book club of yours."

Flossie frowned as she bit her lower lip.

Rebecca went back to giving me directions, directions I felt much less inclined to follow. I wanted to say something to defend Flossie, but I had no idea what the right words might be. I needed time to think.

"No." Flossie lifted her chin defiantly. "No, Miss White. You're wrong. I have life experiences, but at the same time I'm not a bore. I don't feel a need to talk about myself all the time. I know the classics of literature, but I also enjoy reading popular literature. And I'm sure I could cook something that would tempt even your selective taste buds. If you'd only take the time to—"

Hazel breezed through the kitchen door. "How are things going in—?" Her eyes widened as she took in the state of her living room. Her face lost all color and after a moment she muttered, "I . . . um . . . I think something is burning." She disappeared back into the kitchen.

"I'd better go see what that woman is ruining now," Rebecca said after directing me to move the side table, the coffee table, and that heavy armchair to its third location. "No, Trudell. Not there." She pointed to a far corner. "Over there."

As soon as Rebecca left the room, I dropped the armchair where I stood, which happened to be in the middle of the room, and slumped into it. "Are you sure you still want to join this club?" I asked Flossie while trying to catch my breath.

"Of course I do. It's the Arete Society."

"I don't think they deserve you." I blotted at my brow with a tissue I'd found in a pocket. "What club is worth the aggravation of dealing with that dragon?"

"This is the Arete Society we're talking about, Tru. It's been around for generations. My mother and my grandmother were members. And I'm sure it has been run by dragons from time to time."

A loud crash from the kitchen made us both jump.

As we moved toward the swinging door to investigate, the doorbell rang.

"What should we do?" I asked as I automatically moved toward the front door. "Answer the door or offer our help in the kitchen?"

"Kitchen," Flossie answered as she rolled her wheelchair in that direction. "As hostess, Hazel should be the one to greet her guests. She wouldn't thank us for doing that for her." The kitchen door swung back and forth in Flossie's wake.

I hesitated.

The head librarian, Mrs. Farnsworth, might be on the other side of the front door, ringing the bell. She wouldn't appreciate being made to wait outside.

But then there was a second crash in the kitchen.

"Flossie? Is everything all right in there?" I abandoned my quest to open the front door and jogged to the kitchen to find Flossie sitting in her wheelchair next to an enormous kitchen counter lined with sumptuous dishes. Gleaming china platters and crystal bowls added extra elegance to the most creative dishes I'd ever seen in person. The spread rivaled the best of the best on some of my favorite cooking shows.

"Hazel did this all by herself?" I wondered aloud, barely able to restrain myself from taking a nibble out of one of the rainbow-colored mini hamburgers topped with feta cheese. I knew Hazel was a good cook, but I'd never guessed she was this good. My empty stomach rumbled.

Strangely, Flossie wasn't looking at the food but was busy slipping something into her bag.

"What were those crashes?" I asked her.

"I ran into the counter when I saw this mess. Hazel must have dropped her pasta casserole onto the floor. It's everywhere," Flossie said. Her wheelchair made a squishy sound as she rolled through elbow pasta floating in an eggy mayonnaise sauce strewn with cucumbers, pink seared tuna, and chives. "You'd better get a mop."

"We're going to need more than a mop," I said as I stepped farther into the kitchen.

I pointed to the hardwood floor where a pair of legs were sticking out from behind the kitchen counter.

"Is it—?" Flossie asked.

I peered around the counter and followed the legs up to the rest of the woman. Rebecca White was lying flat on her back. Her unmoving eyes seemed to be staring judgmentally at a tiny cobweb hanging from the ceiling.

Flossie looked at the shattered casserole dish lying in pieces next to Rebecca's body. "Tell me she isn't dead."

"Can't do that." I sighed.

Flossie breathed out a long, loud breath. "It looks like there will be an opening for a new member after all."

"An opening? What do you mean an opening?" Hazel demanded. "Did Rebecca say something about my membership?" Our hostess had come into the kitchen through the back door. She was wearing bright yellow dish gloves while carrying an empty garbage can. I was embarrassed that she'd heard Flossie's uncharitable remark about a dead woman. "What's going on in here?" Her voice was filled with suspicion as soon as she noticed the awful mess.

"What did you do to Rebecca?" Flossie demanded right back at our hostess.

Hazel looked first at the pasta salad splattered all over the floor and then at Rebecca, who was lying in the middle of the mess. "Good gracious, Mary and Joseph. She's dead, isn't she?"

The doorbell rang a second time.

"And the rest of the ladies are here. And I suppose the television crew is bound to be out there too. Of course they are," Hazel said before bursting out in a loud peal of laughter. The poor woman laughed so hard she had to bend over and grab hold of her knees to keep from falling over. And she kept laughing.

Chapter Three

———··———

I called the police while Hazel continued to laugh so hard tears poured down her face. It took Flossie threatening to slap her silly before the poor woman managed to get control of herself.

"Sorry, sorry, I've had to put up with this sharp-tongued woman for the past two weeks. She kept telling me that tonight was going to be a disaster . . . and then the dessert burned . . . and I had to take it out to the garbage . . . and . . . now . . . this," Hazel explained between gasping breaths. "She was right, wasn't she? Tonight is a disaster. I bet she died just to make sure she would be right. She would always go to any length to ensure her rightness. I can't tell you how much I hated that." The doorbell rang again. Hazel glanced over at where Rebecca was still on the floor dead. The soles of the former actress's high heels were really the only thing visible from where the three of us were standing. A short laugh seemed to explode out of Hazel's mouth. "Sorry. I can't seem to help myself. Seeing her there reminds me of the Wicked Witch of the East at the beginning of *The*

Wizard of Oz. Smashed by a house. Ding-dong." She
fought back more giggles and more tears. "Gracious, it
isn't funny. I know it isn't. It's just that I worked myself
half to death these past several days trying to make Rebecca happy and then, the moment before the guests arrive and before Rebecca's friend from that television
show comes to set up, that terrible woman drops dead.
And my casserole dish is smashed too. It was a wedding
gift from my sister."

"You didn't do this?" Flossie asked, pointing to the
shattered remains of what I supposed to be the murder
weapon.

"What? Buy that dish?" Hazel shook her head. "No. I
just told you it had been a wedding gift from my sister.
I've had it forever. It's hard to find quality ones that are
large enough nowadays. I don't know how I'll replace it."

"Flossie isn't asking about the casserole dish," I said
gently. "But now that you mentioned it, you didn't happen to, well . . . break it over Rebecca's head, did you?"

"Heavens, no. I'd been working so hard to please
someone who is unpleasable. My membership to the society is still provisional. I wouldn't do anything to mess
that up."

She answered so quickly and so emphatically that I
immediately believed her.

"I could have asked for a provisional membership?"
Flossie slapped her leg. But then she looked over at Rebecca. "I suppose that's not important right now."

"Oh, but it is important," Hazel said. "I've been trying to get into this book club for twenty years."

"Twenty years! I'll be dead and long forgotten before
the society gets around to sending out my acceptance
letter," Flossie cried.

"The Arete Society has always been an exclusive
book club," Hazel said, as if we didn't already know that.

"My mother and my father's mother were both members, and still it's taken me forever to get in."

The doorbell rang again.

"Do you want me to get that?" I asked. I wondered if I should make everyone stay outside. Should I tell the other members what had happened, or would it be better to let the police handle all that?

What would Hazel's son Jace—an ex-NYPD police detective—do?

Jace! I should have called him first. Rebecca had died in his mother's house. He needed to know.

I started to pull out my phone to call him when the doorbell rang yet again. This time whoever was pushing the button decided to push it over and over and over. *Ding. Dong. Ding. Dong. Ding. Dong.*

"The wicked witch is dead," Hazel whispered, and then burst out in hysterical laughter again.

"I'll just go," I said.

Flossie nodded.

The half-dozen ladies at the door didn't give me the chance to decide whether to let them in. As soon as I opened the door, they poured into the foyer. Behind them a smartly dressed woman with perfect makeup and an oversized microphone rushed into the room. Clearly this was Joyce Fellows. She started directing a pair of men with small handheld cameras to where she'd like them to set up. "Who decorated this living room? The setup is dreadful," she said more to herself than to anyone crowding the room. "We're going to have to rearrange."

"It's starting to rain out there, Tru," my boss, Mrs. Farnsworth, said accusingly, as if the rain were somehow my fault. I knew I should have opened that front door right away.

"Where is Hazel? Rebecca hasn't driven her crazy with her little demands, has she?" asked Delanie Messervey, a good friend of the library. She peeled off a stylish tan swing coat and handed it to me. The other ladies followed her example and started piling their coats in my arms too. "Whatever has happened in here? Hazel's living room is a mess!"

All the ladies seemed to be talking at once. I didn't know who to answer first.

From the other room, I could still hear Hazel's wild laughter.

"Sounds like the party is in the kitchen," Delanie said, heading off in that direction.

"No!" I ran to the swinging door and blocked it with my body and the ladies' coats. "No! The police will be here soon."

"The police!" everyone seemed to cry at the same time.

"Ms. Becket, what has happened?" Mrs. Farnsworth said. She glared at me the same way she had when I accidentally jammed the copy machine so badly that it'd taken three technicians to fix it.

"Rebecca is dead," I blurted, because Mrs. Farnsworth's glares always made me exceedingly nervous, and I had trouble thinking whenever I was nervous, which was why I had jammed the copying machine so completely all those years ago. Mrs. Farnsworth had been standing beside me watching me at the time.

"Are you sure?" Delanie cocked her head toward the door I was still blocking. "Sounds to me they are having a party in there."

"I assure you they aren't."

"They?" Count on Mrs. Farnsworth to pick up on that. "Who is in there?"

"Hazel and Flossie," I answered, but the ladies had all started talking over each other again. I doubted anyone had heard me.

"I can't believe it!" cried Annabelle Smidt Possey, the mayor's wife.

"Has someone contacted the authorities?" asked Gretchen Clark, Cypress's new town manager. "I need to inform Mayor Possey."

"I'm texting him now," said Annabelle.

"How did this happen?" Delanie asked. She then added, "Dear, you should put those coats in Hazel's guest room. It's down that hall, the first door on the left."

"Rebecca?" Marigold Brantley sobbed. Fat tears sprang to her eyes. "Rebecca!"

She tried to run into the kitchen, but Delanie—bless her—held Marigold back, hugging onto the thick-armed woman with all her might.

Everyone stopped talking. Marigold and her husband, Sherwood, used to own the town's feed and seed store. They were retired now, and their store had been sold to my best friend, Tori, who had turned it into a coffee shop.

Marigold gulped back several sobs before whispering, "Rebecca is . . . was my best friend."

She was? I suppose Rebecca must have had friends. I didn't know the woman very well. Perhaps she wasn't always *this* awful to everyone.

"What happened?" Mrs. Farnsworth asked again, her voice softer, more compassionate.

"She—" I started to say. But Marigold looked so crushed. I didn't want to be the one to tell her that her best friend might have been murdered. Besides, I wasn't sure I should be saying anything until the police arrived.

"It was probably an accident," I mumbled.

"Probably?" Marigold cried, her voice growing shriller and shriller. "Probably?!"

That was when I noticed that the cameramen who had

been setting up now had their cameras rolling and pointing directly at me. I must have looked quite ridiculous standing there with all those coats piled up in my arms.

"Do you think what happened to former soap opera star Rebecca White could be murder?" Joyce Fellows asked, her voice trembling with excitement. She thrust her microphone in my direction. "And who are you?"

I opened and closed my mouth, not sure what to say. I certainly didn't want to be on camera discussing this.

"Ladies," a deep masculine voice boomed. "I'll need everyone to take a seat in the living room." We all turned as one to watch as the lanky police chief, Jack Fisher, sauntered into the room, his thumbs hooked into the loops of his belt. Two officers followed him into the house along with Krystal Capps, the blue-haired coroner, who winked at me.

"Thank goodness," I breathed. I couldn't remember ever being happy to see the police chief before. But tonight, the sight of his scowling face looked better than finding a new release sitting on a bookstore's sale rack.

Especially after all the cameras swiveled to film him.

Fisher paused when he spotted Joyce Fellows and her camera crew. His grim expression grew even tauter.

"Get the press out of here, now!" he barked, and pushed Joyce's microphone out of his face.

"We're not the press," Joyce insisted. "We're filming a segment on the book club for my television show, *Ideal Life*, and—"

"I don't care if you're filming Santa Claus, you're not doing it here at my crime scene," Fisher snapped back. "Get them out of here," he ordered one of his officers. The officer herded the cameramen and the protesting Joyce back outside.

"I have every right to be here!" we could hear Joyce

shouting. "This is my story. I'll not have someone else steal it from me. Haven't you heard of freedom of the press?"

The second officer directed the rest of us to follow him into the living room. I tried to sneak around him to deposit the coats in Hazel's guest room, but the police officer stopped me. Very well. He could handle where to put them. I dropped the ladies' coats into his arms.

"Why did Hazel move her furniture around like this?" Marigold wondered as she sniffled and dabbed a tissue to her teary eyes. "Her living room used to be so cozy." She'd pushed the heavy armchair that I'd carried all over the room back to where Hazel had originally put it. "The placement of these chairs makes my head hurt. Doesn't it make your head hurt?" she asked the police chief.

"I . . . um . . ." He looked around as if seeing the room for the first time. "It's a room. And we, by gum, have work to do."

His gaze passed over me and stopped at Gretchen, the town manager. "Tell me what's going on here."

"I don't know. We all showed up at about the same time. We had to ring and ring and ring the doorbell before Ms. Becket let us in."

"*Becket*," it sounded like the police chief murmured under his breath. Or perhaps he'd whispered a curse word. His gaze narrowed as he turned toward me. "You're Becket's daughter," he said.

Before my rise to local fame, that was how most people knew me. I was my eccentric father's daughter.

"I am," I confirmed, even though he knew perfectly well who I was.

His gaze narrowed even more. I wondered if I was now just a blur to him with his eyes mostly closed like that. "It's interesting that you'd be here."

"I called dispatch." Another thing I suspected he already knew.

"Then I'll be wanting to talk to you. Where's the woman's body?"

"In the kitchen." I started to lead the way, but he stopped me.

"Go sit down," he said. "Havers, stand watch over these fine ladies. Please, everyone, stay in here until someone takes your statement. Capps and Pitts, follow me."

The three of them went through the swinging door into the kitchen. A few minutes later Flossie emerged. Someone had cleaned the tuna casserole off her wheels, I was glad to see.

"What's going on?" I whispered to her after she'd reached my side.

She glanced around and smiled at the ladies in the room. "The police chief is taking the matter most seriously. He's called in backup from the state law enforcement department. Your friend Detective Ellerbe volunteered to take the case, Tru."

"He's as capable as they come," I said approvingly.

"That he is," the mayor's wife said.

"His mama is a Brantley," Marigold said before blowing her nose. "And Sherwood's cousin. She will make sure her boy finds out what happened to Rebecca."

"I don't understand why the police chief is calling in backup. Wasn't it an accident?" Delanie asked. "Wasn't that what you said, Tru? Wasn't Rebecca's death an accident?"

"I . . . um . . ." What could I say? "It might have been." Not likely. It looked as if someone had hit the poor woman over the head with the now smashed casserole dish, but I sincerely hoped I had misread the clues and that Rebecca's death had been a bizarre accident.

My phone pinged.

Another murder in Cypress? my best friend, Tori, had texted.

How did you hear? I texted back.

It's true??? You have to be kidding me, came her immediate reply.

Wish I was. Who told you?

Everyone is talking about Rebecca's death at the coffee shop.

. . .

I didn't know what to say to that. I mean, I wasn't surprised that Tori already knew. Gossiping ranked higher than fishing or boating as a hobby in our lakeside town. Men and women alike, everyone seemed to get involved when there was a story to be told. And with smartphones and texting, the flow of information only moved that much faster through town.

"Flossie just told me that you found the body?" My friend Delanie shook her head slowly as she sat down on the sofa next to me. She put her arm around my shoulder. "You have to have the worst luck when it comes to these things, Tru." Delanie, who had married into one of the founding families of Cypress, was naturally a longtime member of the Arete Society. "And Hazel was the only other person in the house? I would have never guessed she had it in her to do it."

"She seemed so quiet, reserved," Gwynne Hansy, the high school football coach's wife, said with an excited quiver. High school football was a big deal in Cypress. A successful season meant college scholarships for the boys on the team, which meant a path to a better way of life for many of them. And because of that, the coach and his wife were treated like royalty.

She pulled out her phone and busily tapped away on its screen.

When had Gwynne arrived? She hadn't come in with the original set of women who had pushed their way past me when I'd opened the front door. At least, I didn't think she had.

"It's always the quiet ones," Annabelle said.

"She didn't—" I started to say, but stopped myself. I looked around at the elite women of Cypress crowding around Flossie and me. These women were all dressed in their Sunday finery. Delanie was a strong supporter of the library and a full-time philanthropist. Beside her was her closest friend and my boss, Mrs. Farnsworth. Like always, Mrs. Farnsworth was dressed in an ultraconservative dress with a starched white collar. As much as I wanted to tell these ladies that Hazel wasn't guilty of the crime, I couldn't. Hazel had been in the kitchen. Rebecca had been killed in the kitchen.

One plus one always equaled two.

Didn't it?

This was going to crush Jace.

I pulled out my phone and texted him. Something's happened at your mom's house. You need to get here.

He texted back almost immediately. I'm already on my way. Are you okay?

I'm fine.

How's my mom?

I stared at the screen for what felt like forever, unsure what to tell him. I finally typed, She's talking with the police chief right now. Detective Ellerbe is on his way.

I'm five minutes out.

"Tell him to call a lawyer," Flossie whispered to me.

"Tell him she's going to need a good criminal lawyer from Columbia," Delanie said, shaking her head.

Everyone seemed to be staring at me again. It made my skin prickle.

"I'm sure Hazel will be able to explain what happened. And I'm sure Rebecca's death was a horrible accident," I said.

"Where is Emma?" Mrs. Farnsworth asked, looking around.

"Emma has a stomach bug and decided to stay home," Flossie said.

"I bet that went over well with Rebecca," Annabelle said with a frown. She then leaned forward and whispered, "Rebecca called me this morning. I was attending the bridge club's annual breakfast and couldn't take the call. But she later sent a text saying that we needed to discuss the club's membership."

"What did she want to discuss?" I asked. I remembered Rebecca grumbling about Emma's lack of participation, but she seemed happy to let Emma continue her membership as long as she brought her icebox cake.

"I was under the impression that she was planning on kicking Emma out of the club," Annabelle said with a shrug. She sat back on the sofa and smiled. "Didn't she call anyone else?"

The ladies all looked at each other while shaking their heads.

"Maybe she wanted to tell Emma to tone it down when it came to talking about her travel agency so much," Marigold finally offered. She looked around as if expecting someone to contradict her. When no one did, she continued, "The woman would go on and on about needing to build her clientele and what she had to offer. Don't get me wrong. We all tend to talk about our personal lives a bit before we begin our book discussions, but that's not what the book club is about. Besides, it's not as if any of us are looking to jet off to exotic places every weekend. I mean, who does that?" She glanced over at Flossie. "No offense."

"None taken," Flossie said, even though her shoulders had tensed. "I don't travel nearly as much as I did when my Truman was alive. I haven't been out of the state in over a year."

"Few of us have," Mrs. Farnsworth said with a frown.

"Did Emma ever argue with—" I started to ask.

But Mrs. Farnsworth didn't let me finish. "You have to understand that Emma isn't from around here. Her personality is different from ours. We have to make concessions when it comes to outsiders."

The other ladies all jumped in to agree with her.

"Bless them, they don't know any better. They haven't been raised with proper Southern manners," Annabelle said. "They never attended cotillion. None of them seem to realize when they're being rude, the poor dears."

"I'm not sure that's how regional differences work," I said.

"If she was so ignorant, how in blazes did Emma get invited into the society?" Flossie demanded.

"Now, now." Delanie rushed over to our friend's side. "It's not that we don't want you as a member, Flossie. It's just that you have been so busy with your travels, even if not recently, and your writing takes up a large portion of your time, and we didn't want you to feel like you would have to choose between us and one of your other pursuits. We only have ten members; it would hurt the society if one member regularly missed meetings."

"I don't—" Flossie shook her head.

"This isn't the time to talk about membership decisions," Mrs. Farnsworth said firmly. "Considering the reason we now have an opening—perhaps *two* openings—such a discussion would be unseemly, don't you agree?"

Flossie clearly didn't like it, but surprisingly she let the matter drop. And yet I could tell by the way her brows kept popping up and down that she hadn't stopped thinking about it.

As if by mutual agreement, the ladies shifted the discussion to what Rebecca's death would mean for the book club. Flossie and I listened quietly while they argued about whether the next several meetings should be canceled. A few of the members lamented that I wasn't going to be able to give my presentation. They'd been looking forward to it all month.

Marigold, I noticed, also stayed silent. She stared at her lap as tears rolled down her round cheeks. She appeared to be the only member who was truly going to miss Rebecca.

Chapter Four

———•———

The book club ladies continued to debate what to do about next month's meeting. They didn't know whether they should discuss this month's book next month or skip it and move forward with the book already scheduled for February. A few members wanted to ditch the scheduled list of books altogether and vote on new books since Rebecca was no longer around, and she was the one who had picked out that book list for the year. The discussion came to a quick halt when the front door opened. Officer Havers, who we had all forgotten was standing in the opening between the living room and the front door foyer, sprang to attention.

"Good evening, sir," he said as he tugged on his belt to adjust his pants.

"Good evening—Havers, isn't it?" Detective Ellerbe, a man I knew from past murder investigations, said as he stepped into the foyer. A blast of damp, chilly air along with four crime scene technicians wearing matching dark blue polo shirts entered the house with him. "Good to see you again. How is your wife? The last time we spoke, she was about to graduate from college, isn't that right?"

"Yes, sir." Havers stood taller. He shook the detective's hand. "She's been taking online classes to earn a degree in accounting. She has one class to finish now."

"That's good news, good news." The detective sounded genuinely interested in the officer's home life. He leaned forward and said quietly to Havers, "Keep encouraging her."

"Yes, sir. I will, sir. We're all so proud of her."

Detective Ellerbe patted the man on the arm. He then ran a hand over his salt-and-pepper mustache as he surveyed the situation in the living room.

"There's a film crew outside," he said to Havers. "Why?"

"The lady with the microphone claims to be from some national show filming a piece about the Arete Society. She said the book club, being as old and exclusive as it is, serves as a model for book clubs all around the country."

"Picked one heck of a night to film. Your mayor isn't going to like this."

"No, I don't imagine he would," Havers said.

"Then I suppose we need to get this matter cleared up as soon as possible. Good evening, ladies," Ellerbe said with a dip of his head. He then turned back to ask Havers, "Where can I find the police chief?"

"He's in the kitchen with the coroner," Havers offered.

"Ellerbe, you should have told the local police chief to stay out of the crime scene," complained a tall dark-haired woman who seemed to be in charge of the other crime scene investigators. "I suppose he's stomping all over the evidence."

"Now, Lacy, you know we're here to assist," Ellerbe said. "I cannot go around telling the police chief how to conduct his business."

"Fisher is in the kitchen interviewing the main suspect," Delanie added, trying to be helpful.

"That's even worse!" Lacy pushed past the detective to get to the kitchen. The three others dressed like her followed.

"Aren't you going to go see what happened in there?" Flossie asked Detective Ellerbe, who had remained in the living room instead of trailing his team of crime scene investigators into the kitchen.

"And step into Lacy Daufuskie's crime scene? No way." Ellerbe's mustache bristled.

"You're scared of her, Detective?" Flossie nudged me. "I think I'll like her."

"You should like her. She's one of the best in the state," Ellerbe said with a kind smile. "It's good to see you again, Flossie. How's the book coming? No, don't tell me. I know you refuse to talk about it. But I'm a determined detective. I'll figure out your pen name sooner or later."

"How about you focus on crime, and I'll focus on publishing?" Flossie shot back, but I could tell she enjoyed the attention.

Having Detective Ellerbe on the scene made me feel better about everything. The detective and the crime scene investigators who had accompanied him worked for the State Law Enforcement Division. Small towns like Cypress didn't have the budgets to keep crime scene investigators or even detectives on staff. So when a crime or questionable death occurred, the police chief could request that the state come in to assist.

Police Chief Jack Fisher and the detective were longtime friends. Whenever Fisher needed to call for state backup, he often requested Ellerbe by name.

"The mayor's wife, Annabelle Smidt Possey, is over there," Havers said quietly to Ellerbe.

The older detective gave a shallow nod.

"I assume you'll want to get her statement first, sir," Havers continued.

Ellerbe glanced around the room before zeroing in on me. "Actually, I'd like to interview Trudell first, if you don't mind," he said.

"Ms. Becket?" Havers lifted his brows in surprise. I suppose he didn't understand why someone would want to question an assistant librarian over the mayor's wife. "Uh . . . very well."

"Is there somewhere I can conduct the interviews in private?" Ellerbe asked when the officer had stepped aside without offering any assistance.

"I . . ." Havers glanced around the room.

"I believe there's a small office off to your right," Delanie offered.

"Thank you." Ellerbe moved in that direction, pausing only a moment to gesture that I should follow. "Tru?"

The office turned out to be a neatly organized craft room with a sewing machine and a well-stocked gift-wrapping table. A rainbow array of yarn balls filled a bookshelf that spanned an entire wall, and a small desk with a laptop had been tucked away in a corner. Ellerbe offered me the desk chair, which I accepted.

Ellerbe remained standing. He paced a bit, briefly slowing to study the different hobbies on display in the room. "The house's owner is as neat as a pin."

"Hazel is meticulous in everything she does," I said, enjoying the strict tidiness of the room. "She also takes great pride in playing hostess."

He stopped pacing and frowned at an untidy pile of scrap material that seemed quite out of place with the rest of the room beside the sewing machine. "Trudell, please tell me Fisher is wrong about why we're here."

"Why did he say he needed you?" I asked as I watched him.

He picked up one of the scraps and studied it. From where I was sitting, I could see that someone had forcefully ripped the threads from the cloth. He put the cloth into a small paper bag, which I recognized from past crime scenes as one of the evidence bags Ellerbe liked to use. "For Jace's sake, how about you just tell me what happened tonight?" he asked as he jotted a note on the side of the bag before tucking it into his pocket.

The first time Ellerbe had questioned me about a crime, he chatted about the weather and current events, taking the time to put me at ease before asking any questions. Now that we knew each other and were—in a way—friends, I suppose he didn't feel the need for niceties.

"How do you know I was in the house when it happened?" I asked him.

The tilt of his head deepened as he glanced in my direction. "Even if you weren't here at the time of death, you were just now in a room with all of those women, which means you've been gathering as much information from them as possible and surely know more about the victim's death than anyone else in this house."

"Save for the murderer," I said, not trying to be glib, but after the words came out of my mouth, I realized that was exactly how I sounded.

Ellerbe closed his eyes and sighed. When he opened them again, he said, "Where were you when the death occurred?"

"I was in the living room. Unfortunately, I didn't see anything important," I quickly added.

He pulled out his notebook. "What exactly did you see?"

I explained what had happened and where everyone

was in the house at the time. While I did this, he jotted notes, asked clarifying questions, and occasionally groaned.

"So, Flossie and you were in the living room when you heard a crash," he said, summarizing what I'd told him. "And then Flossie went into the kitchen to investigate while you went toward the front door. That's when you heard a second crash?" He paused and looked at me.

"Yes. It wasn't the same kind of crash, though."

He nodded. "You went into the kitchen to find Flossie and the victim? You had said Flossie and Rebecca White were arguing before this happened?"

"No, I didn't say they were arguing." I didn't like how Ellerbe was twisting my words. "It had to have been an accident. And what I said was that Flossie wanted to know how to get an invitation to join the Arete Society, and Rebecca made it sound as if there was nothing Flossie could do to get invited. They weren't arguing, though."

Ellerbe nodded again. "But Flossie and the victim were in the kitchen alone together?" he asked for a second time. "And you heard a crash?"

"Flossie told me she ran into the kitchen counter with her wheelchair. And I don't like the way you're looking at me. The only way Flossie would be able to hit anyone over the head with a dish of tuna casserole would be for her to miraculously get out of that wheelchair of hers and stand up, so you can get whatever thoughts you're having at the moment right out of your head."

Ellerbe's eyes softened just a bit before he continued his questioning. "And the owner of this house, Hazel Bailey, who happens to be Detective Jace Bailey's mother? She claims to have been outside when this all happened?"

"Yes, she came through the back door after Flossie

and I discovered Rebecca's body." My voice was growing more and more clipped. "She told us that she'd been taking out the garbage."

"I see." He closed his notebook with a snap. "Death by tuna noodle casserole pretty much sums things up, don't you agree?"

"Don't say that around Betty Crawley unless you want that to be the headline in the morning paper," I warned. Betty was the local newspaper reporter who liked to add extra drama to her articles in the hopes that a national newspaper would see one of them and offer her a position. Her favorite thing to do was to quote people out of context to make her stories sound that much more exciting. I'd been the victim of her misquoting more than once. So had Ellerbe.

"Once the details of Ms. White's death become known, I'm sure Betty will come up with that exact headline all on her own," Ellerbe grumbled. "What rotten luck that there's already a camera crew on the scene. I dislike too much publicity before we get all our facts together. Too much reporting on the crime scene can change eyewitnesses' memories. Speaking of which, do you have any thoughts on who might have wanted the book club president dead, besides our Flossie?"

"Could have been anyone. From what I saw tonight, Rebecca was a hard woman to like."

"But the only people in the house were Flossie, Hazel, yourself, and the victim? And you were in the living room when the death occurred, is that correct?"

"No." I didn't like how he kept going back to pointing the finger of blame at my friend. "*Flossie* and I were in the living room," I corrected, but as soon as I'd said it, I realized Ellerbe or anyone with even half a brain in their head would then conclude that Hazel killed Rebecca before running outside. I threw my hands into the air. "But

I didn't go into the kitchen until after we heard a loud crash. Anyone could have been in the kitchen."

"You heard two crashes," he reminded me. "Did you see anyone else either outside the house or anywhere nearby?"

"No," I hated to admit. "But don't take that to mean there wasn't someone else in the kitchen. It wasn't as if I'd been staring out the windows, watching for people. And you must have noticed on your way up that long sidewalk that the house is in the middle of the cypress forest. There could have been dozens of people going in and out of the kitchen door and neither Flossie nor I would ever know."

"Is that so? You, Tru? You wouldn't have known?"

I nodded.

Slowly.

"Is it likely that other people were coming in and out of the house without you knowing?" he asked.

"It could be." For Jace's sake, I hoped like a child hoping for Santa on Christmas Eve that that was what had happened.

Ellerbe asked a few more questions before telling me I could go home. When we returned to the living room, Annabelle stood up, clearly expecting to be the next person called in to give her statement.

Ellerbe didn't seem to notice. He turned to Havers. "Ms. Becket is free to go."

"Yes, sir." Havers opened the door for me.

"Actually, Flossie and I came in the same car," I explained as I returned to my place on the sofa.

"Of course the two of you did," Ellerbe said. "Well, you can leave as soon as I get her statement. Flossie"— he gestured toward the craft room—"if you don't mind coming with me?"

"Whatever I can do to be of assistance," Flossie said with a smile.

This set off a firestorm of complaints from the book club members, all of whom were respected members of Cypress society who weren't used to being told they needed to sit around and wait while others went before them. "Were any of the rest of y'all in this house when Ms. White died?" Ellerbe asked them.

The ladies looked at each other. After a moment, they shook their heads.

"In that case, I appreciate your patience," he said. "And I promise we'll get you all home as soon as possible."

In the silence that followed after Ellerbe left with Flossie, my stomach growled. I put my hand on my middle and blushed. Since I wasn't going to get dinner at the book club tonight, all I wanted to do was go home and find something to eat. Not that I looked forward to eating the bland food sitting in my refrigerator. Nothing would compare to those lobster tacos Rebecca had waved under my nose. Their spicy aroma had made me want to sing with joy.

"These things can take a while," Delanie whispered to Annabelle.

"These things shouldn't be happening. Not in Cypress. Not to me," Annabelle replied angrily.

"Not to anyone of us," Marigold said. "This is the Arete Society, not a bingo hall. If this institution isn't safe, nowhere is." She dabbed her nose with a tissue. "Poor, poor Rebecca. This shouldn't have happened. Not to her. Not to our own—"

"You can't come in here!" Havers shouted as he blocked the front doorway.

We all turned to stare.

Despite her brave front, Delanie pressed a shaky hand to her mouth.

"This is my parents' house," the man on the wrong side of the doorway shouted right back.

I stood up.

"Sir, I have my orders."

I rushed to the door.

"I cannot let him in," Havers said to me in a quiet panic.

"Jace, can we talk on the porch?" I put my hand on my boyfriend's broad chest. I could feel his heart pounding beneath my palm. "Officer Havers, if I promise to keep Jace outside, would you run and get the police chief out here?"

"I'm not supposed to—" Havers started to protest. I didn't let him finish.

"What would you do if this was your mama's house?" I asked him.

He opened his mouth and shut it again right away. "I'll go get Fisher."

"Thank you," Jace said through clenched teeth.

Jace Bailey stood a little over six feet tall. He was dressed in khaki pants and a crisp white cotton shirt with a dark blue blazer on over it. He'd been the football quarterback and a track star in high school. Unlike some of our classmates, he'd kept in shape since graduation. And like in high school, his dusty blond hair was still slightly too long and in need of taming. I liked it that way.

I put my hand on the side of his handsome face, hoping to ease some of the pain in his tight expression. The blond stubble covering his square chin scraped against my palm. "Your mother is holding up." Barely. But he didn't need to know that.

"Where is she?" he demanded as he stepped out onto the porch with me. Thankfully, the camera crew had grown tired of waiting in the rain and had packed up and left. I spotted Betty Crawley, the local reporter, huddled under an umbrella about one hundred feet away. She

leaned toward us, as if trying to hear what we were saying. "Where is my mother?"

"In the kitchen with the police chief and the crime
scene technicians," I answered, keeping my voice low.

"Alone? Without a lawyer?" He started to charge toward the door again.

I held up my hand, but he didn't give me the chance
to say anything.

It looked like he was going to push me out of the way.
But instead, he tugged at his hair, making it that much
messier. "She shouldn't be talking to anyone without a
lawyer. Please, I need to get her out of there."

"She's not going anywhere," Police Chief Fisher said
as he came out onto the porch.

"Then I'm going in there." Jace started toward the
door again. "My mother is a strong woman, but no one
should be going through something like this alone. I'm
all the family she has in town right now."

That wasn't true. Hazel had a sister, a gaggle of cous-
ins, and a cranky old great-aunt who all lived within the
town limits. Not only that, Jace's mom had an extremely
generous husband who treated her like a queen. Neither
I nor Fisher pointed this out to Jace, who was making a
face that reminded me of a rabid possum spoiling for a
fight.

"Where is your father?" I asked him instead.

He shook his head. "With all the hubbub going on at
the house leading up to the book club, he hightailed it
out of here to go fishing in the Everglades. He was planning to be gone for the entire week. I've been trying to
get ahold of him all night, but he's not picking up. Not
that I'm surprised. He often turns his cell off once he
gets out to his fishing spot so no one from work can call
and disturb his peace."

"Oh no! What are you going to do?" I cried.

"I called a buddy on a police force in a nearby town. He's heading out to the cabin my daddy rented to let him know that he needs to call. But until we can get in touch with him, I'm all my mama has. Fisher, you have to understand why I need to be with her now."

"Son, I'm sorry, but you can't be here." Police Chief Fisher blocked his entrance into the house.

"She's my mother," Jace said quietly.

"That's more reason why you can't be anywhere near this homicide investigation."

"Homicide investigation!" Jace exclaimed. "You mean accidental death, sir? This is my mother's house."

"I'm sorry, son," the police chief repeated. And it sounded as if he was honestly sorry.

Jace appeared all the more desperate to rush through the doorway and get inside. "This is my mother's house," he repeated. "It's always part of the garden club's spring house tour. Not because my mom hires a designer to decorate for her. No, that showroom look in there is one hundred percent her doing. Plus, she loves throwing parties. She can make anyone feel comfortable at her table. No one is murdered in her home. No one. Not even Rebecca White."

"There are witnesses." Fisher pointed to me. "This one and Flossie Finnegan-Baker were here when it happened."

"Not witnesses." I threw up my hands. "We went into the kitchen and found Rebecca. She was already dead. Hazel wasn't there. She had been outside taking out the trash."

"Well, not *eye*witnesses, but close enough," Fisher amended. "Rebecca's death was not an accident. And Jace, you know as well as anyone that we cannot have investigators related to either the victim or our main suspect anywhere near the crime scene. You cannot work this case. You cannot be part of this investigation."

Jace started to argue.

"Go home," the police chief ordered. "And while you're at it, I suggest that since your father isn't around to do it, you get on the phone to get your mother a good defense attorney."

"I'll leave, but only if you promise you'll stop interrogating her until the lawyer I hire for her arrives."

Fisher wrinkled his nose and appeared ready to object. He surprised me when he said, "It's a deal, son."

With that promise made, Jace reluctantly left.

My heart walked down the path with him.

Chapter Five

———·———

It was long after midnight by the time I drove up to my house, a small clapboard bungalow that sat among a row of similar homes. The first thing I saw as I pulled into the driveway was Jace's green Jeep. I then spotted my boyfriend sitting on the front stoop with his head buried in his hands. The porch light seemed to shine on him like a spotlight.

"Let me brew some coffee," I said as I approached. I figured neither of us was going to get much sleep tonight.

He rose slowly to his feet, looking as if he were battling against the weight of the entire world. "Thanks, Tru. I hope you don't mind that I waited for you." He hesitated. "I can go if you want. You must be exhausted after—"

"Heavens, what kind of friend would I be if I sent you away?" I grabbed his arm and pulled him toward the front door. "You must be crazy with worry for your mother."

He swallowed hard and nodded.

"Have you been able to get in touch with your father?" I asked.

"Not yet. My buddy got lost and headed down the wrong dirt road. He says he should reach him within an hour or so."

I unlocked the front door and pushed him inside before following.

"Yeow!" Dewey Decimal, my friendly tabby cat, greeted us at the door. His tail, held straight in the air like a flagpole, trembled with kitty delight. He wove his long, lean body between my legs and then Jace's, pausing several times to butt his head against our calves.

"Hey there, little guy." Jace reached down to scratch Dewey behind his ears. "I'm afraid I don't have a toy for you today."

Jace nearly always brought a cat toy with him whenever he visited. "Sometimes, I wonder if you like my cat more than you like me."

Instead of answering, Jace simply smiled in that make-me-breathless way while still petting my kitty behind the ears.

"I'll start that coffee." I moved through the living room toward the kitchen.

Jace stopped me with a hand on my arm. "Thank you," he said. "I mean it, Tru. Thank you for opening your home for me like this."

"You'd do the same." And despite the doubts I'd been having about our relationship, I knew that much was true. If the tables were turned, he'd do anything to help me.

Jace gave a curt nod, as if accepting help—anyone's help—came hard for him. He followed me into the kitchen. Dewey, meowing happily, came too.

I put a few liver-flavored treats on the floor for Dewey before measuring grounds into the coffeemaker.

"Tell me, Tru." Jace leaned against the kitchen counter. "Tell me what happened tonight."

"Didn't you talk with your mother's attorney?" I asked, wondering why he needed to hear the story from me. "Didn't you talk with *your mother*?"

Shortly after Jace had left his mother's house, Percy Redi-Finch showed up. According to Delanie, Percy was a high-powered defense lawyer in Columbia—South Carolina's state capital. He was a partner in the firm Finch, Finch, and Twist. Delanie had called him the best of the best, a lawyer other lawyers called when they needed representation. While Percy was officially an outsider to Cypress, he did own a vacation lake house in town, which was why Delanie knew and approved of him.

Percy, a man who was both tall and broad, had taken up quite a lot of space in the front foyer. Annabelle had gushed over his carefully fitted navy-blue suit, which she insisted had to have been custom-made. Nothing off the rack would fit such a tall man so perfectly. Although he resembled a giant, his eyes looked kind and his voice was soft. He had spoken briefly to Detective Ellerbe and Police Chief Fisher before leaving with Jace's mom.

We had all watched from the front window as he used his massive body to shield Hazel from Betty Crawley, who'd pursued the pair while shouting questions and snapping pictures with a camera with a long telephoto lens.

"Yes, I talked with the lawyer," Jace said. He sounded miserable about it. "I didn't get a chance to talk with Mom. Redi-Finch checked her into a hotel out on Interstate 95 for the night and will take her to his office in the morning to strategize. He kept her away from the phone, saying he wanted her to get a good night's sleep before the police come to arrest her for murder." Jace looked up at the ceiling and took several deep breaths. "I can't believe it. My mother is almost certainly going to be arrested for killing that cranky woman and there's nothing Dad or I can do to stop it. My father probably won't even be in town when it happens. Please, Tru, I need you to tell me what went on at her house." He shook his head. "Because I don't understand how any of this can be happening."

"We can't do this without chocolate cake." I pulled out a decadent three-layer dark chocolate cake with raspberry filling from its hiding spot under the sink. My mother, who often popped by unannounced, was a fanatic when it came to healthy eating and would toss out anything she deemed junk food. I'd learned the hard way to hide my snacks well.

I cut two large slices. Of course they were large. I still hadn't had dinner. I put the slices on dessert plates and slid the larger of the two over to Jace.

"It'll take the edge off," I said before taking a few bites of the moist, fruity cake.

After devouring the slice on my plate, I told Jace everything I'd seen and heard at his mother's.

As soon as I finished, Jace insisted rather firmly, "I know my mother. She wouldn't hurt anyone. She couldn't."

"Not even in a fit of anger? Rebecca was being simply awful. And I only saw a fraction of their interaction together. Perhaps she pushed your mom over the edge," I said, playing devil's advocate.

"No!" Jace dropped his fork with a clatter. "No. That's impossible. The worst she ever did when she and my dad were going through a rocky patch was to wash all his wool pants in the washing machine. Ruined them all. She did it because she'd been furious with him." He lowered his voice. "My dad had been threatening to leave her for his young, pretty secretary."

"That was six years ago?" I asked.

"Seven." He smiled ruefully. "Both my parents would call hourly to tattle on what the other had done. It was . . . memorable . . . and not in a good way."

"I can imagine." My parents had gone through a rocky patch of their own that had ended in divorce when I was in high school. The experience had only hammered home my love of libraries and the escape they could provide to anyone in desperate need of quiet.

I put my hand on Jace's and gave a gentle squeeze of support.

My slinky little tabby jumped up onto the kitchen counter, a place he knew he wasn't allowed, interrupting our intimate moment. Dewey looked me square in the eye as if annoyed with something I'd done before pushing a pile of library books I'd left near yesterday's mail onto the floor. The books landed with a page-wrinkling, cringe-inducing crash.

"Naughty kitty!" I scolded as I gently lifted the scamp off the counter. "You know better than to do that. And look at these books. Their pages are crumpled."

"Let me help you." Jace crouched down and helped me gather up the books. They were the paperback historical romances I'd loaned to my neighbor Cora. She'd read them almost faster than I could pull them from the shelves.

Jace paused to study the cover of one of the books. The hero, his shirt ripped and dripping wet from the sea behind him, stood with his arms akimbo as he stared confidently forward with one eyebrow raised.

"Should I be jealous?" he asked.

I snatched the book away from him and added it to the stack I'd gathered in my arms. "Don't be silly. Despite that cover, nearly all of these books are brilliantly written."

He raised an eyebrow, perfectly copying the sexy hero's expression. "You've read them?"

"I'm a librarian. I read everything." And I enjoyed reading everything, including genre fiction. Well, *most* genre fiction.

As soon as I put the books back on the kitchen counter, Dewey jumped back up and was batting at them again.

"I don't know what's gotten into Dewey. He's usually careful around the books. Cora must have spilled some perfume on them." I carried my kitty to the living room and left him on his favorite chair, where I knew he'd stashed at least five catnip toy mice.

When I returned to the kitchen, I found Jace with his nose next to the books, sniffing.

"Are they perfumed?" I asked.

"If they are, only a cat can smell them."

I picked up one and inhaled deeply. The book smelled slightly sweet, not like perfume, though. It smelled like ink and paper and adventure. It smelled like a library. I smoothed a crease in one of the pages before placing the books back into my tote bag. I then stuffed the tote into a lower kitchen cabinet. "That should keep Dewey from messing with them. I was planning on returning the books to the bookroom tomorrow anyhow." I glanced at the clock on the stove. "I mean, this morning." I yawned. "Today. Um . . . what were we talking about?"

"You were telling me how you thought my mother was capable of murder," he said, sounding about as exhausted as I felt.

"No, that wasn't what I was saying." I closed my eyes as I remembered the look of shock on Hazel's face when she came in through the back door to find Flossie and me standing near Rebecca's body. "I was pointing out how circumstances look bad for her. Really bad."

"Trust me, you don't have to tell me that," he muttered.

"But I don't think it's all hopeless, Jace. There was something about the way your mother acted when she saw what had happened in her kitchen. She immediately demanded to know what *we'd* done. She practically accused Flossie and me of murder. I don't think someone guilty of murder would be able to pull off the look of pure anger and then shock so sincerely. I don't think it was faked." I touched his hand. "Unless your mother has a split personality, I don't believe she is guilty." I put another slice of chocolate cake on my plate. It tasted too good on my empty stomach. "Detective Ellerbe is on the case. He's a good man. He'll get this all sorted."

Jace took my hands in his. "Tru, Ellerbe is a good detective, but you and I both know justice doesn't always happen."

"But—"

"Tru, I need you," he said with great feeling. "I need you," he repeated. He rubbed his stubbly jaw. "My mom was alone in the kitchen with Rebecca. No one else was in the house. That all sounds dodgy. I understand that Detective Ellerbe has other investigations. He's not going to spend much time on what must obviously seem like an open-and-shut case."

"But he's—" Ellerbe was a good man, a careful investigator.

"The detective is not going to go looking for a needle in a haystack when he thinks he's already holding that needle in his hand. Would you? Of course not. No one would."

Jace might have been right about that. "What do you need me to do?"

"The police chief can order me to stay away from the investigation." Jace started pacing. "But he can't stop you from being you. I need you to do your thing. I need you to poke your nose into everyone's business, ask your questions, and prove my mother's innocence."

Could I do that? Could I prove that Hazel didn't kill Rebecca? "But she was in the kitchen."

"That's why I need you."

"Your mother was in the kitchen," I repeated. "Rebecca had followed her into the kitchen. How do I prove someone else was responsible? Where do I even start?"

"My mom wasn't in the kitchen when you went to investigate the loud crash you heard. She wasn't there," Jace repeated, as if desperate to convince himself that it was true. "That's where you start."

He was right. Hazel hadn't been in the kitchen. Plus, there'd been that second crash when Flossie was in there. Despite how badly she had wanted an invitation to join the Arete Society, she couldn't have hurt Rebecca. Not like that. And—

"No one else was in the house," I reminded Jace.

"That we know of. I need you, Tru. You see things no one else sees."

I see things that are out of place, probably because I love making sure my library shelves are always neat and orderly. But this was different. I shook my head. This was impossible. What we had on our hands was a murder that could rival the best locked-room mysteries of classic literature.

My heart started to beat a little harder.

If Hazel had been outside at the time of Rebecca's death, no one had been in the room with our sharp-tongued victim.

My mind started to whirl a little faster.

Unless someone had slipped in the back door after Hazel had taken the burnt remnants of her dessert out to the garbage bin that she kept in the shed.

I could do this.

I reached for a notebook to start jotting down my thoughts. Any one of the Arete Society members could have arrived early and set out to watch the house for an opportunity to strike.

But who else had a motive?

I set down the pencil I'd only just picked up. "Your mother couldn't have been the only one Rebecca had been tormenting. Although, according to Delanie, Rebecca apparently had been dictating her demands to your mother about how to host the book club meeting all week, and then she started to snipe at Flossie nearly right after we'd arrived. It was like she couldn't help herself."

"I wonder why?" Jace frowned at the cake in front of him.

"Maybe Rebecca was angry with someone and lashing out at everyone. My mother does that when she's upset with something my father has done."

Jace sat back in his chair and smiled. "So, you are going to help me? You're going to investigate?"

I smiled back. "Did you ever think I wouldn't?"

"Honey, I didn't doubt you for a moment. But my mama raised me right. You know that. It would be impolite to assume you'd help without being asked nicely."

"Your mama is a wise woman. Now let's get to work."

Chapter Six

———·———

The next morning arrived far earlier than I was prepared for. I would have totally overslept if not for my phone. It buzzed loudly, jolting me awake.

I CAN'T FIND YOUR FATHER, my mother shouted in her text message with all caps. She only text-shouted when talking about my dad. The hurts they'd inflicted when going through their divorce still festered all these years later. And Mama Eddy still had no qualms against pulling me into the middle of their battlefield.

I haven't talked with him since I had lunch with him last Thursday, I texted back as soon as I managed to get my tired eyes to focus. I wondered why she needed to find him. I would have asked, but I honestly didn't have the emotional energy to deal with whatever trouble was brewing between them. I'll let you know if I hear from him, I texted instead.

That fool man has gotten himself into trouble. I just know it, she texted back almost immediately, which meant she must have already typed the words before I'd sent my reply.

I didn't know what to say, so I set my phone back down on my dresser and started to get ready for the day. Thirty minutes later, I gave Jace a goodbye kiss on his forehead without waking him and then fought jaw-cracking yawns as I headed down Main Street toward Cypress's public library.

Along the way, I couldn't stop thinking about my mom's text. My dad was probably out fishing. But why would she care?

I stared at my phone. And why hadn't she mentioned Rebecca's murder in her texts? Certainly she'd heard about it by now. I was sure half the state must have heard about it. And she knew I was going to be at Hazel's house. We'd talked about it over Sunday's supper.

Perhaps since members of the town's elite were also at Hazel's house last night, she didn't feel as embarrassed that I was at the scene of a murder as she usually would have. Perhaps she even considered my being there a good thing, since it meant I had spent time rubbing noses with women Mama Eddy respected and wished to keep as close friends.

I bet she wouldn't feel quite as pleased after I proved that one of those socially high-powered friends of hers had murdered the town's starlet. Jace and I had stayed up until nearly dawn speculating on what might drive one of the other book club members to murder.

"I bet all the members conspired together to kill her," I had declared at about three in the morning. (Nothing rational ever happens at three in the morning.) I'd then slapped the dining room table with a smack so loud it made poor Dewey, who'd been napping on the rug under the table, jump. "They all arrived at your mother's house at the same time, which is evidence enough for me. Yes, that must be it! Those women pulled off a *Murder on the Orient Express* murder right under my nose. Oh, they must have thought themselves so clever. But they didn't realize I'd read and reread all the classic murder mysteries. I know them practically by heart, the arrogant fools."

"Um, I don't know, Tru," Jace had said. His head had bobbed a few times, and I was sure he had been sleeping and hadn't really heard my brilliant deduction. Sleep must have been why he wasn't singing my praises. I'd solved the case without even having to investigate.

My own lack of sleep must have turned me into a crime-solving genius!

A few minutes later, I led Jace to the living room sofa, covered him with a blanket, and then shuffled off to bed believing I'd solved Rebecca's murder, only to wake up the next morning with the realization that nothing I'd written in my notebook (or crowed to Jace) last night made much sense.

In the cold light of day, I understood that I would have to conduct a real investigation, the likes of which I'd never conducted before. But first, I needed to get to work.

I was a block from the library when the church bells started to chime, marking the half hour.

"No. No. No." I started to jog.

The town could set their clocks by Mrs. Farnsworth's punctuality. Without fail, she would walk up the steps leading to the library and unlock the front door at precisely eight thirty every morning. And she expected her support staff to be at the door waiting for her to let them in. Then, after we all shuffled inside, she'd lock the door behind us, keeping it locked until the library opened at ten.

Tardiness was not tolerated.

I needed to get to the library.

But as I sprinted toward the building with its elegant marble columns across the front that made the library look like a Greek temple plopped in the middle of our very Southern town, Mrs. Farnsworth was nowhere in sight. She must have already gone inside the library.

And that wasn't the worst of it. A bigger obstacle than a locked front door stood between me and my job. Joyce Fellows and her camera crew were jogging down the library steps. Joyce looked about as happy as a child who'd just dropped her ice-cream cone. Betty Crawley, looking nearly as miserable, chased after them.

I would bet a month's salary that Mrs. Farnsworth had scolded them soundly before sending them on their way. No one scolded better than Mrs. Farnsworth.

At first, the sight of the reporters didn't worry me one bit. I doubted any of them would have any interest in talking with me. I wasn't a member of the Arete Society, nor had I known Rebecca very well.

But then I heard Betty call out to Joyce Fellows, "Who you need to talk with is the assistant librarian, Trudy Becket! She calls herself our local sleuth. She's solved all the recent murders here in Cypress."

Thanks bunches, Betty. She made it sound like there were murders in town all the time. *And my name is Trudell, not Trudy.*

But I didn't correct the local reporter (aka the thorn in my side). Especially not after Joyce shouted to a woman dressed in jeans and carrying a clipboard, who hadn't been at Hazel's house last night, "Get me this Trudy person." I certainly didn't mind that Joyce and her film crew would be looking for the wrong person.

"She should be here," Betty declared, and started looking around the street. "You need to ask her about how she pretended to be pregnant this past fall. What a hilarious story."

Oh, good grief. Why did Betty have to tell them *that*? I ducked behind a large mailbox and hoped no one would look out their window and notice—I hated it when the townspeople talked about me. It'd taken months to get that pregnancy rumor to die down. I didn't need any of those silly rumors to pop back up, and I certainly didn't need to have any of those same rumors repeated on national television. If that happened, Mama Eddy would die of embarrassment. Or rather, she wouldn't *actually* die. She'd just claim to have died and spend the rest of her days telling me about how she'd died of mortification thanks to me, her ungrateful daughter.

No, thank you. I'll just stay right here and hide even if I do look ridiculous crouching here.

After a few seconds, I peeked out over the mailbox.

Good news! Joyce hadn't seen me. She and her camera crew were making a beeline toward the Sunshine Diner across the street, where several prominent elected officials liked to take their breakfast. Betty continued to chase after them while waving what looked like a résumé in the air.

As soon as they had all disappeared into the diner, I made a mad dash for the library's front door and tapped frantically on the glass.

"*Let me in, let me in, let me in*," I whispered desperately.

Anne Lowery, the library's young and trendy IT tech, walked into the foyer, spotted me, and smiled.

Thank goodness.

"You're going to hate that you were late this morning," she said as she pushed open the door. "Why were you late, anyhow? Never mind why. Follow me. You're going to love what's happening. It's amazing. It's, you know, like the future, but today?"

"What is?" I asked.

What kind of bizarro world had I walked into? Why didn't Anne mention Rebecca's death or the fact that reporters were waiting at the library's entrance this morning?

Did no one in town know about Rebecca? I was about to ask Anne about it when I heard the murmur of voices coming from her office.

"It's unconventional"—Mrs. Farnsworth's whispery voice sounded uncharacteristically friendly—"but if you say it's a good idea . . ."

The rest of what she said and the deep-voiced reply were muffled, as if someone had closed a door.

"What's going on? Is someone getting the tour this morning?" I asked. Ever since the library's transition into a technology center, town leaders would ask Mrs. Farnsworth to give tours for business entrepreneurs in the hopes that they would locate their companies in Cypress. The most recent tour had been given to a start-up called Tech Bros. The company had taken over an old barn in the middle of a cotton field. No one was sure what the company hoped to produce in a termite-infested, rotting barn. The company hadn't hired many locals and had turned away any looky-loos who just happened to stop by. The two twentysomething co-CEOs had taken Mrs. Farnsworth's library tour twice already, both times scribbling notes on their tablet computers.

"Tech Bros," Anne said with a goofy smile.

"Again?" I started to ask why the CEOs might be so interested in our library. But Dewey was wiggling around in the tote bag I was carrying. "Oh! I'd better get this little guy downstairs before anyone comes this way. I'll be back in a few minutes."

"But—" Anne sounded disappointed that she wasn't going to be able to tell me all about the excitement brewing down the hall.

"Sorry." I hated to be rude but getting Dewey downstairs couldn't wait. "I'll be back in no more than fifteen minutes." She could tell me what was going on then. When Dewey got restless in his bag, he'd sometimes complain. And I mean he'd complain in a *loud* screeching voice.

He wiggled around as if winding himself up to fuss.

"I really need to get him settled." I hurried toward the back of the library, where a flight of stairs led to the basement.

I hadn't made it much farther than a bank of public computers when a large metal monster rounded a corner. It whirled and sputtered and made an odd sucking sound as it maneuvered itself directly into my path.

The shiny beast had two red LED lights for eyes. A series of green LED lights formed an openmouthed smile that looked more menacing than friendly. It had a large electronic screen for a chest. It rolled toward me, moving with surprising speed for a heavy machine that was slightly taller than my five feet six inches.

"This must be the surprise Anne was trying to tell me about," I muttered to myself. "I should have known. First, we go all digital. Naturally, the town manager would then bring in robots to replace the librarians. 'Why look,' she'll tell the CEOs of the companies she's trying to woo, 'there's nothing but computers in this library. Isn't it wonderful?' But it's not wonderful," I said to the robot bearing down on me. "You are faceless and mindless and scary."

I tried to step out of the robot's way.

The mechanical librarian adjusted its path to follow me.

"Shoo. Leave me alone."

It kept coming closer.

"Go away," I said, feeling like a fool for talking to a machine. "Back up. I need to get around you so I can go to the basement."

"In-tru-der," it answered in a flat metallic tone. Its chest lit up with INTRUDER written across it in bold red letters.

"No." I patted my own chest. "I'm a librarian."

Dewey stuck his head out of the tote bag, meowed worriedly, and then dove back inside when the robot lifted its vacuum hose of an arm as if pointing an accusing claw in our direction.

I backed away from the menacing thing until my legs bumped into a table.

But the robot continued to roll right at me. The sucking sound grew louder.

Was this how things were going to end for me? Done in by technology?

Chapter Seven

My cell phone pinged. Someone had sent a text. But I couldn't get to my phone to check my messages. I was too busy trying to keep away from that menacing vacuum-hose arm the killer robot was waving at me.

My cell phone kept pinging. And then my phone started ringing.

Mama Eddy, I guessed.

"In-tru-der," the robot said again in that flat, but chilling, metallic voice.

"No," I repeated, tapping my chest some more, as if that would make a difference. "Librarian. I work here."

It rolled closer, and I had nowhere to run. It had me cornered with a wall to one side and a table behind me. In a desperate attempt to avoid whatever it meant to do once it caught me, I climbed onto the table, pushed the tote bag containing Dewey until it was tucked behind my back, and then huddled next to one of the public computers.

By this time, my phone had stopped ringing. The call must have been sent to my voice mail. Another ping told me a text had arrived almost immediately after the ringing had stopped.

I hated to ignore whoever was desperately trying to get in touch with me. I worried it might be Jace with bad news about his mother. But I couldn't take the call or reach for my phone. The robot swung its massive vacuum-sucking arm at me.

"Hello? Anne? Anybody? Help!" I shouted, not caring that I was breaking Mrs. Farnsworth's cardinal rule of never raising my voice within her hallowed halls of literature. This was a life-and-death situation, after all!

"Tru? What in the world are you doing up on that table?" Anne asked when she found me. She scrunched up her nose as she peered in my direction. "And why are you shouting?"

"That . . . that . . . that . . ." I wagged my hand at the robot that was still trying to hit me with its vacuum-like arm.

Anne shook her head. In her hands was what looked like a game controller with a broken cord. She held it up as she walked closer.

"Anne, please, do something before I get chopped up by that oversized paper shredder." My voice squeaked. "Help me."

She hit a few buttons on her game controller. The robot's menacing red eyes went dark, and the loud sucking sound stopped, but its creepy green grin remained.

"What is that thing?" I demanded, shaking my finger at it. "And what is it doing here?" Dewey meowed and peeked his nose out of my tote bag again. He took one look at the robot and shot back down to the bottom of the bag for a second time.

"That . . . is . . . a . . . robot," Anne said slowly, as if she were speaking to a Neanderthal who had never witnessed the miracle of modern technology before. The IT tech, who was about a decade younger than me, often acted as if I grew up during the age of the dinosaurs. She loved her technology and was (sadly) one of the twenty-seven percent of Americans who hadn't read a book in the past year. She preferred podcasts. I felt sorry for her. "Actually, it's not simply a robot. It's a technological marvel," Anne said with a happy sigh. "It's the librarian of the future."

"*The what?*" I didn't want to believe that I'd heard that correctly, but what else could it be?

"I'm not whispering. If you can't hear me, I think you need to get your hearing checked. They say it starts to go once you reach a certain age." She raised her voice. "I said, it's the librarian of the future, or LIFU for short."

"Shh. You don't have to shout." I'd done enough shouting for the both of us. I expected Mrs. Farnsworth to arrive to scold us in any moment. "It's not that I can't hear you. It's that . . ." I waggled my finger at the robot again. "Why would a librarian of the future go around attacking people? That's not proper librarian behavior."

"It's all very advanced. I'll show you." She tapped the screen on its chest. It lit up with Cypress Library's catalog search page. "You can do your research right here. It'll send the books directly to your tablet or to your phone if you press this button." She pressed a red button next to the screen. The robot lurched forward. "Or perhaps this button." She pressed a green button next to the screen. The robot toppled over backward. It then whirled and sputtered as it tried—unsuccessfully—to right itself.

Seeing it lying on the ground like a turtle teetering on its back, I felt safe enough to climb down from the tabletop.

"It shouldn't have done that." Anne frowned at the machine as it continued to flail around. "It also vacuums and mops the floors and carries supplies. Plus, it has an advanced AI capacity."

When I continued to stare at her as if she'd lost her mind, she huffed. "AI means artificial intelligence, Tru, which means its programming acts like a human brain and can make decisions independent of its formal coding."

"I know what AI means, thank you very much. What I don't understand is why that thing was shouting 'intruder' at me. And why would a mechanical librarian chase me into a corner? What was it going to do to me?"

"Keven must have left it on night patrol duty. I just have to press this yellow button here."

"No! For goodness' sake, don't press any more buttons!"

Anne ignored me. She pressed the button.

I jumped back.

The robot screamed "INTRUDER!" as it shot a stream of yellow dust into the air. The powdery dust rained down on Anne.

"That's a theft deterrent measure," Anne said, sounding surprisingly calm for having just been covered from head to toe with the bright yellow dust.

I covered my mouth with my hand to hide my smile. I really shouldn't find any of this funny. But poor Anne suddenly looked like Big Bird, which was *kind of* funny. "We need a robot to patrol the halls to stop all those thieves who prey on our library? Yep. That makes sense." No, it didn't, but who was I to argue with Big Bird?

"Obviously, there are still some bugs that need to be worked out," said my yellow friend.

I handed Anne a couple of tissues. "If it's buggy, what in the world is it doing here? We open to the public soon."

She wiped her face with the tissue, which only smeared the yellow dust around without taking any off. "LIFU is a prototype for Tech Bros. You remember Keven and Trey, don't you? They're the company CEOs?"

"Yes, Anne, I remember who they are." Did she think I was becoming forgetful along with losing my hearing?

"Well then, you must understand that those two men need to give LIFU some real-world testing. And Cypress, with its state-of-the-art library, is the perfect place to test the machine. You would know all of this if you'd been on time this morning. Anyhow, Keven is the brains of the operation. He can make this robot sing. And I mean literally. You should hear LIFU sing."

"Please, I'm begging you, don't push any more buttons." I didn't want to see what else it could do. "I don't want to hear it do anything. How in the world did you get Mrs. Farnsworth to agree to let this . . . this . . . ?" I waggled my hands in its direction.

"It's not my doing." Anne frowned down at the robot again. "The mayor and the town manager were the ones who agreed. They're all in my office with Keven and Trey discussing the arrangement."

"Why don't you go back to your office? I'm sure how you look right now will convince Mrs. Farnsworth to send this metal monster and everyone else away," I said with a smile.

"But I don't want LIFU to go away."

"Really? Even after what it did to you?" I couldn't believe that. "It looks like that yellow stuff got on your computers too."

Anne whirled around in alarm and gasped when she saw how the row of public computers to the right of her was all tinged a bright yellow hue. "I bet it got onto the motherboard." She breathed loudly for a few moments before pasting on a fake smile. "It'll be okay. It's worth the inconvenience. It's not every day I get the chance to work with a genius like Keven. And LIFU is a marvel. You should hear Keven talk about the technology that's being used in it."

"Uh-huh." Dewey started wiggling around again. "I have to get to the basement."

"Wait. But I wanted to tell you—"

"Can't talk now," I said. Dewey stuck his head out of the bag. He looked ready to jump out and make himself at home upstairs, which I couldn't let happen. If Mrs. Farnsworth discovered I'd been sneaking a cat into her library . . . Well, I shuddered to imagine what she might do!

"I heard what happened at the book club last night," Anne said as she followed me toward the basement, leaving a trail that looked like pine pollen. "It's a shock, isn't it? Jace's mom? And Rebecca? The Star of Cypress will be sorely missed, won't she?"

Dewey looked at Anne and meowed as if he could understand her and was trying to provide kitty comfort, which I'd discovered sometimes involved a nip to the hand.

Anne smiled and scratched Dewey's head. "It's fitting that you adopted a kitty with a skull on his head seeing how death trails you around like it does. You found Rebecca's body, didn't you?"

"Death doesn't follow me around. And I don't know why everyone says Dewey has a skull on his head. He has tabby markings just like any other run-of-the-mill tabby cat. You know, stripes?" I kept heading toward the basement.

Anne ran in front of me and blocked my way with her bright yellow body. "Yes, his markings are stripes. But they also form what looks like a skull, and one of these days all this rule-breaking you're doing around the library will catch up to you, Tru."

I cringed. I'd long prided myself as a rule follower. Breaking the rules, even for a good cause, bothered me like a sore tooth. Anne knew all about my secret bookroom in the library's basement, a bookroom where I let Dewey stay when I was at work during the day.

She enjoyed teasing me about it, telling me she would expose my secrets if I didn't do her bidding. For a while I had lived in fear, thinking she would say something to Mrs. Farnsworth that would get me fired. But just a few months ago, Anne had gone out of her way to protect the secret bookroom, proving her teasing had been just that—teasing.

Anne looked down at my little kitty and cooed softly as she wiggled her bright yellow fingers in front of Dewey's face. His eyes darkened, and he lifted a paw to bat at her.

"Please, don't encourage him," I said, gently pushing him back into the tote bag. "Was Mrs. Farnsworth upset that I was late this morning?"

"What do you think? Whoops, you can ask her yourself."

Like a demon conjured by speaking her name, Mrs. Farnsworth rounded the corner.

Anne, bless her, put herself between Mrs. Farnsworth and the tote bag where Dewey wiggled impatiently.

When the wiggling didn't get him the attention he'd been hoping for, he let out a long, unhappy meow. Clearly, I was taking too long to get him down to the bookroom. He loved walking through the stacks and sniffing the books. Apparently, he enjoyed sniffing *some* books more than others, going by his odd behavior around those historical romances last night.

"Good morning, Mrs. Farnsworth," I said loudly to cover up my feisty kitty's complaints. "Another sunny day. And much warmer than it was last night, don't you think?" I knew I sounded like a ninny, but my sleep-addled brain couldn't think of anything clever to say. There really were two thoughts in my head at that moment—get my noisy kitty settled in his favorite place and prove that Hazel didn't kill Rebecca White. Neither of which were proper topics of conversation for my boss. "The forecast calls for rain, but I think they're wrong. Don't you agree? Gracious, when walking here this morning I didn't spot even one cloud in the sky."

Mrs. Farnsworth, dressed in conservative black, didn't say anything. She simply looked at me as if I'd lost my mind.

Anne poked me in the side hard enough to make me yelp.

"What in blue blazes has happened to *you*, Anne?" Thank goodness for Anne and her new bright yellow tint. Mrs. Farnsworth's attention had only stayed on me for that one very awkward moment.

Anne looked down at herself and acted as if she hadn't noticed that she looked like a giant banana until that very moment. "The LIFU glitched."

"That oversized robot thought I was an intruder," I said, rushing to Anne's defense. "Anne saved me when it tried to attack me."

"Attacked? Where's Keven?" Mrs. Farnsworth whirled around and started back toward Anne's office.

"Now, Mrs. Farnsworth." Gretchen Clark, the town manager as well as a member of the Arete Society, rounded the corner and blocked the head librarian's path back to Anne's office. "Just a moment ago, we all agreed that allowing LIFU to work at the library would provide good press for the town. Plus, it would be fun for the kids to interact with a robot."

"Did you see the mess it made?" My boss pointed at Anne. "And it attacked my librarians. Attacked them! This is unacceptable. What if it had attacked a patron? A child, even? Playing with the robot before the library opens is one thing. I cannot have these disruptions during operating hours. Just look at Ms. Lowery. She's yellow! Yellow! She's going to have to go home and change, taking time that she could have used to do her work."

"I understand, but—" Gretchen started to say.

"Oh, my stars!" a man with a thin mustache and wearing a tan porkpie hat exclaimed as he approached us. "It worked!"

"Shhh!" Mrs. Farnsworth hissed. "Please, don't forget you are in a library, Mr. Verner."

"How many times do I have to tell you to call me Keven, dear?" the man said in a near whisper. "It's just my excitement. It bubbles over. I've never seen the theft deterrent system deployed. It is amazing, don't you agree?"

"I don't know why you insist on having us whisper, Lida. The library isn't even open," Mayor Possey said as he joined the group.

His wife Annabelle had her arm looped through his. "Gracious sakes, Lida, what happened to your assistant?"

"Your husband's miracle of technology happened," Mrs. Farnsworth said in her whispery yet forceful voice. "And we keep our voices down inside these walls out of respect for the institution. This place deserves at least that much, especially after what y'all over at town hall have done to it. Removing all of the books and turning it into a glorified cybercafé, indeed." She clicked her tongue.

I looked at Mrs. Farnsworth, then at Gretchen, and finally at Annabelle. All three had been at Hazel's house last night. And yet none of them looked as if they'd lost any sleep over Rebecca's death. It was as if last night hadn't happened. Did life truly move forward so quickly for everyone?

It seemed as if they were more concerned about a robot that barely worked than they were about the murder of a neighbor. Granted, that robot had just turned one of us yellow, which was quite impossible to overlook. But still . . .

Weren't they upset that the president of their book club was dead? Hadn't they considered Rebecca their friend?

"Keven, dear," Annabelle said. "Perhaps if you made it look softer, more feminine, the robot wouldn't be so intimidating. You could put a big pink bow on its head."

"A bow? That is something we had not considered," Keven said.

"Well, you should," Annabelle pressed. "It would make a world of difference, I believe."

At the same time Gretchen turned to Mrs. Farnsworth. "You must agree that using LIFU suits the forward-thinking, technology-minded image Cypress is trying to project. Plus, we're supporting one of our first start-up businesses by letting our library be used as a proving ground. It's a win-win for Tech Bros and the town." Gretchen glanced in my direction. "Good morning, Tru. You missed the presentation." She then looked over at Keven and blushed. "It was spectacular. It's amazing what these young men have done."

None of the women were even talking about Rebecca or the shock they'd suffered last night. Shouldn't they be talking about her?

I could barely think of anything else.

"They are bringing the future to Cypress. It's exciting," Annabelle said. She too looked over at Keven and blushed. "Gretchen, are you available for lunch today? Maybe we could entice this young man to spend some time with us if we promise him a free lunch. I also think he would be a wonderful speaker for next month's Arete Society meeting."

"Oh, that's a splendid idea," Gretchen said. "Can we take you to lunch today, Keven?"

"I'll have to—" He looked over at the fallen robot and sighed. "I should say no, but for you two lovely ladies, I'll make an exception. You can buy my lunch."

Dewey wiggled impatiently in his tote.

Sorry, Dewey, I've not forgotten about you.

Keven turned to Mrs. Farnsworth. "My partner and I thank you from the bottoms of our hearts for letting us test out LIFU in your library," he said, with a tip of his hat.

Mrs. Farnsworth looked ready to object. But then Keven smiled at her. He was rather handsome.

"You are kind and wise." His smile grew. "I would not ask you to do anything that makes you feel uncomfortable. I am only asking that you give LIFU a chance. I will do anything you ask to make you feel assured of its safety, my dear Lida."

"I'm not saying you cannot test its operations here," Mrs. Farnsworth said, blushing a bit. "But the machine needs to be safe. Our patrons—"

"It will be. I promise. I will make the adjustments personally." He bowed with the flourish of a knight-errant, which made Mrs. Farnsworth smile in a funny way I'd never seen before. He then rushed over to Anne. "My dear girl." He took her bright-yellow-stained hands in his. "This is wonderful. You'll have to tell me exactly what happened and how it felt to be blasted by LIFU's theft detection powder."

Anne's cheeks turned deep red, or rather, a deep orange given the combination of red and yellow. Like Mrs. Farnsworth, Anne smiled stupidly up at the maker of that killer robot. "I . . . I . . ." she stammered. "It was amazing. How do I wash this off?"

"I'm afraid it is impossible. The yellow will stay for several days. That is the point of the dust. It stains the villain."

"What if it had stained one of our patrons?" I demanded, surprised I was being the voice of reason while Mrs. Farnsworth continued to smile and nod at Keven. "The library could have a lawsuit on our hands if that thing glitches and hurts someone."

"Naturally, Keven will turn off the patrol feature, won't you, Keven?" Gretchen said. She, too, wore an idiotic smile for the inventor.

Keven nodded somewhat absently and then squatted down next to the now lifeless LIFU. "It shouldn't have fallen over like this. Its gyroscope must have stopped working." He opened a panel and started fussing with the robot's insides.

"Can it be fixed?" Gretchen asked as she peered over his shoulder. Mrs. Farnsworth, Anne, and Annabelle were all hovering over the handsome inventor.

"Ladies, back up and let the boy do his work," Mayor Possey said sharply.

"I do have some adjustments to make," Keven said without looking up from the robot. "I am going to have to take it back to the factory."

"Good," I grumbled. I hoped he kept it at his factory forever.

Keven looked up at me. "Are you afraid of new

things?" His voice had a patronizing note to it. He smiled at me in a way that made me feel like I was a silly backwoods ninny.

"No," I protested. "No, I'm not afraid of new things." Which might have been a lie. I was rather partial to the comfortable and known. "I am, however, afraid of large mechanical creatures that attack me in my own workplace."

"It mistook Tru for an intruder," Anne explained needlessly. LIFU still had the word INTRUDER emblazoned across its screen in red block letters. "It wouldn't have happened if she had been here when the rest of us had our pictures scanned into LIFU's database."

I wished she hadn't reminded everyone that I was late to work. But there was a bigger issue. "That robot attacked me, even after I showed it that I posed no threat. Is that really what we want roaming the halls of our library? An armed Robocop?"

Mrs. Farnsworth seemed to seriously consider my question. "I'm not—" she started to say.

"I'll retool patrol mode," Keven said, his blazing smile back in full force. "I promise it will work better than ever when I bring it back."

Annabelle sighed loud enough that I could hear her from across the room. "Isn't he the best?"

The mayor helped Keven get the robot back onto its wheels. Together, the two men pushed the now deactivated robot toward the entrance. "Let me get the door for you," Mrs. Farnsworth offered as she ran after them.

"I can get the door. I'm closer," Gretchen said as she ran ahead of Mrs. Farnsworth.

"Oh, for gracious sake," Annabelle said as she tried to match the other ladies' speed. "I'm the one who should go. It is my husband who is helping Keven. And don't you ladies have jobs to do?"

I looked over at Anne.

"Aren't you going to join the race?" I asked her.

She shook her head. She was staring down at her bright yellow hands. "It's not going to come off?" she whimpered.

Dewey peeked his head out of his tote bag, looked at poor Anne, and meowed sympathetically.

Chapter Eight

———•———

The library's basement has always held secrets. During Prohibition in the 1920s, one area of the basement had been transformed into an elegant speakeasy with live music where the residents danced and drank bootlegged alcohol. During World War II, the basement had been renovated to accommodate a sturdy bomb shelter sporting thick walls and heavy double doors.

As I stood in front of those large doors, Dewey poked his head out from the tote bag to peer at me.

"Hold your whiskers," I said with a smile for my book-loving kitty. It always took me a moment to fish a set of keys from my pocket.

Mrs. Farnsworth might not trust me with the key to the library's front door, but she had assigned me as keeper of the keys to the storage areas in the basement. In all honesty, though, it really wasn't as big an honor as I'd often pretended. She had handed over the storage room keys so I could fetch items that she might want to use on the library's main floor such as tables, chairs, or bookshelves. Or if she needed me to sweep or mop up a mess.

It was amazing (and by amazing, I mean *gross*) how many children threw up at the library. I wouldn't mind if a robot took over that responsibility.

The heavy doors to the old bomb shelter opened with an ear-piercing *creeeeaaaak*. I made a mental note to find some oil for the hinges. Squeaky doors and secret bookrooms did not go together.

As soon as I was inside, Dewey jumped out of the bag and went straight to the fiction section. He rose onto his hind legs to stand like a person and then started to paw at the books on the shelves. He moved with care, as if searching for a particular title.

I left him to his browsing and set my second tote bag—the one filled with the returned library books—on the old and scarred circulation desk. I knew I couldn't linger long. Anne would come looking for me if I didn't make her a pot of strong coffee right away. That is, if she hadn't already taught the robot to do that.

We all had our peculiarities. Anne needed her coffee. I needed my books.

I planned to check back in and shelve the returned books after brewing the coffee and finishing any tasks that needed to be completed upstairs.

On my way out, Dewey jumped up onto the desk. With a quick swat, he managed to tip the books out of my bag and onto the floor. He jumped down and batted at the same paperback historical romances he'd attacked the night before.

"Stop that," I said. After gathering the books from the floor, I sniffed them. They must have an odor on them to explain Dewey's fascination with just those books. Like last night, I couldn't smell anything out of the ordinary. The books smelled like, well, books. Slightly musty and richly flavored with promise.

I placed them back on the desk and then hurried back

upstairs, fully expecting to find them on the floor again by the time I returned. Dewey, after all, was a cat. Need I say more?

Upstairs, I staffed the front desk while working on a children's program that was scheduled for a little later in the week. I sipped my coffee. I'd brewed it extra strong, but nothing would be strong enough to make up for a night with almost no sleep.

After yet another jaw-cracking yawn, I stared mindlessly at the handwritten notes in front of me. My hands remained idly wrapped around my warm coffee mug as I realized I wasn't going to get anything productive done. I looked toward the front door and then over to the large, gray institutional clock near Mrs. Farnsworth's office. The library had been open for a little over a half hour, and foot traffic had been unusually low. I yawned again. My eyes started to drift closed.

"Trudell! Why aren't you answering my calls?" a voice that was both whispery and angry startled me.

I jerked awake and fumbled for my phone. I'd completely forgotten about those texts and calls that had come through during the robot attack. How could I have forgotten them? What if Jace had been trying to get in touch with me? Lack of sleep had to be the reason for my forgetfulness. I was useless without a good night's sleep.

I scrolled through the notifications. All the texts and calls had been from one person.

I looked up to find that same person standing on the other side of the front desk with her hands on her trim hips and her perfectly painted red lips slightly pursed.

"I am sorry, Mama," I said. "Things have been crazy around here."

She glanced around. The library was nearly empty.

"And I barely got any sleep last night," I added.

She harrumphed at that.

"What's wrong?" I finally asked her.

"It's your daddy," she cried.

"You still haven't been able to get in touch with him?" According to Mama Eddy, my daddy lived to torment her. They'd been divorced for over two decades, but it didn't matter. They still hadn't figured out how to live in the same town without acting like it was a war zone.

"No, I haven't. He's gone! Disappeared!"

I reached for my phone. "I'll text him."

"Don't bother. I went to his house this morning after texting you. There's mail piled up on the front porch. And that nosy Mrs. Carsdale next door told me that she hadn't seen him for the past three days."

"That's . . . odd." Even though Mama Eddy had told me not to, I sent my father a text anyway asking him to give me a call. "Do you think we should call the police?"

"No! I mean, maybe? Just don't let your daddy know that I'm worried about him. He'll get all puffed up with conceit, and we all know that man has enough conceit as it is. But when you do find him, make sure to tell me. I have a bone to pick with that man."

She pivoted on her high heels with the grace of a ballerina and hurried out of the library.

I, dutiful (and *concerned*) daughter, gave the police station a call.

"Oh, hey, Tru," Janie Curry, the police dispatcher, said. "Saw that Jace's Jeep was parked in your driveway when I drove into work this morning. That boy must be cut up something awful about what happened at his mother's."

"He is," I agreed. "But why I'm calling is—"

"You know I can't tell you what's going on here," she whispered into the phone. "Wish I could. I know you're wanting to help and all. But Fisher already warned me that I need to keep my mouth shut around you."

"I understand, but I—" I tried again to report that my father was missing.

"You can try and try, Tru. But I can't tell you that the state forensics teams found Hazel's fingerprints all over the broken casserole dish and no one else's. Nor can I tell you that they're saying that Rebecca died of injuries sustained from a blow to the back of her head. Furthermore, I can't tell you that they found pages from a book, of all things, in the kitchen. And here's the odd part—it was a novel, not a recipe book. And Hazel says it's not hers, but if it is hers, it might prove motive."

"Wait. What was that last part? A book? What could that mean?"

"Do you have wax in your ears? I told you I can't tell you. But if you're on the case, I'm sure you're going to prove the experts wrong. Hazel is innocent, isn't she? Of course she is. That's why you're getting involved. Now, I'm going to hang up before Fisher comes over here."

"Wait! Don't do that. I need to report something. My—"

"Well, why in the world didn't you say so? Have you uncovered something interesting? I knew you would. I was just telling Cora that you were more effective than half the trained police force in the state. I bet you already know all about the stuff I'm not allowed to tell."

"Janie, please let me talk." I paused, fully expecting her to jump in and interrupt me before I could say more.

"Well, what are you waiting for, girl? Talk already."

I drew a breath. "My father seems to be missing. There's mail piled up on his porch, and his neighbor doesn't know where he went."

"Marianne doesn't know?" Janie gasped. "Well, that is worrying. That old busybody doesn't let anyone in her neighborhood walk much more than two steps out of their house before she gets the wheres and whats and hows of their plans. Don't worry your pretty head none. I'll make sure Fisher sends someone by your daddy's place to check things out. It's probably nothing." But she suddenly sounded just as worried as Mama Eddy had.

"Thank you." I disconnected the call and added "missing father" to my rapidly growing list of troubles.

Chapter Nine

———— · ————

I closed my eyes and tried to remember a time when the library had books, robots weren't chasing me, no one in town was ever murdered, and my father always answered my texts in under five minutes. Talk about a bunch of mis-shelved books! Nothing in my life seemed to be in its proper place.

My father wasn't at his beloved lake house. Hazel should have stayed in her kitchen last night. Mrs. Farnsworth was hiding in her office this morning instead of making sure the library was running properly, which really wasn't all that unusual. And Flossie. Dear book-club-obsessed Flossie. Where was she this morning? She should have come in by now. And why had she gone into Hazel's kitchen by herself last night? What about the second crash I'd heard? Flossie couldn't have hit Rebecca over the head with the casserole dish from her wheelchair, not unless Rebecca was already on the floor.

Oh dear, I was far too tired to organize that jumble.

"Merciful heavens, Tru! It looks like you smeared swamp mud under your eyes," Delanie cried.

My hand jerked as my heavy eyelids popped back open, and my coffee toppled over.

Delanie's light blue knee-length A-line dress swirled like a cloud around her as she skidded to a halt in front of my desk. "Didn't you get any sleep last night?"

"No, not really. And could you give a girl some warning before sneaking up on her like that?" I grabbed a few tissues out of the box on the desk and mopped up where I'd spilled my coffee on the mostly blank paper in front of me.

"Here. Let me help with that." Delanie, who looked as fresh as a cover model with her perfectly styled blond hair, dug around in her purse until she produced a small makeup compact.

"Thanks, but I have emergency cover-up in here somewhere," I said, reaching for my own purse.

"No, hon, this is *industrial* strength. I have it flown in directly from France. And you need it. Believe me, you need it. A few dabs will perk you right up."

Since she insisted, I took the compact. The makeup might hide my puffy eyes, but nothing short of a text message from my daddy and a full night's sleep would perk me up. Still, I looked in the compact's tiny mirror. (Yikes, I looked worse than I had when I'd left the house.) I quickly dabbed the makeup under my eyes and then tried to hand it back to Delanie.

She refused to take it. "You need to keep that so you can reapply throughout the day."

"Are you sure you won't need it?" Surely, after the shock we had all suffered last night, she should have to apply the cover-up as heavily as I had.

"No, dear, I had my beauty sleep. Never miss it."

"How?" How had she managed to sleep? "Aren't you upset over—?" I looked around the empty library before whispering, "Over what happened last night?"

"Of course I'm upset. I went home in a state of total shock. I considered Rebecca a dear, dear friend. Everyone in the book club did. But I took one of those tiny little blue pills the doctor gave me a few years ago for my nervous condition and ended up sleeping like the dead." She paled. "Poor choice of words."

"Wait. Rebecca was a dear friend of yours?" Something about that didn't ring true. "Last night, Rebecca's death seemed like an inconvenience to everyone, save for Marigold, who was clearly grieving. Am I missing something?"

"Tru, what did you want us to do? Scream and pull at our hair?" She smiled kindly at me. "That's not how we act in the South, and you of all people should know that. We present a strong front. Hollywood even made a movie about it, *Steel Magnolias.*" Delanie sighed. "Rebecca could have been as great as any of the actresses in that movie, if only she hadn't walked away from her acting career."

"Why *did* she walk away from acting and move to Cypress?" I asked. "Did she know anyone here?"

Instead of answering me, Delanie waved at Gwynne Hansy and Marigold Brantley, who were coming into the library. Gwynne told us that she was coming in to have a coffee. She had a gleam in her eyes and a sly smile that I took to mean that she was anxious to share what she saw last night at Hazel's with the gossipy bunch that liked to gather in the library's new café. Marigold was heading in the other direction. She held up a tote bag. "My sewing machine has never worked right," she told us. "I have some mending to do, and the sewing machines in the makerspace are computerized, which makes everything that much easier."

I wasn't sure about that, but I told her to come get me or Anne if she needed any help. She assured us that she knew what she was doing and hurried away.

"Life goes on," Delanie murmured as she looked over at Mrs. Farnsworth's closed door. "Was Lida upset this morning? She does hate having to deal with any kind of drama. My poor friend doesn't know what to do with those kinds of emotions."

"What kind of emotions?" I asked. "Were Rebecca and Mrs. Farnsworth close friends as well?"

"Goodness, no," Delanie blurted without hesitation. "Lida had no patience for Rebecca's . . . um . . . strong personality. Especially not after she'd taken over the Arete Society. Granted, Lida had no desire to lead it. Too much drama, you know. But she hated how Rebecca had turned the book club into her personal fan club of sorts."

"How do you mean?" I asked.

"Oh, you know." Delanie gave an elegant flick of her wrist. "Rebecca liked to talk about her life in New York or Hollywood. I enjoyed hearing about her exciting, fast-lane lifestyle," she quickly added. "Her moving to Cypress added a bit of glamour to our lives, don't you agree? She will be sorely missed."

Would she? She wasn't a frequent visitor to the library. I couldn't remember ever speaking with her before last night.

At Hazel's, Rebecca had mentioned her work on the soap opera a few times. I found it interesting, but I suppose after a few book club meetings her musings about her former life as an actress might be annoying. If Mrs. Farnsworth didn't enjoy listening to Rebecca's jaunts down memory lane, others in town probably felt the same way. Had someone gotten annoyed enough with our former small-screen star to silence her completely?

That didn't seem likely.

"Keep dabbing on that makeup while I go knock on Lida's door and check on her."

"Wait. I—" I said. I wanted to ask her some more questions about the book club members.

"I know, dear," Delanie said with a wave, "you don't have to tell me. Lida doesn't want to be disturbed. But she'll thank me for rushing by to warn her."

"Actually, I was going to ask about—"

"Yes, dear. Unfortunately, you do need the makeup. Quite a bit more, in fact." She pointed to her own left eye. "Especially there."

It felt like I'd put on too much already, but Delanie always looked amazing, so I dabbed more of her magical concealer on under my eyes. I liked how it made my skin feel tingly. And I wasn't sure if it was my imagination or not, but it seemed to make me feel more awake. "What do you need to warn Mrs. Farnsworth about?"

"Haven't you heard?" she asked over her shoulder as she knocked on Mrs. Farnsworth's office door. "The coroner has officially ruled Rebecca's death a homicide. The police will be coming by to question Mrs. Farnsworth." She knocked on the door again. "They are going to question all of the other book club members. Again. Can you imagine?"

"Did Rebecca have any enemies?" I tried again to ask, but Delanie had already pushed open the door to Mrs. Farnsworth's office. She stepped through the door without waiting for Mrs. Farnsworth's invitation.

I suppose there was nothing wrong with her boldness. While I would never barge into Mrs. Farnsworth's office (the head librarian would lecture me for hours about how she needed to be left alone so she could perform her duties), Delanie had been Mrs. Farnsworth's dearest friend since childhood. She could dance a jig while singing at the top of her lungs in the middle of the library, and Mrs. Farnsworth would do nothing more than laugh. Not that

Delanie would ever do either of those things. She was much too refined a lady to dance a jig.

I leaned forward and tried to listen in on Delanie and Mrs. Farnsworth's conversation. Mrs. Farnsworth was complaining that the police should have taken better notes last night, since she'd been thorough with her answers, when my cell phone rang.

"Tru." It was Jace calling. "We need to talk."

"What's wrong? What's going on?" He sounded worried.

"Fisher has arrested my mother. My father is still eight hours out. I just got off the phone with him. He's getting ready to head home now. But even when he gets here, there's nothing he can do. My mom is being taken to the police station right now. She's alone." His voice cracked with emotion.

"Where's her lawyer?" I asked, alarmed to hear that Hazel didn't have her legal representation with her.

"Oh, the lawyer is with her."

"Thank goodness." I breathed a deep sigh of relief.

"But I'm still worried. Fisher wouldn't tell me any details because I'm not allowed to be involved with the investigation. But he did say that things looked bad. And he's put me on leave and told me to stay away from the police station until . . . well, I don't know if he'll ever let me come back. He told me that I'd be fired on the spot if I tried to interfere."

"Where are you now?" I asked him.

"At home." I heard his dog, Bonnie, bark in the background. "But I can't stay here and wait for the police to carry out their investigation. I have to do something. This is my mother we're talking about."

"Delanie just told me that someone—I'm guessing Detective Ellerbe—will be coming by to ask some additional questions. You stay put and let me see what I can find out. We can compare notes when I get off work."

There was a long pause before he said, "I don't know if I can wait that long."

"I don't think you have a choice. Not if you want to keep your job. Let me help you."

"But Tru . . ." he started to say, then sighed. "I've never liked to be sidelined. Not in football and definitely not now when someone I love needs my help. I need to do something."

"Well, I do have something important that you can do." I explained to him how my father had gone missing.

"Oh, Tru, I'm so sorry. You must be beside yourself with worry."

I was. "But I'm not so distraught that I cannot help you and your mother. Let me help you." Investigating Rebecca's murder was a good way to take my mind off wondering why Daddy *still* hadn't returned my text.

"I suppose I could do that. You find out what really happened at my parents' house last night, and I'll go searching for your wayward father. I'll start out by heading over to his house to see if there's anything there that might explain where he's gone." Jace sounded relieved to have an important task to keep him busy.

"I can't tell you how much that would mean to me. Oh, I've got to go. Flossie has just come in the door. There are a few things I need to ask her." Perhaps she'd tell me more about that second crash I'd heard. And the pages of a book the crime scene techs found. Did she know anything about that?

Flossie, dressed in various shades of pink, wore a look of determination as she rolled toward the front desk.

"I'll call if anything happens," I told Jace. "Otherwise,

meet me at my house after the library closes, and we can compare what we've found."

"Have him bring dinner. I'm in the mood for fried chicken from the Grind," Flossie said, too loud for inside a library. "Enough for five."

I was sure he heard her, so I didn't repeat it. "Keep the faith," I told him instead. "We'll get through this."

I prayed my words were true.

Chapter Ten

————— • —————

I thought you might need an extra pick-me-up this morning," Flossie said once I'd disconnected the call with Jace. She placed a steaming hot coffee from Perks on the desk in front of me.

"I do." I took a deep sip. Tori's coffee shop brewed the best coffee in the state. "And perfect timing too. I just spilled my cup."

"Glad to help. It's Tori's special eye-opener blend." Flossie tilted her head to one side. "Are you wearing makeup? Is that for Jace? Or is there some other reason you're all smartened up?"

"Smartened up?" I laughed at the term. "Delanie told me to put the concealer on. She made it sound like I'd scare away the patrons if I didn't."

"There's no way you could look as bad as that. You're as cute as a kitten, even on your worst days. Did you have a bad night's sleep, dear?"

"More like a no-night's sleep."

"I thought you might." She tapped the desk next to the drink she'd brought for me. "Sleep deprivation can make a girl's eyes puffy." Flossie rolled away from the desk and then started to swing around a large, spiked metal ball on a chain. "That's why I always make sure to have eight hours." She swung the spiked ball one way. "Even when I'm under deadline. I stop myself from writing in order to give myself eight hours." She swung the spiked ball another way. "Science recommends that—"

"What's going on here? What in the world is that?" I demanded after having to practically duck under the desk when the spiky ball arced in my direction. The memory of seeing Rebecca dead on the floor after being knocked upside the head with a casserole dish had already made me flinchy.

Did Flossie have that weapon with her last night? (I cannot tell you how much I hated myself for even thinking *that*.)

"Oh, this thing?" Flossie pretended to be surprised that anyone would notice that she was flinging around a deadly weapon. "It's called a meteor hammer. Isn't it a beauty? It was used in ancient China. This one isn't ancient, mind you. It's a replica, and not at all valuable."

She gave it another swing. "Whoa, this is harder than they make it look in the YouTube videos."

"What's it for?" I asked while ducking under the desk again to get out of the spiky ball's path.

"Never you mind," she said, which meant she was researching her next book. This wasn't the first time she'd come into the library with a strange weapon. In the past couple of years, she had brought in things like throwing darts, a claymore, and a boomerang, all in the name of research.

"Don't hit anyone with it," I warned. A few months ago, she'd struck Delanie in the back of her head with the boomerang. Flossie had claimed it was an accident, and I'm sure it was . . . *maybe*. The two of them had been arguing at the time about who wrote the best mysteries—Agatha Christie or Sir Arthur Conan Doyle. Like me, Flossie has been and always will be on Team Agatha. She'd been trying to convince Delanie that while Sherlock Holmes had been described time and again as a genius, his stories hadn't withstood the test of time as well as those featuring the deductive prowess of either Miss Marple or Inspector Poirot.

Delanie had refused to listen to reason.

A few seconds later the boomerang had slipped from Flossie's hands—or so she'd claimed—and whacked Delanie in the back of her head.

Flossie had a temper. Plus, she had been alone in the kitchen with Rebecca for a few moments before I rushed into there. And I had heard a second crash.

Certainly Flossie hadn't—?

"You didn't bring that meteor thingy with you to the book club last night, did you?" I asked.

"Are you kidding? I was trying to convince the other members that I was Arete Society material. You know I didn't bring it." She started to fling it around again. "Not that it mattered."

"Perhaps you could practice mastering your weapon later?" I ducked as it came at me again. "Jace just called to tell me they've arrested Hazel. His father is eight hours out, and even if he were here, I doubt he could do anything other than worry as much as Jace is worrying. And the police chief won't let Jace investigate. So, he's out searching for my daddy, who has suddenly gone missing. While he does that, our attentions need to be focused on how to prove Hazel didn't kill Rebecca even though the evidence really makes it look as if she did. What was that crash I heard shortly after you went into the kitchen?"

"Crash?" Flossie frowned as she shook her head. "I-I

might have knocked over a dish when I ran my wheel-chair into the kitchen counter. I don't really remember. Seeing the kitchen in such disarray had flustered me."

"The only mess in the kitchen was the casserole on the floor." *Along with Rebecca*, I didn't add. "The rest of the dishes were in perfect order."

"They were? Well, I must have knocked something over if you heard a crash. What do you need me to do to help Hazel?"

I stared at Flossie. My friend, who could remember every detail of every trip she'd ever taken, should have been able to remember the state of Hazel's kitchen last night. I then looked at the weapon she still had in her hand. Did I wonder if she might have swung the meteor hammer in frustration and accidentally killed Rebecca?

No. No. That couldn't be possible.

"Did you see a novel on the kitchen floor?"

"A novel?" Flossie asked, but she wouldn't look me in the eyes. "Why would there be a novel in Hazel's kitchen? The book they were reading this month was a biography."

"I don't know why there'd be a novel on the floor. I certainly didn't notice it. But the crime scene techs found some pages of a novel, at least that's what Janie let slip when I called to report my father's disappearance."

"Hmm . . ." Flossie shuddered. "I don't know. I didn't see much beyond the mess. I suppose it could be a clue."

"It must be," I said. "I'll ask Hazel about it as soon as I can. It's a shame you didn't see it there, so I could mention the title to Hazel. Janie has been instructed not to tell me anything about the investigation."

"How rude. I bet Fisher is worried you're going to upstage him for a third time. People will start to wonder if the man is even capable of doing his job."

"He's not capable of investigating murders, he doesn't

have the staff or the technology. That's why he calls in the state to help. He shouldn't get upset that I'm lending a hand too."

"Your blossoming popularity burns him up something fierce, though. And you know it. We're lucky he's not been taking his jealousy of you out on Jace."

"Yeah, I'm lucky," I mumbled, remembering how Jace had been acting secretive lately. Was our relationship falling apart even before it really got started? Did Fisher know about our floundering relationship? I was about to ask Flossie for dating advice, but she had turned her attentions back to the murder investigation, which was what I needed to be focusing on as well.

"Besides us, Hazel was the only other person in the house." Flossie frowned at the spiky meteor hammer. "But I can't imagine Hazel harming anyone. Yes, we do need to figure out how to help her. I suppose I could hone my flinging skills later." Flossie gave the meteor hammer one more swing. I had to dive out of the way to keep from getting whacked in the kneecaps. "There must be something wrong with its balance. It doesn't go anywhere I want it to." She weighed the ball and chain in her hands for a moment and then slid it into the tote bag she kept hanging from the arm of her wheelchair. "For Hazel's sake, I can worry about its construction later. The poor dear must be devastated. Should we head downstairs to discuss how we can prove her innocence?"

"I want to. But my Wednesday morning Moms and Tots program begins in ten minutes. I can join you afterward. If you'll excuse me, I need to go read about a cranky rabbit before helping the kids create their own cranky animals out of recycled materials."

"Ah, that explains the pink milk-jug pig sitting beside the stapler. It's scowling at me."

"She *is* mighty cranky," I agreed.

As we were talking, a steady stream of mothers led their children past the front desk, all heading in the direction of the children's area.

"Looks like you're going to have a full house today," Flossie said with a nod toward the brightly colored room, which was growing louder by the moment.

"That cranky little rabbit is one popular gal." I glanced at the cover of the rabbit book and noticed that its kaleidoscope of bold colors resembled the kind of tie-dyed dresses that Flossie often wore. "You didn't happen to write and illustrate this book, did you?"

"If I did, would I tell you?" she said with a sly smile.

"No, you tell us nothing about your writing life." I honestly wished she would. We were friends. Plus, she knew I could be trusted with a secret. After all, I'd been successfully keeping a giant whopper of a secret directly under our feet. "You do know you can trust me, right?" I said quietly.

"Don't be silly. Of course I trust you."

"Then why—?"

"Fine. Fine. I didn't write that book. I wish I had. It has probably one thousand words, tops. I could write that many words with my eyes closed. And yet the cranky rabbit book has outsold most of the full-sized novels on the best-seller list."

"Care to name the title of one of those best sellers that you wrote?" I asked. From the sparse details Flossie had let slip over the years, I knew she had written at least a few thriller novels.

Flossie wagged her finger at me. "You know I can't answer that."

"Can't or won't?"

"Honey, take your pick," she said with a laugh.

At the same time, a shout came from the children's

room. And then a crash. "I'd better go take charge. Will you still be around in an hour?"

"I'll be in my regular spot in the basement. Maybe I'll use the time while waiting for you to practice my skill with the meteor hammer some more."

A vision of toppled bookcases and scattered books suddenly flashed before my eyes. The aisles in the secret bookroom weren't wide enough to give Flossie proper space to fling her weapon around. "Please, don't."

"If I don't practice, I'll never get better."

"Practice outside. Away from people. And books. Away from books," I said as I hurried away. I hoped she would heed my advice.

I also hoped Flossie had nothing to do with Rebecca's demise.

The cranky rabbit book was indeed a hit. After the reading, the preschoolers managed to get glue everywhere as they created their own adorably grouchy creatures. All in all, the program had been a smashing success. I smiled as I scrubbed up glue (How in the world did those gobs of glue end up on the windows?) while the mothers and their adorable tots moved to other areas of the children's room to play with the computers or find a tablet that had been loaded with picture ebooks.

I still hadn't given up on trying to get the mayor and town administrator to agree to return hardcover picture books to the children's room. Young children needed to hold books in their hands, not tablets. But for the moment, I was concentrating on cleaning up the sticky messes the kids had made.

"There's a mountain of glue on that table over there," Sissy Philips said as she thrust her finger toward the table

where her twin boys and their baby sister had been playing. Her boys were dancing around her, tugging at her
arms, whining about wanting ice cream. Her daughter
plopped down on the floor and started to suck her thumb.
A thumb, I noticed, that was drenched in the (*thankfully*
nontoxic) glue the library had provided for the project.

"Thanks for the heads-up." I went back to scrubbing
the glue off the window. Sissy and I were not—nor had
we ever been—friends. In high school, she'd been the
popular beauty queen with perfect clothes and makeup.
I'd been the bookworm. Now, all these many years later,
she still wore perfect clothes and perfect makeup. And I
was still a bookworm. But unlike in high school, she
clung to her popularity with an ugly desperation that
made me feel sad for her.

Although we clearly had nothing more to say to each
other, she didn't leave.

I scrubbed harder.

She huffed a few times.

"Is there something else you want to tell me?" I finally asked.

She tilted her head to one side as if posing for a camera. "You want to talk to me," she said.

I glanced over my shoulder at her. "I do?"

"*I'm* a member of the Arete Society," she said with a
note of pride in her voice. Not the good sort of pride,
either, but the kind ministers liked to warn us about
from their Sunday pulpits.

I set the cleaning rag on the window ledge and turned
to her. *Really? I didn't realize you could read* were the
unkind words I kept locked behind my teeth. "But you
weren't at Hazel's last night," I said instead. Nor did any
of the members mention Sissy or take note of her absence. They *had* noticed Emma Guerin's absence.

"Well, I . . . I'm not officially a member. Not yet.

Rebecca had invited me to come to last night's meeting, but I decided to stay home. Because, well, I thought my presence might be awkward for you."

"Awkward?" What was she talking about?

"I was doing you a kindness. You know, since the meeting was being held at Hazel's house?"

"Yes?" I asked, still not understanding why she felt like I wouldn't want her to come to the meeting.

"Really, Tru? You can't be that dense." She huffed when I continued to stare blankly at her. "I mean, it wouldn't have been fair for you to have to sit in your boyfriend's mother's house next to me." She ran a hand down her snug sweater and form-fitting jeans and then tapped her blue high-heeled boots against the terrazzo floor. "Hazel would look at this and despair that her son didn't end up with me. Half the town expected us to get married after high school. So, you'd understand why Hazel would end up hating you for being, well, your dowdy sweater-set self when compared with me."

Really? This was the kind of thing Sissy thought about? "Sweater sets are practical for work. I wasn't wearing a sweater set last night."

"Good for you," Sissy said in a condescending way that made my cheeks feel hot.

"What do you want, Sissy?" I asked, tired of her games. "I'm busy."

"What do I want?" She chuckled.

"Other than Jace," I said somewhat unkindly. But she couldn't have him since she was married and Jace had enough self-respect to keep himself away from bored housewives. At least, I thought he did.

"I was going to help you with your little investigation, but if you're going to be rude . . ." She started to walk away.

Good riddance.

Who needed her?

I could solve this murder with my eyes closed.

Scratch that last thought.

And the one before that.

Hazel needed our help.

So did Jace.

"Wait," I said, hoping I wouldn't regret calling her back. "How well did you know Rebecca?"

"Rebecca was a star. A real star." She sniffled a little. "And I understand why you might be rude to me. I've heard talk around town that Jace is growing restless. I heard he's going out at night . . . without you." She tsked. "That has to hurt."

"Sissy," I said sharply. Her words had hit the mark, especially since she'd echoed the worries I was already having. "What did you want to tell me about Rebecca?"

"Oh, Rebecca. I'm going to miss her. She recognized quality when she saw it. That's why she befriended me."

"Sissy," I warned.

"She told me the Arete Society needed younger members."

I nodded.

"She told me that she planned to push out some of the members to make room for new, fashionable members like myself."

"I see."

"I don't think you do. Joey! Stop punching your brother!"

"Okay, Sissy. I'll take the bait. What don't I see?"

"I like Hazel. She's always been kind to me. I don't want her blamed for something she wouldn't do. Hazel was one of the newer—not younger, but *newer*—fashionable members that Rebecca had handpicked. Plus, Hazel would never commit a murder before a dinner party. She would have waited until the party was

over. Anyone with any kind of party-planning experience would know that. But if some of the other members
discovered what Rebecca had intended to do last night—
you know, kick them out of the book club—they would
have had ample motive to kill off the book club's president *before* the meeting started."

"Who?" I asked. "Who was upset?"

"I don't know, exactly. Rebecca didn't give me names.
Is this how you solve mysteries? You have others do the
work for you? I should have known you weren't as clever
as everyone says you are."

"What makes you think other members of the book
club might know what Rebecca was planning?" I asked,
focusing on helping Hazel instead of on Sissy's insults.

"Well, I knew because Rebecca told me. We were
close like that. We texted each other all the time. In one
of her last texts she assured me that she would make
room for me in the society. It said that she was going to
kick someone out of the club at last night's meeting to
make space for me. But I think someone else in the club
also knew about Rebecca's plans. You see, I found a note
someone had slipped through my mail slot yesterday
morning, warning me to skip the meeting. I assumed
because it would be awkward to be there when the person I was replacing was being told to leave." She leaned
closer to me. "If you must know, I think Rebecca was
going to kick out Marigold Brantley. She was so clingy
around Rebecca. And she isn't the least bit fashionable.
She comes to events dressed as if she's just walked off
the farm, which is ridiculous. Her family doesn't own a
farm, and they don't even have the feed and seed store
anymore. Why in the world does she dress like that?
Anyhow, she acted as if she was Rebecca's best friend.
So embarrassing for Rebecca."

"Do you have the note with you?" I held out my hand.

"No, of course not. Why would I carry something like that around with me?"

I closed my hand into a fist and lowered my palm. As much as I wanted to get my hands on her note, I forced myself to do the right thing. "You need to call Detective Ellerbe and tell him what you just told me and give him that note and show him your texts," it hurt to say.

"But I told you," she whined.

"And I'm telling you to take what you know to the authorities. If I text you the detective's phone number, will you promise me that you'll call him?"

"I'm not a child," she said. "I don't have to promise you anything."

Then stop acting like one. I didn't say that. Nor did I say, *And stop whining.* Instead, I said the one thing I thought would persuade her to do the right thing. "I was hoping you'd refuse to cooperate. Do you really think I want you helping Jace or his mother? Honestly, I don't want you having anything to do with him."

"Well, if that's how you feel." With a huff, she pulled her children out of the children's room. But as she made her way through the library, I saw that she was checking her phone.

I texted her Ellerbe's contact information. There were still no texts from my father.

Sissy didn't spend much time studying the messages on her screen before placing a phone call. I hoped it was to Detective Ellerbe. But even if it wasn't, that was okay too. I already planned to call Ellerbe myself and provide him with a few specific questions he should ask Sissy.

Hopefully, with Sissy's help, he would finally start looking beyond Hazel for a murder suspect.

I yawned deeply and pulled out Delanie's compact to dab some more cover-up under my eyes. It really did make me feel better.

Chapter Eleven

———— • ————

Detective Ellerbe arrived at the library to personally interview the Arete Society members for a second time instead of sending one of his officers to do the task for him. He headed straight for Mrs. Farnsworth's office without even glancing over toward the front desk where I was working.

"I think he did that on purpose," I whispered to Flossie, who had come back upstairs—thankfully without her weapons—and was sitting at the table with me.

"He's embarrassed," Flossie said.

"He knows we're going to prove him wrong," I said.

"No, Tru," Ellerbe said over his shoulder. "The facts aren't on your side this time."

"The man must have eagle ears. Are eagle ears a thing?" I'd have to look that up. I mean, I knew eagles had ears. I just wasn't sure if an eagle's hearing was sharp enough to warrant an idiom.

"The saying is eagle eyes, dear, not ears," Flossie whispered.

"Oh, right. That makes more sense." And I knew that.

My lack of sleep must have dulled my ability to think properly. "You cannot even see an eagle's ears."

Ellerbe turned, looked at us, and shook his head.

"Be careful, Detective. You might think you know what happened at Hazel's house last night. And yet 'there is nothing more deceptive than an obvious fact,'" I said.

"Very nice," Flossie said, beaming at me with pride. "Sir Arthur Conan Doyle wrote that, did he not?"

"He did," I answered, feeling smug that I was able to pull out an appropriate literary quote despite my desperate need for sleep.

"I would have preferred an Agatha Christie quote," Flossie said. "How about this one? 'Instinct is a marvelous thing. It can neither be explained nor ignored.'"

"That works too," I said. "My instincts are telling me that Hazel didn't commit the crime. And yet the police arrested her this morning. A travesty of justice, don't you agree, Detective?"

"We're not living in one of your confounded books," Ellerbe grumbled before heading into Mrs. Farnsworth's office.

About fifteen minutes later, he emerged. Flossie had left to help a patron use the card catalog in the secret basement bookroom. Our younger patrons had no idea how to look up a book the analog way.

"That was fast, Detective," I said as he approached the front desk. I dabbed a little more of Delanie's cover-up under my eyes.

"These are follow-up interviews. They don't take nearly as long." He tilted his head to one side and studied me for a moment. "Are you okay, Tru?"

"I didn't get much sleep last night," I admitted as I continued dabbing the makeup under my eyes. "I think it's making me loopy."

"No, I don't think that's it. Your hands are shaking. I don't think they were shaking like that when I came in. And your eyes are jittering around. How much caffeine have you had this morning?"

"How much—?" While trying to remember, I closed my eyes.

Ah, that felt nice. Like floating on the water as gentle waves rocked me.

"Tru?" Ellerbe rapped on the front desk with his knuckles.

I woke up with a jerk. "Sorry. I think I dozed off there for a moment. What were you saying?"

"I was asking about how much caffeine you've had. Some of those energy drinks have too much and aren't really that safe to drink."

"I only had a few cups of coffee. Maybe three?"

"Four," Anne corrected as she hurried past.

"Four," I amended. "But that's only three more than I usually have."

He crouched down until he was eye level with me. "Have you taken any new medications?"

"No. I rarely take anything more than headache medicine. Why?"

"Because I think you've overdosed on something."

"You think I—?" Now that he mentioned it, I did feel overly warm. My heart seemed to be beating faster than usual, but I'd assumed it was just my anxiety over trying to prove Hazel innocent. "That's ridiculous," I said as I hid my trembling hands underneath the desk. "I heard the forensics team found some pages of a novel in the kitchen. I don't remember seeing them. Where were they? Which book were they from?"

"Who told you that? You shouldn't know anything about that." He stood back up. "And we're talking about you and your strange behavior, not the investigation."

"There's nothing wrong with me that a good night's sleep won't solve."

He didn't look convinced, but he let the matter drop. "So you are poking your nose into my investigation," he said.

Why deny it? "Yes. I'm investigating. But by the sound of things, I don't think my nose will be anywhere near *your* investigation."

"'If you place your head in a lion's mouth, then you cannot complain one day if he happens to bite it off,'" Ellerbe said.

"Did you just quote Agatha Christie to me?" Because it sure sounded like he had.

He smiled. "I figured it would be the only way to get you to listen to me." He leaned in closer. "And did it work? Are you listening?"

"I hear you," I hedged. There was no way in the world that I wasn't going to keep asking questions and investigating.

He grimaced. "That's what I figured. Whatever you do, be careful. I don't want anyone to get stabbed or shot or whatever else trouble you and your friends have found in the past. Do you hear me?"

"Loud and clear." I saluted him with my trembly hand. "But you have to understand, Detective, Rebecca died at Hazel's house while I was there. Something about the circumstances surrounding her death doesn't feel right. It's like when I find a book that's been put on the wrong shelf. I can't rest until I put that book back where it belongs."

He gave a sharp nod. "In that case, I have two requests."

"Sure. Shoot."

"First, share whatever you learn with me. I'm just as interested in figuring out what exactly happened at Hazel's house last night as you are."

It was my turn to press my lips together. "I'll try" was the best I could promise. "What's the second thing?" I asked before he attempted to perform one of his Jedi mind tricks on me and pry out of me a promise to tell him everything I learned. He could be awfully persuasive when he wanted to be.

"I need you to take care of yourself, Tru." His brows crinkled with concern again.

"Always." I crossed my fingers as I said it. In the past, I hadn't always been careful. The last time I tried to solve a murder, things went horribly wrong and Jace had almost died. "Did Sissy Philips contact you?" I asked, deciding to change the subject to something I wanted to talk about.

His brows crinkled even further. "I believe someone by that name left a message on my phone."

"You need to talk to her. Even though she wasn't at Hazel's last night, she told me she had been invited and had been told she would soon be a member of the Arete Society. She also mentioned several other things that might help with your investigation."

"What did she tell you?" He sounded wary.

"Well, apparently, Rebecca was planning to kick out a few members of the club last night to make room for some younger blood. And Sissy thinks Marigold Brantley, who was apparently one of the members who were going to be removed last night, should rank pretty darn high on your suspect list. See? I can share information."

"Never doubted that you could. I'll give your friend Sissy a visit right now." He rapped on the desk again before he headed for the door. "And please, Tru, take care of yourself."

"Tru?" Jace sounded worried.

I opened my eyes. I must have been dreaming. Either

that, or someone had installed a roller coaster in the middle of the library. Knowing Anne and some of her outlandish ideas, she *would* put a roller coaster in a library. On the upside, an amusement ride would be better than an aggressive robot with a creepy smile. And the kids would love it. My eyes slid closed again.

"Tru?" Jace repeated louder.

Mrs. Farnsworth shushed him.

"Ellerbe called me, Tru. He told me he was worried about you," he said, speaking softer.

"What? Why?" I jerked my head up. My heart was beating extremely hard again. Or perhaps it had never stopped thudding as if it were being abused by a deranged drummer. "I'm fine. I'm overly tired, but I'm fine."

"You don't look fine." That was Mrs. Farnsworth speaking. She'd come out of her office and was standing next to Jace with her arms akimbo. "You look like you have your finger in an electric socket. Your entire body is shaking. What's wrong with you?"

"I need a nap," I said.

Jace hooked his hands under my arms and pulled me to my feet. "I'm going to drive you over to the urgent care center to get you checked out." He paused and looked over his shoulder at Mrs. Farnsworth. "If that's okay with you, ma'am."

"Go. Go. She's no use to me here, not looking like that."

Cypress's small rural hospital had closed several years ago. Luckily, an urgent care center had opened recently in the strip mall next to the laundromat, giving residents access to some desperately needed health care services.

My racing heart rate got me admitted into the urgent care center's examination room straightaway.

"Did you take something to wake yourself up?" Jace asked.

I curled up on my side on the elevated table. The paper covering made loud crinkling sounds. "I drank a couple of extra cups of coffee. And I'm tired. We didn't get any sleep last night. I can't do that. Can't stay up all night. Never could." I yawned. "I need my sleep."

He frowned. "We'll see what the doctor has to say."

Apparently, Dr. Lewis didn't think my elevated pulse and blood pressure could have been caused by a lack of sleep. Nor did she think a few extra cups of coffee would create such a dramatic reaction. She ordered several tests to figure out what was making my system go haywire. She then had her nurse administer intravenous fluids to help flush out any poisons. She also gave me a shot of something that made my heart calm down, which only made me feel sleepier.

"I could sure use a cup of coffee," I said as I stifled a yawn.

"No!" Dr. Lewis and Jace objected in stereo.

"Then how about a nap?" I asked.

"Will you be able to stay with her?" the doctor asked Jace.

"Yeah, I can. I'm on vacation right now."

"Because of your mom?" Dr. Lewis asked gently. This really was a small town where everyone always knew everybody else's business.

"My mom is innocent," he said forcefully.

"Well, then." Dr. Lewis signed some papers. "Go home, Tru. Drink lots of water. Eat foods that are high in fiber. And get some rest. But first, give Mama Eddy a call before she hears about your visit here from someone else."

Chapter Twelve

———— ·· ————

My cell phone rang before I could make that call to Mama Eddy. "You poisoned yourself by drinking too much caffeine?" my mother screeched into the phone before I'd barely had a chance to say hello. "How many times have I told you? Many, many times, that's how many. Our family cannot drink alcohol or anything laced with drugs like that. Do I have to remind you how your uncle Richard died? He drank himself into the grave. That's how."

"He was your uncle, not mine, and he lived to be ninety-seven. He died after entering his peach tea recipe at the county fair. And there wasn't anything in the tea that did him in. He slipped on a lemon peel on the way up to the stage to collect his blue ribbon." They had draped his blue ribbon over his casket at the funeral. As a child, I'd been horrified that I might one day win a blue ribbon and end up like dear Great-uncle Richard. You know, dead? I considered myself lucky that I never excelled in crafts or sports and was never really in danger of having to risk my neck climbing up stairs to collect a blue ribbon.

"You're only proving my point, Tru. If poor Richard had stayed away from tea, like I do, he'd still be alive today."

"He'd be over one hundred and twenty years old if he was still alive," I pointed out. "And that would be an amazing feat."

"That's not what I meant, and you know it. I won't drink anything other than water and neither should you."

Mama Eddy also liked wine. But I knew my mother well enough to know when not to correct her.

"I'm going to come over right now and go through your cabinets and fridge. With my help, you can get a clean start."

"No, you don't need to do that!" I'd just gone grocery shopping. And while I had hidden most of the junk food, I didn't want her tossing out my coffee or tea or who knew what else she would deem unhealthy. Gracious, my mother ate like a bird lately. And that wasn't a figure of speech. When I had Sunday supper with her last week, she literally ate seeds.

"An intervention is needed," she insisted.

"No. No. No interventions. The doctor said it couldn't have been the coffee I drank."

She'd stopped listening. "I will not lose my daughter to an unhealthy diet! Do you hear me? Your body is a temple. You need to start—"

Jace lifted the phone from my ever-tightening grip even though he was driving. "Mama Eddy," he said smoothly, which was for him a brave act. She intimidated him just like she intimidated anyone who had endured her cotillion classes, which was pretty much anyone under the age of forty who grew up in Cypress. "The doctor wants your daughter to drink water and rest. I'm going to see to it that she does just that. What she needs right now is quiet." He paused. I could hear Mama

Eddy's voice, but I couldn't make out what she was saying. Jace winced. "Yes, ma'am. I understand. But this is the doctor's orders. You can have your intervention after she's recovered." Mama Eddy's voice got louder. "No, ma'am. We don't know what caused her reaction. It could be an allergic response or even poison. We have to wait for the test results to come back."

"Poison?!" I clearly heard Mama Eddy yell.

"Lack of sleep!" I shouted. "Not poison."

"Probably not poison," Jace said. "No ma'am, I'm not putting your daughter in danger again. I've never put her in danger in the first place. No ma'am, I'm not trying to be smart with you."

As soon as he ended the call, he tossed me the phone as if it were on fire. "I now understand why you weren't dating anyone when I moved back into town. Your mama must have scared off anyone worthy of you."

"Has she scared you off?" I wouldn't blame him if he no longer wanted anything to do with me or my crazy family. Maybe that was why he'd been pulling away from our relationship. My crazy family had scared him.

"I'm braver than the average bear," he said in a corny Yogi Bear voice that made me laugh.

When Jace pulled up to my house, I spotted Tori waiting on the front porch. She was holding a tote bag, its strap slung over her shoulder. A Perks T-shirt and jeans hugged her trim body like a glove. She'd finished the outfit with chunky-heeled boots and a faux-fur-lined black puffy coat. I knew the coat's lining was faux fur because Tori made a point of telling anyone she saw that it wasn't real fur every time she wore it, which wasn't really that often given how short our winters were in Cypress.

She'd pulled her long blond hair up into a high pony-tail, a style she often used when working at her coffee shop.

A large brown paper bag with grease stains on the sides was sitting on one of my porch chairs.

I smiled when I saw it. Tori knew me well enough to bring me something wickedly fried and heavenly delicious from the Grind. Fried foods were my go-to whenever I felt the need to stress-eat. Well, that and chocolate.

She took one look at me as I made my way up to the front of the house and frowned. "Girl, you look sick."

"That's a compliment, right? Sick means good?" I teased.

"Not when I'm looking at you when I'm saying it. You look pale as a haint." She grabbed my arm as if she thought I couldn't manage to get myself up the few steps onto my porch, which was ridiculous. Jace had my other arm, not that I needed his support either.

"I'm sure I'm not that pale."

"What's a haint?" Jace asked.

"Boy, you've been gone from the South for too long if you can't remember that a haint is a ghost," Tori said, and gave Jace a thump on his chest with the back of her hand and then a wink in my direction.

"No one uses that word anymore," I said.

"Yes, they do. Tru's just saying that so you won't feel stupid. But really, go ahead and feel stupid. That's how I usually feel when I'm around her. She's always been the brains of our friendship."

"If I'm the brains, which I'm totally not, that would make you the beauty." Which she totally was.

"At the moment, I am. Let's get inside before your cat tries to claw his way out of this sack again."

"You have Dewey in there?" I tried to get the tote bag from Tori's shoulder, but she wouldn't let me.

"Flossie helped me catch him. We figured you'd feel better having him home with you. She wanted to bring him, but I told her to stay and keep her ear to the ground at the library. It's her day to volunteer at the basement's circulation desk anyhow."

"And it's your day to work at Perks," I reminded her.

"When I heard something had happened to you, I knew I needed to be here. Especially after last night. And your daddy is missing too? Have you heard from him yet?"

"I haven't." It hurt in my chest to admit it.

"I have some friends out looking for him," Jace said.

"And I have Dewey to bring you comfort," Tori added.

"Thank you." I was touched she'd bring my kitty to me.

"You're my bestie." Tori hugged my arm. "I'd do anything for you."

I smiled as I unlocked and pushed open the front door. Dewey sprang out of the tote bag and across the threshold into the house in one graceful leap. He then looked over his shoulder at me and gave a ferocious meow that seemed to say *What's taking you so long? Get in here and pay attention to me.*

He bounded across the room to where he'd left a bright green crinkly ball and batted it with his paw.

"Hey, little buddy," Jace said. He'd brought the crinkly ball with him about a week ago.

Dewey picked up the crinkly ball in his mouth and tossed it up in the air. It flew across the room and smacked Tori square in the forehead.

"Hey! He did that on purpose!"

"How is that possible?" Jace said with a laugh. "He was playing with his ball."

"I saw the sly look he gave me before he threw it," Tori said. "He wanted to hit me in the head."

"Why would he do that?" I asked. "I'm sure he's trying to play with you."

"He's upset I took him away from those books he keeps pulling off the shelves." She watched Dewey as if she expected him to throw something else at her.

"Let's get you off your feet, Tru," Jace said. "Dr. Lewis wants you to rest."

"I can rest after I eat whatever is in that bag of food Tori brought. Isn't it lunchtime yet?"

"It's two o'clock," Jace said.

"It's already two?" Mrs. Farnsworth must be having a fit that I'd been gone so long. "No wonder I'm feeling so hangry. Let's get into that bag you brought, Tori. It smells soooo good."

I tugged Jace along with me to the kitchen, where Tori unloaded her greasy bag. Out came a tub of gooey macaroni and cheese, fried onion rings, and chips made from sweet potatoes with a creamy avocado lime dip.

"Oh! Oh! Oh! I love you, Tori," I cried as she pulled out each treasure.

"What about me?" Jace complained. "I'm the one who rushed to your rescue and got you to the doctor's."

"You're pretty great, too." I gave him a quick peck on the cheek. "But Tori brought me . . . Is that fried okra?"

"You know it. But slow down a minute. I still don't understand what happened," Tori said as she started piling food onto three plates. "All I know is what Flossie told me, which wasn't much. She called Perks frantically shouting that Jace was taking you to the hospital."

"Not the hospital. Just to the urgent care center to get me checked out," I scoffed. "There wasn't anything that wrong with me."

"Her heart rate was so high, the doctor considered calling an ambulance to transport her to a proper hospital," Jace tattled.

"But she didn't call an ambulance. And my heart rate did get better." I dipped a chip into the smooth avocado sauce and took a bite. Hot and spicy, while also cool and tangy. Delicious.

"The intravenous fluids helped get her vitals back in order," Jace said, suddenly frowning as deeply as he had at the urgent care center. Also, he hadn't touched the plate of food Tori had placed in front of where he was standing. "Why don't we take our plates to the table so Tru can sit down," he said. "She's supposed to be resting, not standing around eating fried foods."

"You're sounding dangerously like Mama Eddy," Tori warned. "And I still don't understand what happened." My friend settled in her chair at the table. She sat on one side of me. Jace sat on the other. "What was wrong with you?"

"We have no idea." I shrugged.

"She might have been poisoned," Jace said at the same time. He still hadn't even tasted the creamy mac and cheese. The Grind made it with pimento cheese and paprika and sprinkled crushed Italian-spiced croutons all over the top. It was a brilliant combination.

"I wasn't poisoned." I turned to Tori. "He told Mama Eddy the same thing about the possibility of poisoning."

"Oh, gracious. Why did you go and do a foolish thing like that? Do we need to start gulping our food to get it down before she arrives?"

"No need to gulp," Jace said. "I explained to Mama Eddy that Tru needs quiet and rest. Doctor's orders."

"In that case, we probably have an hour before she arrives," Tori said.

"Surely she'll let Tru rest for more than an hour."

"She won't if she thinks her daughter's life is in grave peril." Tori shook her head. "You should have told Mama Eddy that Tru had had a bad case of her monthly cramps. That would have kept her away."

"I couldn't have told her mama *that*."

Tori dragged a sweet potato fry through the avocado

dip. "It would have kept her away. Tru, do you think someone slipped you something poisonous to stop you from doing what comes naturally and asking questions?" Tori asked.

I'd started eating quicker than usual just in case Mama Eddy showed up at the door, so it took a moment for me to chew and swallow what I'd stuffed into my mouth before I could answer. "That's silly. I'm not the only one around here asking questions. Detective Ellerbe has been thorough, as always. And then there's that Joyce Fellows who wants to turn Rebecca's tragic death into a docudrama. I had to hide from her this morning in order to avoid being ambushed by her camera crew."

"But you're the one who has a reputation for catching murderers in this town," Tori said with one eyebrow artfully raised.

"Not just me. We're all a team. You, me, Jace, Flossie, and even Delanie. We've solved the past mysteries together. Is there more mac and cheese?"

"You know it." She left to go get the pasta tub.

"I wasn't poisoned," I said to Jace when we were alone. "I wish you'd stop telling people that."

"The doctor said that drinking too much coffee wouldn't cause the reaction you had. Lack of sleep wouldn't either. So, you tell me. What happened, Tru?"

"We've already been through this. I don't know." I wished I did.

"Exactly. That's why we need to keep our minds open to all possibilities until Dr. Lewis gets the blood tests back. In the meantime, I hope you're going to be extra careful."

"I'm always careful." I didn't like how everyone kept telling me to be careful. It wasn't as if I were recklessly running around with a pair of scissors in my hand.

"You know what I think happened? I think whoever

killed Rebecca tried to kill you this morning," Tori said as she returned with the tub of mac and cheese and a big serving spoon. "Were any of the members of the Arete Society also at the library this morning?"

"Well . . ." I had to think about that for a moment. "Delanie and of course Mrs. Farnsworth and Gretchen Clark and Annabelle Smidt Possey, and Sissy Philips. Oh, and Gwynne Hansy and Marigold Brantley came in this morning, too. Gwynne came in to talk about last night with the regulars who spend their mornings in the café while reading newspapers from around the country. And Marigold had come to the library to finish a sewing project. She then headed down to the secret bookroom in search of some light reading material."

"Wait. Did you say Sissy? Well, despite her being a wretched person, I think we should focus on Arete Society members," Tori said.

"I am. Sissy told me that Rebecca had promised to make her a member." I then told them what she had told me about Rebecca planning to push out a few of the older members.

"Can she do that?" Tori asked.

I shrugged. "I'm not a member. Nor did I ever care to be, to be honest. That's not my crowd."

"It's not mine either," Tori said. "Too uppity and the books they read are dreadful. People are always dying in them."

"They are not dreadful books," I argued. "They are all highly acclaimed. And may I remind you that people are always dying in the books we read for our book club since we read exclusively mysteries?"

"Oh . . . yeah, you're right." Tori never actually read the books for our book club meetings. She'd occasionally watch a movie adaptation if there was one. But that wasn't the same thing. "Were any of the other book club members at the library this morning?"

I closed my eyes and tried to picture everyone I saw this morning. My head still felt muzzy. All my mind's eye could see was Flossie swinging around that spiky meteor hammer. "No, I don't think so."

"Well, then." Tori clapped her hands. "Those are our suspects. One of them poisoned you. Find out which one, and we'll know who killed poor Rebecca White. This might be our easiest murder investigation yet."

I shook my head. "Why poison me?" It was preposterous to think that someone would want to kill me just because I was at the book club meeting last night.

"You tell us, Tru," Tori said. "Why poison you? What do you know that you aren't sharing with your bestest of best friends?"

"N-nothing," I stammered. There was something. I'd personally brewed three cups of coffee I'd drunk that morning, but Flossie had brought me the other cup. And I hadn't eaten anything since getting to work. So, if I had been poisoned, it would have had to come from Flossie. But I trusted Flossie. She was one of my closest friends.

"It's a shame to lose Rebecca White, really," Tori said sadly. "What a talent she had."

"You were a fan? Of Rebecca's?" That surprised me.

"Did you ever watch *Desiring Hearts*? Rebecca was: The. Best. Character. I wish I had that kind of backbone."

"You already do. Believe me, you do," I said between bites. "Did you get to know her after she moved back to Cypress?"

"She never made herself accessible, did she? I mean, she never came into Perks." Tori frowned at that. "I wonder why. Why move to a small town and then keep to yourself?"

"She was active with the book club. So I suppose that's something," I said.

"No one liked her," muttered Jace, who'd been unusually quiet up until then.

"What's that?" Tori asked.

"I said, no one liked her."

"Did you know her?" I asked.

"Not personally. But I talked to my mother about her this morning. Everyone had been so excited when Rebecca moved to town."

"When was that?" I interjected. "About six years ago?"

"Seven," Jace said.

"I remember some of the council members wanted to hang up banners in her honor," Tori said. "Luckily, calmer heads talked them out of it. Talk about tacky."

"Why did she even move here?" I asked. "Why Cypress? Did she have family in town?"

Tori shook her head. "I don't know."

"I wish she hadn't moved here," Jace said as he stared at the tabletop.

I put my hand on his. It made my heart ache to see him hurting like that. "Well, that's one of the first things we need to find out. What was she doing in Cypress? And if she was so popular, why did she give up on acting?"

"And why was she so nasty to everyone in town?" Jace added.

"Did she have any friends?" Tori wondered aloud.

"Marigold Brantley broke down and sobbed when she heard what had happened," I recalled. "And although she didn't show it last night, Delanie told me this morning that she and some of the other members were mourning Rebecca's loss too. But Marigold had seemed truly devastated. She claimed to be Rebecca's best friend."

"Then I suppose Goldie is who we really need to talk to," Tori said, standing up.

"You took the words out of my mouth." I stood up too. "Let's go."

Jace cleared his throat.

I grabbed my purse. "Since I'm still feeling shaky, Tori, I think you should drive."

Jace cleared his throat again.

"Do you need some water?" I asked him.

"No. But I think you're forgetting something," he said quietly.

I was? "What's that?" I had my purse and my phone and, oh yes, there was my notebook. "Do you think I'm forgetting you? I know you want to come along with us, but Fisher seemed adamant that you were banned from getting involved with the investigation. I wouldn't want you to get in trouble."

"Aww, I bet he's thinking you forgot to give him a kiss. The two of you are so cute," Tori gushed.

"I don't want to come with you. I mean, I do want to come, and Tori is freaking right about my wanting a kiss, but that's not what the two of you are forgetting. You were poisoned, Tru, remember?" He patted the chair I'd just vacated. "The doctor grounded you until tomorrow."

Chapter Thirteen

———•———

I wasn't poisoned, but nothing I said to either Tori or Jace that night convinced them that no one wanted me dead . . . this time.

And by the time I was getting ready for bed, my father still hadn't returned my text, or any of the twenty increasingly frantic other texts I'd sent him. Sure, Daddy had left home without warning before, but he'd always stayed in contact by phone or text. I tried to get Jace to leave and go driving around, searching for my father. But he refused to leave me alone.

He sat up in an armchair in my living room all night to protect me from any bad guys who might try to break down the door to get to me. His buddies, he promised, would keep searching for my father. They'd call with news.

That was how, for the second night in a row, Jace stayed over. I was sure my neighbors, who were some of the biggest gossips in town, would be thrilled to call and text everyone they knew in the morning with *that* news. By lunchtime, everyone in Cypress would be talking about how the two of us were now in a serious relationship. As I lay in bed thinking about that, the panic I'd expected didn't come. Who cared if that was what people thought? It wasn't as if they'd be wrong. At least I hoped they weren't wrong. I still needed to talk to Jace about why he kept canceling our dates without good reasons.

He's here with you now, a kind voice in my head reminded me. *He's here when it counts.*

Perhaps that was what serious relationships were all about. Perhaps we didn't have to know everything about the other person. How boring would that be?

Besides, I kind of liked giving the neighbors something to talk about. And even if none of them spread the gossip around, Jace's neighbor Agnes Knickerbocker, who took care of his dog Bonnie, would tell her friends that Jace spent two nights away from his home.

I still hadn't met Bonnie, I might add, because Jace was worried his dog might not like me. Apparently, his dog liked very few people. When I asked him why he let Agnes meet Bonnie, he explained that Agnes always smelled of sausages and I didn't.

I supposed that was a compliment.

Wasn't it?

I decided to take it as one.

Tori stopped by the next morning. She had coffees and an assortment of pastries from Perks. She'd also brought Charlie Newcastle—her latest stupidly handsome boyfriend—with her.

I grabbed my friend's arm, pulled her inside the house, and had the bag of pastries open before she could tell me good morning.

"Have I ever told you that I love you?" I asked Tori just before I gobbled down an almond croissant that packed an explosion of nutty flavors in my mouth.

My friend laughed. "Not often. Just every time I bring you food. And I love you too, my dear."

"We all love you and are worried about you," Charlie said, looking nearly as serious as Jace had all night. Today, he was dressed in a dark blue suit with little typewriter cuff links, a humorous touch that offset his tall, dark, and dangerous vibe. "I brought you a feel-better gift." He handed me a tattered old clothbound book.

Charlie owned the local used bookstore, the Deckle Edge. Over the past several months, he'd gifted me several valuable first edition books, saying he knew I'd take care of the books properly.

"Are you serious?" I breathed. My heart skipped a beat when I read the title on the plain yellowed cover aloud. "'*Rebecca* by Daphne du Maurier, Uncorrected Proof.'" I opened the book to the title page and read the publication date: 1938.

"*An uncorrected proof?*" I whispered.

"That's right," Charlie said with a big grin. "I do apologize for the coincidence of the title. I hope it doesn't cause you distress. I'd been meaning to gift the book to you for a while now. It's one of the proof copies, sometimes called advance reviewer copies, that the publisher sent out to newspaper reviewers prior to publication. I came across it in a used-book auction last month."

"Oh my goodness, thank you," I said, hugging the book to my chest. Charlie's enthusiasm for books, especially old books, matched mine. "I seem to remember that the hero of this book is accused of killing Rebecca, his wife. He sets off to prove his innocence."

"Just like Hazel has to prove her innocence," Tori said.

"Only, the husband—" Charlie started to say.

"Shush!" Tori swatted Charlie's arm. "Don't ruin the ending for Tru!"

I chuckled. "It's okay. I've read the book before."

"My mother didn't kill anyone," Jace said.

"If y'all will excuse me, I need to get ready for work. I'm afraid if I'm late again, Anne's robot librarian will hunt me down and spray me with its theft detection powder. Let me tell you, being cornered by that metal menace yesterday felt like I'd stepped into a warped version of our future. And it wasn't pleasant."

"What happened?" Jace exclaimed at the same time Tori cried, "Robot librarian? You have to be joking. Mrs. Farnsworth would never allow such a thing in her library."

Charlie was the only one who didn't act surprised. He leaned back on his heels and smiled. "I see those kids at Tech Bros finally got it up and running."

"You knew what they were doing?" I spun around to Charlie. "You do know that everybody in town has spent weeks trying to figure out what that company was making."

"She's right," Jace said. "How did you find out?"

"You know him," Tori said with an eye roll in his direction. "He's the town's secret keeper. Everyone tells him their secrets and then swears him to keep that exciting knowledge to himself. It's maddening, really."

"Not this time, dear," Charlie said. "I wasn't the only one who knew. Tru could have asked her father what those boys over at Tech Bros were up to. Ashley has been working for them ever since they opened."

"He has?" I asked, surprised my dad didn't tell me about his latest venture, especially considering he was building a machine to take my job. Maybe that was why he'd decided to keep quiet. I checked my phone for the fifth time that morning. Still no texts from him. There were two new texts from Mama Eddy demanding an update on the search for my father as well as asking for an update on my health. I quickly texted her a reply, promising her that the police as well as Jace's friends were still out searching for Daddy and that I'd had a hearty breakfast. "Maybe someone at Tech Bros knows where my father has gone."

Just then, Jace's phone pinged.

I held my breath while he peered at his phone's screen.

"News?" I asked, feeling somewhat queasy.

"Hmm." He tapped out a reply to the text before looking up at us. "My dad is back in town." Jace sounded like he was having trouble catching his breath. "He's . . . he's at the courthouse. They're letting my mom out on bail."

"That's good," I said. "Isn't it?"

"But the evidence against her is bad," he continued. "Her attorney has advised Mom to negotiate a plea deal."

"But she didn't do it!" I cried.

Jace shook his head and walked out of the room.

Tori put her hand on my arm when I started to go after him. "Give him a moment."

I swung around to confront Charlie. "So, secret keeper, has anyone come into your store and confessed to killing Rebecca White?" I figured it wouldn't hurt to ask.

"I wish! Everyone who comes in is just as perplexed about her death as we are. She didn't seem to have any close friends, but at the same time no one thought she had any enemies, either. No one knew her well enough."

"Except for the book club members," I pointed out. "And the young, fashionable wannabes like Sissy who had been promised entry into the Arete Society as soon as the less fashionable members were kicked out."

Dewey sauntered into the room, purring loudly.

"Where have you been?" Charlie asked as he bent down to scratch my little kitty behind his ears. "Aren't you supposed to be greeting visitors at the door?"

Dewey, as if understanding the question, meowed and looked at me.

"What?" I said, with mock indignation. "I haven't stopped you from doing anything you want, even though I think I should. He's been playing rough with the library books lately. He damaged a few of our historical romances."

"Naughty kitty," Charlie said softly while still scratching Dewey's neck. "You know books aren't playthings. You'd better not try that the next time you visit my store, or I won't give you a liver treat."

Dewey stood up on his hind legs and nipped Charlie's hand. Then, being the fickle kitty that he is, he turned around and slinked over to Tori, purring even louder as he rubbed against her legs.

Dewey then looked over his shoulder and meowed loudly again, as if to say *I don't care for your threats.*

"Let's circle back around to this killer robot of yours, Tru," Jace said when he came back into the room. He crouched down to lure Dewey over to him, which totally worked. My kitty bounded over to his favorite guy. Dewey then lifted his chin so Jace could scratch him there. "What happened? And why didn't you tell us about this attack yesterday? It might be related to someone trying to poison you."

I shuddered at the memory of how LIFU had chased me down. "No, it's not related. The robot mistakenly thought I was an intruder," I said, and then told them what had happened. "Keven Verner was on hand. He took the robot back to the factory after it malfunctioned. Even though it may have ruined several of the computers,

Anne is still gaga over the mechanical menace . . . and its creator."

"Wait? It turned Anne yellow? At least that's a good color on her," Tori said with a smile. "And believe you me, I understand why she's gaga over Keven. He's come into the café a couple of times. He is one handsome man with that thin mustache."

"Is he?" Jace asked me.

I shrugged. "I was too busy worrying about what his robot might do next to really notice."

"He is," Tori gushed. "Oh, he definitely is."

"Hey!" Charlie said with what was clearly feigned jealousy. Tori and Charlie had been spending a great deal of time together lately and had started acting like an old married couple. I looked at my friend and wondered when the two of them would announce their engagement. Usually, by this point in Tori's relationships, she's already said "I do" and is away on an extended honeymoon.

For my sake, I was glad she wasn't away on a honeymoon.

I was also glad that Tori was taking this relationship slower than usual. I liked Charlie and genuinely believed he was a good match for my best friend. I wanted things to work out between them.

Tori waggled her hips at Charlie. "Just because I'm devoted to you, lover boy, doesn't mean I don't still have eyes in my head." Charlie started to say something in response, but Tori didn't give him a chance. She whirled toward me and demanded, "Did you and Jace make any progress coming up with possible motives for killing Rebecca after I left yesterday? Or did you make kissy faces instead?"

I blushed. We hadn't pursued the investigation.

"Tru slept off the poison while I sat up and worried," Jace said with a yawn.

"I wasn't poisoned. It was too much caffeine," I countered.

"We will see, won't we?" Jace said. "She's expecting a call from Dr. Lewis this morning with the lab results telling us what poison Tru had been given."

"I wasn't poisoned," I repeated. I had an urge to stomp my foot for emphasis, but I figured doing something so silly would accomplish nothing more than startling my cat.

"So you say," Jace said in that calm voice that never made me feel calm. "Please humor me and let me drive you to work."

"Work!" I jumped, managing to startle poor Dewey, who had wandered over to his bowl and was finishing up his breakfast. "I'm going to be late . . . again! And that robot is going to come after me again, I just know it."

"But I thought we were going to Goldie's house to question her?" Tori cried. "That's why I came over this morning. I want to hear for myself what she has to say about Rebecca. I cannot believe more people aren't broken up over her death. You really need to watch a few episodes of *Desiring Hearts* with me, Tru. Rebecca was wonderful on that show."

"I'm sorry, Tori. I can't go this morning. I agreed to lend an extra hand during Anne's tai chi class at ten, plus Mrs. Farnsworth would lecture me until my ears bled if I missed a second day of work, especially if she discovered I'd spent the day not sick in bed but conducting a murder investigation."

"But we have to help poor Hazel. Surely you haven't forgotten about her," Tori said as she bounced on the balls of her feet, clearly anxious to get moving.

"No, of course I haven't forgotten about Hazel. And we can visit Marigold after I get off work."

"But that's not until five," Tori complained.

"I'm not giving up on the investigation. Far from it. The best bits of gossip always find their way to the library. So that is clearly where I need to go."

Little did I know how true that would prove to be.

Chapter Fourteen

———•———

Whew, I made it to the library on time. I dashed up the steps as Mrs. Farnsworth was unlocking the door. Anne seemed pleased to see me. Mrs. Farnsworth acted indifferent. But I suspected by the way her sharp gaze kept coming back to me that she was relieved to see me as well.

"Excuse me!" Joyce Fellows from *Ideal Life* came running up the steps behind us dressed in a crisp blue suit. A full camera crew chased after her. "Excuse me! I'm trying to get information about Rebecca White's murder. I understand you were there. Excuse me! Trudy? I need to speak to you. The interview will be aired nationally," she hastily added, as if that would interest me.

"No, thank you!" I rushed through the door as soon as Mrs. Farnsworth opened it.

"We don't open until ten," Mrs. Farnsworth informed them. "Plus, we don't allow cameras inside the library." She slammed the door closed and locked it before Joyce could push her way inside.

I drew in a long, shaky breath. "I don't want to be on national TV."

"Who would?" Mrs. Farnsworth hurried away from the glass doors. "I will not allow our library to be turned into a circus. It was inconsiderate for Ms. White to invite the press to our book club meeting. And without telling anyone." She clicked her tongue. "It's also inconsiderate for that television crew to act like they have a right to thrust their cameras in our faces."

I rushed after Mrs. Farnsworth.

"Wait. You didn't know that Joyce Fellows was coming the other night? Rebecca didn't warn you?"

Mrs. Farnsworth whirled back toward me. "That Rebecca was a pot-stirrer. She likely thought it'd be fun to watch us squirm when a national television crew ambushed us. There she'd sit with a new outfit, professionally done-up hair, sharply manicured nails, smiling while the rest of us looked like we always did—nice, but not *national television* nice. She was always stirring the pot like that. Putting herself at an advantage. And then, if we dared complain, she'd act all offended that we didn't recognize how much trouble she'd gone to for us. But . . . but . . . I really shouldn't be saying any of this, should I? Speaking ill of the dead and all." She pinched her fingers together and flung her hand as if she were tossing salt over her left shoulder.

With her eyelids snapping, she spun on her heel and hurried toward her office. "Try to do something about all that yellow, Anne. I don't want your neon coloring distracting our patrons. Did you bother to wash at all after you left yesterday? You look—" Mrs. Farnsworth shook her head and disappeared into her office. She closed the door with a loud slam.

"Well, you certainly put her in a mood, didn't you?" Anne said.

Dewey stuck his head out of his tote bag and meowed in the judgmental, scolding way that he'd mastered so well.

"I didn't mean to," I said to both kitty and Anne.

Anne looked down and shuffled her feet a bit. "I washed ten times last night, and I'm still as bright as a highlighter pen."

"That dark purple you put in your hair pairs nicely with the yellow," I said. "It kind of softens the effect." Yesterday the streaks in her hair were aqua blue, which had made the yellow stand out more.

"Thanks," she said. "I had hoped the change in color would help."

"Well, I suppose I had better start the coffee." Anne always complained if I didn't brew a pot first thing in the morning.

Anne jumped in front of me, blocking my path to the employee lounge. She held up her hands. "I'll do that. How about you skip drinking coffee for a while? Or maybe we should get two pots. One could be strictly for decaf."

"Dr. Lewis said whatever made me sick yesterday couldn't have been from drinking too much coffee." Did we really have to rehash this?

"Then you were poisoned!" Anne cried. Her eyes grew wide. "Someone tried to poison you? Here? In our library?"

"Shh. No, I wasn't poisoned. No one is trying to hurt me. It was lack of sleep and perhaps a bit too much coffee. I didn't get any sleep the night before and clearly my body shut down." Since Anne didn't want me to brew the coffee, I made a U-turn and headed toward the basement instead.

"Is that what the doctor said?" Anne asked as she followed along with me.

"Not exactly. We're still waiting for the blood tests to come back. But when they do, that's what she's going to say. I'm sure of it."

"Well, I'm not." Anne seemed determined to follow me to the basement. "Whenever there's a questionable death in this town, you get yourself wrapped up in it."

I kept walking. "I don't care who killed Rebecca White," I said. "All I'm doing is trying to prove that Hazel is innocent."

"I knew it! You can act all unconcerned. But everyone knows that the only way to prove Hazel is innocent is to find evidence against someone else. And that someone else is worried about the questions you're going to ask, the secrets you're going to dig up. Gah! I'm going to have to be careful about what I eat or drink around you."

"I wasn't poisoned!"

Mrs. Farnsworth stepped out of her office and cleared her throat. Nothing about her movements or her throat-clearing had been overly loud, but the head librarian was someone who could command the attention of the room with merely the shift of her hand.

Both Anne and I stopped and waited to be admonished for making too much noise.

"Tru, how are you feeling after yesterday's ordeal?" Mrs. Farnsworth asked in that whisper-soft voice of hers. Before I could assure her that I was fine, she said, "If you need to take time off to get some rest, do it. I can't have you accidentally erasing any databases today."

That happened once. Once! During my first year on the job, I accidentally erased one electronic catalog. You'd think she would have forgotten about that by now. But no, Mrs. Farnsworth had a memory as sharp as a sword's blade.

I was prepared to take her up on the offer and go home. Perhaps I could search a bit for my father on the way over to Marigold's house. It wasn't as if I was needed at the library today. I didn't have any children's programs scheduled, and I could use the time off to talk with some of the other members of the book club as well.

"Let's not have Tru rush home yet," Anne said, sounding a little panicked. "She's promised to help with the tai chi classes. You are feeling better, aren't you, Tru? So many people are coming to the classes now, Mrs. Farnsworth. I really depend on Tru lending an extra hand."

"Can't the robot help you?" I asked.

"Don't be silly. It's not programmed to help out like that," Anne shot back.

Mrs. Farnsworth shrugged. "If you think you can manage working here today without setting anything on fire, Tru, stay. Work."

Again, I'd worked for the library for nearly fourteen years. And I hadn't set anything on fire in the past twelve of them, thank you very much.

Admittedly, my first few years at the library were rocky ones. For one thing, Mrs. Farnsworth terrified me. Nearly everyone who grew up coming to her library would quake in their shoes whenever she was around, even as adults. The stern librarian rarely held back her bone-chilling, teeth-rattling, you'd-better-straighten-yourself-out glares. It had taken me several years to get used to working alongside her without suffering a panic attack that often ended with me breaking, dropping, erasing, or setting something on fire. It wasn't until I learned deep breathing exercises from a how-to book I'd found in the 610 section that I conquered my anxieties and began to show Mrs. Farnsworth I could be an asset to her library.

"She looks fine, doesn't she? Of course she does. She's fine. She's staying," Anne kept saying. "I mean, we want life at the library to appear as normal as possible, don't we? What with Rebecca White's murder, we can't have anyone thinking her death might be somehow linked to the library, can we?"

"I don't see how—?" I started.

"Doesn't the library order the Arete Society's book club books every month? Don't the members come here to pick them up? Aren't the sales of those books a fundraiser for the library? It sounds like the library and the book club are tied tightly together in a way that . . ." Anne shook her head.

Mrs. Farnsworth clacked her teeth together, a sure sign that she was about to lose her temper. "I don't know what Ms. Becket has been telling you about the Arete Society, but—"

"I didn't hear any of this from Tru," Anne was quick to clarify, much to my relief. "I read all about it in the local newspaper. It's front-page news." She held up her phone and turned the screen so both Mrs. Farnsworth and I could read the headline of the online edition of the regional newspaper.

"'Death by Tuna Noodle Casserole,'" I read aloud, and then shook my head. "I warned Detective Ellerbe not to mention how Rebecca died around Betty."

Mrs. Farnsworth gasped. "It's terrible. Terrible. If anyone needs me, I'll be in my coffee. I mean, office. Office!"

She retreated back to her office, the heels of her sensible shoes clacking on the terrazzo floor. She closed the door with an uncharacteristic bang for the second time that morning.

"And *you* were complaining that *I* upset Mrs. Farnsworth not ten minutes ago? What were you thinking?" I poked Anne in the arm.

"Ow." Anne rubbed her arm. "It's not as if the two

women got along. You heard Mrs. F talking about Rebecca this morning. She called her a pot-stirrer, which isn't a name I'd ever heard anyone called before, but it doesn't sound good."

"It isn't good. It means that Rebecca liked to stir up trouble," I said. "And you should be more sensitive to Mrs. Farnsworth's feelings. Couldn't you tell she was on edge when she came in this morning?"

"One," Anne said with a great deal of sass, "Mrs. Farnsworth has been on edge since the moment I met her. She's got to be the most irritable woman I've ever met. And two—Mrs. Farnsworth hated Rebecca White."

"Are you sure? As in hate-hate? Not just that she disliked how Rebecca was a pot-stirrer?" How in the world would Anne know that . . . *and I didn't*?

Instead of answering me, Anne said, "So is it true? About how Rebecca White died? It sounded so unbelievable that I had assumed Betty was making things up for her articles again. But neither you nor Mrs. Farnsworth seemed at all surprised by the headline, which means it must be true, doesn't it?"

"That's how it looks," I said. "Did Rebecca ever do or say anything to Mrs. Farnsworth directly to upset her?"

"I don't know. You'll have to ask Aunt Delanie. She's the one who mentioned it. I loved watching Rebecca on *Desiring Hearts*. One year for Halloween, I even dressed as her character, Delilah Morris. Do you remember how everyone wanted to be Rebecca White . . . or maybe they had wanted to be Delilah?"

"I do remember that." Although I never wanted to be someone who wore tight dresses with high heels and stabbed their friends in the back. But I supposed it was that kind of twisted but elegant drama that made shows like that so popular. "Everyone was watching it at the time. *Desiring Hearts* topped the list of favorite shows in Cypress because Rebecca had a Southern accent that wasn't at all twangy. She made it sound as if she was actually from around here and not somewhere in the mountains."

"The twang is an upstate trait?" Anne asked.

I shrugged. "Probably not. But that's what we all say around here when we hear a bad fake Southern accent. There's no one Southern accent. There are many, many regional variations. But Rebecca did sound like she came from somewhere around here. I wonder if she had roots in the area."

"I seem to remember reading somewhere that she was from the Midwest," Anne said. "But I could be wrong. I used to read everything I could find about her. Wasn't she the best? I think I still have a copycat version of the white purse Delilah carried when she confronted Prissy and Hank about their affair when she was carrying Hank's baby. Oh, that brings back memories. The show has really lost its pizzazz. I wonder if Rebecca will get her picture featured in the memorial section of the Daytime Emmy Awards. She would like that."

"I think she'd rather still be alive," I said as I headed toward the stairs that led to the basement.

Anne followed. "Duh. But she was a star. A true star. Are you sure it was a tuna noodle casserole that killed her? Like poisoned her? Like you were poisoned?"

"No, she wasn't poisoned, and neither was I," I said. "She was hit over the head with a casserole dish. The impact shattered the dish."

Anne shook her head. "Poor Rebecca. She'd hate to be done in by something as common as a tuna casserole."

"Again, I think she'd rather be alive," I said.

But Anne ignored me. She hugged herself and smiled. "It's like a plot from *Desiring Hearts*. Aunt Delanie always told me that the ladies hosting these book club events served the most creative gourmet food. Tuna noodle casserole sounds more like something you'd find at a church picnic. This town certainly has tons of church picnics, and there's always a tuna casserole. It's so, so cliché."

"Rebecca said the same thing after Hazel told her that was the main dish."

"And Hazel lost her temper and killed our famous Rebecca for disparaging her church casserole? I suppose when you stop and think about it, that makes sense. People in this town are deadly serious when it comes to their recipes."

Although Anne had spent summers visiting her aunt Delanie at her lake house, she grew up on the West Coast. She'd suffered terrible culture shock when she'd first moved to Cypress but was quickly learning the ins and outs of our community.

"It's kind of poetic too," Anne continued. "To die in a way that echoes how her character was killed off the show, I mean. Wasn't Delilah poisoned by a quiche, a food Hank later swore Delilah would never eat? And here Rebecca was killed with a food she said she wouldn't eat?"

"Really? Her character was killed by a quiche?" I had only watched a handful of the episodes. It wasn't that I didn't want to watch the show. It was simply that Mrs. Farnsworth's lunch hour corresponded with when it aired, and mine didn't.

Anne nodded. "Life imitating art, don't you think?"

Perhaps someone who like Anne—not Anne, but *like* her—knew all the episodes of *Desiring Hearts* had decided to cleverly take her revenge against the aging television star by copying her on-air death, while framing Hazel by making it look like she'd committed the murder in a moment of frustrated passion.

Someone like, say, Mrs. Farnsworth, who made sure to take her lunch hour when *Desiring Hearts* aired. Someone who, after meeting the actress behind Delilah, decided she wasn't as charming and glamorous in person. Someone who once had loved Rebecca but now hated her.

Now that was something I could work with.

But not right now. I needed to get Dewey to the basement before the library opened for the day and before it was time to help Anne with her tai chi class.

Chapter Fifteen

———·———

One of the perks of working in a state-of-the-art high-tech library was that the databases were vast and deep. As soon as Anne's tai chi class had ended, I spent the rest of the morning stationed at the front desk's computer reading plot summaries of *Desiring Hearts* episodes. And wow, what convoluted plotlines, especially in the scenes where Rebecca White appeared. I had to start taking notes just to keep it all straight. Her character continually made enemies, badmouthed everyone she met, and finally was killed off at the end of her first season.

I remember that at the time, the town had been abuzz with talk about the show, certain that her character's death was a ruse and that the writers would ultimately bring her back from the dead, despite having been poisoned, drowned in a nearby river, then stuffed into a wood chipper. But the best TV soap operas routinely brought back popular characters from even worse fates.

It wasn't until Rebecca White had settled in our town

that the die-hard fans finally gave up hoping for her return to their favorite show. For a few years after that, fans from all over the country would come to Cypress hoping to catch her in the act of backstabbing a friend or scheming against a foe. But Rebecca had become a recluse, leaving her lake house only to attend her exclusive book club meetings. She had a maid who handled all her shopping and had erected a tall privacy fence around the perimeter of her property. Slowly, the interest in her waned. The fans stopped coming. And the excitement of having a celebrity living in our midst faded away.

Faded, but didn't completely disappear. There were some in town—like Tori, Anne, and Marigold—who still idolized her, which made me wonder: Who else idolized the former star? Did Rebecca have a stalker? Did a crazed superfan kill off the very human Rebecca White for not living up to the star persona she had once been known for?

That was another possibility worth looking into.

By midafternoon, life at the library felt normal. A group of women were working with Anne on a computer, searching genealogy databases for long-lost ancestors from all over the world. Mrs. Farnsworth was teaching a sewing class. And I was teaching a teen how to find literary criticism in our online database. I had just finished explaining how to cite a source in her research paper on Poe's "The Raven," which was due tomorrow, when someone screamed.

Oh no!

I knocked over my chair in my haste to get out of it.

What if Rebecca hadn't been done in by a crazed fan? What if the murderer was systematically targeting the members of the book club?

I ran in the direction the scream had come from.

I had seen Marigold heading toward the library's café

not that long ago. In my gut, I knew the scream had been hers.

I sprinted toward the café.

Please, please, please. Not another dead body. I didn't think my heart could take it.

"Enter your request," a metallic voice demanded.

I skidded to a halt at the café's entrance.

"Get away from me!" Marigold yelled at the same robot that had attacked me yesterday morning.

Oh, thank goodness. Marigold was still alive. All of the patrons in the café were healthy and alive.

"Enter your request," the metallic voice repeated, sounding more determined than before.

When had Keven returned that thing? And why hadn't I been warned? The robot clearly wasn't ready to be interacting with the public. I couldn't be the only person around here who realized that!

I marched into the café to find the barista huddled behind the counter and Marigold backed into a corner; LIFU, the most aggressively helpful robot in the world, was rolling toward her with its tube-like arms raised.

"Stop!" I shouted at the oversized tin can. Mrs. Farnsworth would forgive me for shouting when a patron's life was in jeopardy. Unfortunately, my shouting at it didn't slow the robot down. It kept rolling toward poor Marigold.

I had to do something, so I took a flying leap and tackled the robot from the side. I squeezed my eyes shut, hoping I didn't trigger its powdery defense mechanism. With a whirling, grinding cry, the robot toppled over on its side.

I scrambled back to my feet and scurried away from it, pulling Marigold along with me.

"It already dyed Anne yellow," I whispered. I didn't want the robot to hear me and react.

"What . . . what . . . what . . . is . . . ?" Marigold stammered. Her entire body was shaking.

"LIFU," I said. "It's supposed to be the librarian of the future that Tech Bros is developing. Let me buy you a calming herbal tea."

"That-that's what Tech Bros is making?" Her eyes grew large as she turned back to the robot. "Just wait until Cora hears about this! She'll be furious that I learned the secret of that place before she did."

Her mouth forgot its outrage. She smiled as she frantically tapped out several text messages. While she did that, I ordered two large chamomile lavender teas and then sent a text of my own to Anne, asking her to do something with the tipped-over robot, which kept demanding "Enter your request" on an endless loop.

"What is going on in here?" Mrs. Farnsworth hurried into the café, looking ready to scold everyone involved. "Ms. Becket, what is the meaning of all this noise?"

"That—" I thrust my finger at the flailing robot. "I had to physically stop that *thing* from attacking a patron."

"You must be mistaken," Mrs. Farnsworth whispered. "Keven assured me that LIFU's programming follows Asimov's three laws of robotics." She held up a finger as she summarized each law. "It is incapable of harming people. It must obey orders. And it must protect itself as long as it doesn't harm people in the process. It's all very straightforward."

"Straightforward or not, Lida, Tru is telling the truth," Marigold said, coming to my defense. "She was very brave. I thought your robot was going to strangle me."

Marigold Brantley was a plain woman, with broad shoulders and muscular arms. Even so, she looked terribly vulnerable standing there with her hands protecting her neck.

Mrs. Farnsworth pursed her lips. "It did?"

Marigold and I both nodded.

"Well, that isn't acceptable," Mrs. Farnsworth said after a long span of silence. "I'll give Keven a call and have him fetch LIFU. Clearly, something so large needs more safeguards."

"It was quite a harrowing experience," Marigold said. "If Tru hadn't tackled your robot and then pulled me away, I shudder to think what might have happened."

Mrs. Farnsworth looked over at the metal menace. It was still flopping around and demanding that someone enter a request. The head librarian then gave an emphatic nod. "I'll make the call now."

After Mrs. Farnsworth left, I handed Marigold an oversized mug of tea. "This should calm your nerves. And I do apologize for what happened. The library is supposed to be a safe space."

She patted my hand. "I don't hold this against you. You're not the one pushing all these modern ideas down our throats. It's shameful, really. Rebecca didn't agree with what the elected officials were doing with the library, either. At one of our meetings, she told Annabelle to tell that puffed-up husband of hers to leave our town alone. Like the rest of us, Rebecca wanted the town to stay quiet and quaint. That was why she moved to Cypress, after all."

Annabelle and Rebecca had been feuding? Interesting. "What did Annabelle do? Did she defend her husband?" I asked.

"Annabelle got all huffy and then tightened up her lips, like she does when what she really wants to do is stomp and scream. But that woman is too much a lady to carry on and show her true self. Besides, she wouldn't want to follow in Ginger Faraday's footsteps, kicked out of the society and shunned by her friends."

"What do you mean?" I asked.

"About Ginger? That foolish woman couldn't follow the rules, so—this was a few years ago—Rebecca led a vote to expel her from the society. She ended up leaving Cypress altogether, which was one of the reasons Rebecca suggested Emma open a travel agency. Ginger had been the only travel agent in town, as you'll recall, not that she was a good one. She couldn't have been. I heard her business went bankrupt."

"No, not about Ginger. I'm more interested in hearing about Annabelle and her true self. What did you mean by that?"

"Didn't you know? Annabelle has a nasty temper. She tries to hide it, but it pops out often enough that we all know it's there, despite her sickly-sweet charm." Marigold clicked her tongue. "It's a good thing the police already know who killed our . . . our . . . dear friend." She paused to blink back tears. "Otherwise, Annabelle might have found herself in the awkward position of being a prime suspect even though she wasn't there."

"Really? Do you think Annabelle might have sneaked—?" I started to ask.

"Oh, no. No. No. No. It was Hazel. She must have gone mad, like one of those dogs that attack for no reason, you know?" She tucked a loose strand of gray hair back into the tight bun that was the only hairstyle she ever wore. "I wish I had known Hazel was unstable. I would have warned Rebecca." She blinked back more tears. "Surely there was something I could have done to keep this from happening."

"You and Rebecca were close friends, weren't you?" I asked gently.

"Oh, yes." Marigold took a long sip of the tea. "We were like sisters." She took another sip. "I cannot believe . . . I mean, it's like a bad dream that she's gone."

Marigold and Rebecca were as different as my best friend Tori was from me. But I'd known Tori since kindergarten. We'd always been friends. Rebecca had only been in town for the past seven years and seemed to hold herself above the rest of us.

Marigold, on the other hand, used to run the local feed and seed store with her husband. She often wore homespun gingham dresses with frills at the shoulders and thick-soled waterproof boots. Today's dress was a forest-green-and-white checked pattern. I'd never seen her wearing makeup or jewelry of any kind.

"Why were the two of you close? Did you have anything in common?" The pairing of a glamorous ex-actress with a strong but plain farm girl seemed like an odd couple. "I mean"—I tried to soften my question—"I might have been too much in awe of someone like Rebecca to feel comfortable becoming her friend. How could I compete with someone who was friends with big-name Hollywood stars? I wouldn't know what to say."

"Oh, I thought the same when I first met her." She leaned toward me and whispered, "She liked everyone to think she was this top-shelf princess, but, in reality, she was as common as you or me. When I discovered that her father had been a farmer back in Iowa, I realized we had loads to talk about. My father farmed cotton. Her father had farmed potatoes, corn, and sweet peas. When we were alone together, she liked to reminisce. She really added something special to our town, didn't she?"

"I wish I had gotten to know her," I said. Investigating the murder of a stranger felt like I was wandering around lost in a corn maze. I didn't know which way to turn.

"I believe she would have liked you, Tru. You both share a love of fine literature. Before I met her, I was reading what Rebecca called trash. You know the books, commercial romances and thrillers? She showed me that books shouldn't entertain me. Books are meant to challenge us, she liked to say."

"Romances and thrillers can challenge the reader, while also entertaining them," I pointed out. "There's nothing wrong with enjoying a book you're reading."

"That's kind of you to say. I know that as a librarian you must be diplomatic. You can't judge the readers who come looking for this book or that. But you can be honest with me, we know some books are superior to others."

I shook my head but decided not to make a big deal about disagreeing with her. For one thing, Marigold was clearly grieving. It would be cruel to argue with the viewpoint of someone Marigold had obviously idolized. And for another thing, Rebecca's literary snobbery wouldn't drive anyone to murder. There were plenty of literary snobs living in Cypress. And they were all alive and well, which made me wonder . . .

"Did Rebecca ever talk about any overly aggressive fans? You know, like someone who might have been stalking her?" I asked.

Marigold closed her eyes and sighed deeply. "Rebecca used to have fans following her around everywhere. She hated that. Said it made her feel so uncomfortable. But, in time, the fans went home and I fear she missed it. She'd always look around when we'd go somewhere together. But there was never anyone there. Not anymore. She tried to hide it, but she was disappointed, I could tell. She'd been sad lately. Terribly sad. Broke my heart to see that."

So, no stalkers. "There had to be something . . . some*one* . . . who was unhappy with her. Do you know if there was anyone in the community who was jealous of the attention Rebecca always got? Perhaps someone saw Rebecca as a threat to their membership in the Arete Society, for example?" I hoped my prodding would spark some ideas.

But it didn't. Marigold shook her head quite forcefully. "No! Everyone loved her. That hothead Hazel must be mortified by what she's done."

"I'm not sure she is—"

She sucked in a sharp breath. "Don't you fret, dear. I'm sure we won't hold the actions of your future mother-in-law against you or that handsome beau of yours. Every family has its black sheep."

"Wait. What?" *Mother-in-law?* "We've only just started to date—"

"We all agree that y'all make an adorable couple." She was nodding to herself. "It breaks my heart what happened. It's all a tragedy for everyone involved, a terrible, terrible tragedy. I still cannot believe I'll never see Rebecca again. She was like my sister. We shared all our little secrets."

"What kind of secrets?" I asked, eager to move away from talking about my relationship with Jace and back to discussing the investigation.

"Now, I can't be telling you that. That's why they're called secrets, you know? They're bits of a person's life that aren't supposed to be retold. They're like sacred pieces of our souls that we share with only those nearest and dearest to us." Tears welled in her eyes. "I'll miss that the most." She sniffled. "The sharing of our secrets."

"Did she ever tell you about anyone in town being upset with her?" I asked, desperate to get a peek at those secrets of hers. "You don't have to tell me exactly what she told you, you could just point me in the right direction."

"Everyone loved Rebecca." A tear rolled down her cheek. "She-she was like the sun. People liked basking in her warmth. If anything, she was too generous, too giving to those around her."

"How do you mean?" I asked gently. I hated upsetting Marigold like this, but I needed something . . . anything.

"She liked to help people and make sure they succeeded."

"Who did she help?" This was like pulling teeth.

"Honey, she helped Hazel so much that she had to skip her weekly lunch with me. Hazel had found herself so far in over her head, she needed Rebecca to hold her hand through every step of the book club planning."

"But Hazel is an accomplished hostess." There was no way Hazel needed anyone to hold her hand.

"That's what we all thought. She talked as if she knew what she was doing and made us believe she could meet the Arete Society's high expectations, but when it came time to show off her abilities, she completely fell apart." Marigold dabbed at her damp cheeks with a tissue. "Rebecca told me how she'd had to spend hours over at Hazel's house to supervise the book club preparations. I don't understand why Hazel took offense and lashed out like she did. She-she should have been grateful." The last part came out as a loud sob.

"But Hazel is innocent," I argued. "I was there. And I'm sure of it."

Marigold's voice trembled as she spoke through her tears, "You're investigating, aren't you? Of course you are. Cora told me just the other day that you had to be feeling restless, what with how quiet things have been around town lately." She sniffled. "You haven't had an opportunity to exercise your . . ." She tapped her temple. "I'm sure once you satisfy your curiosity, you'll agree with the rest of us. Hazel snapped and did the unthinkable." Her tears were really flowing now. "I'm sorry. I have to go."

With a tissue pressed to her eyes, she ran from the café.

I sat back, took another sip of my tea, and worried.

Every road I took kept leading me back to Hazel. But there had to be someone else who didn't idolize our local celebrity. Someone who wanted Rebecca dead.

Chapter Sixteen

———— • ————

What did you do to LIFU?" Anne demanded. I'd been so wrapped up replaying the conversation I'd just had with Marigold, I hadn't noticed that Anne had come into the library's café to look after the fallen robot. She was standing next to my chair at the café counter with her bright yellow fists propped on her hips. "It's completely messed up. And now we're going to have to explain to Keven how we broke his expensive prototype."

"I didn't break anything on that defective piece of metal. All I did was push it over," I said.

"You pushed it over?! I know you don't like technology, but don't you think attacking a defenseless robot is going too far?"

I held up a finger. "One, that thing isn't defenseless. The unnatural color of . . . of, well, all of you is proof enough of that." I lifted a second finger. "Two, I didn't attack it."

"You just told me you did!" Anne cried.

"No, I told you that I knocked it over. Which was necessary in order to save one of our patrons from becoming that thing's next victim. Why did Keven bring it back? It's a menace."

She cocked her head to one side and looked at me. "That's what happened? Really?"

"Ask the barista. He was cowering behind the counter when I came in."

"I was," the barista said, and he turned a bit red.

Anne bit her lip as her gaze ping-ponged between me and the robot. "I don't understand. It was never even supposed to come into the café. It's only supposed to roam around the main library floor aiding anyone who needs it. And Keven promised he fixed the other . . . um . . . problems and disabled the security features."

"Look on the bright side, this gives you an excuse to see Keven again," I said.

"I don't—"

"Everyone seems to be gaga over him," I said, not unkindly.

"He is dreamy," the barista agreed.

"Well, I've never met someone that brilliant," Anne confessed while turning a bit red—er, orange—in the cheeks as well. "I worked with bona fide geniuses in Silicon Valley, and Keven makes most of them look stupid." She smiled to herself for a moment before sobering again. "I don't understand what's going on. LIFU was working beautifully this morning when he brought it over."

She returned to the robot and knelt beside it. "What did that mean lady do to you? You can tell me," she cooed to the machine in a sugary-sweet voice I'd never heard her use before.

"I didn't do anything to it!" I protested.

"Ah!" Anne looked up at me and smiled.

"What?" I asked. I wasn't sure why I'd stayed to watch her treat that thing as if it were alive and in possession of feelings. I had work to get back to and, more importantly, a murderer to find. "What is it?"

"It looks like whoever last used the robot jammed it up with several nonsense requests. Most of them are strings of letters that don't even form words. All this gibberish probably overloaded LIFU's AI system. It's been programmed to figure out requests, even if they are misspelled, you know? There are five gibberish ones here that happened within several seconds of the others, almost like someone was banging on the screen."

"Who would do that?"

"One of your technology-hating friends?" Anne asked with her bright yellow eyebrows raised.

"My friends don't hate, they just prefer—"

"I'm just yanking your chain." Anne stood and brushed off her pants. "If I had to guess, a child was playing around with it. Did any of your tots sneak away from your program?"

"I didn't have a program this morning. And I haven't seen any children in the library today, at least none that could walk or reach that thing's screen."

"Hmm . . ." She pushed a few buttons on the robot. I stepped back as it groaned as if in pain. "It's trying to reboot," she said as she continued to fiddle with it. "Hold on. Let me try to stop it." She pushed even more buttons. "That's interesting. The last real request produced an article about Rebecca White landing a role on a television show. Everything after that is gibberish. Look here. The article was still on the screen when someone started banging on it. Who was this patron of yours who LIFU supposedly attacked?"

"It went after Marigold Brantley. She used to run the feed and seed store."

"Goldie? Had she been using LIFU?"

"I don't know." Had Marigold been using the machine to look up something about Rebecca? "And why does everyone know that Marigold's nickname is Goldie? I've never called her that, or even knew to."

Anne shrugged. "Don't know. That's how she introduced herself to me the first time we met. She had come in right after our grand opening and wanted to see all the equipment. She's a whiz when it comes to computers. Knew more about some of the components than I did." That admission couldn't have come easily for Anne.

"Are you saying that Marigold would know better than to pound on the screen like that?" I asked.

"Definitely."

"Marigold is a computer whiz?" I felt like I needed to say that aloud. It was yet another thing I would never have guessed about her. Apparently, I didn't know anything about this woman who lived in our small town my entire life. It made me wonder what other things I'd missed about my neighbors. "Marigold told me that she and Rebecca were close. Why would she look up an old article about Rebecca landing the role on *Desiring Hearts*? And if she's such a computer expert, why would she come to the library to look up the article? Why not just use her own computer or even her cell phone to do her research?"

"Tru, haven't you been paying attention at the staff meetings?" Anne sounded hurt. "I explained more than once that our database includes paid subscriptions to hundreds of publications."

"I knew that." I'd forgotten. "I just wasn't thinking."

She shook her head as she peered closely at the robot's screen. "Anyhow, a straight Google search wouldn't get her access to what we have. And we don't have the funds to make the subscriptions available to our online patrons. She'd have to come to the library to find this article." She swiped her finger across the screen. "Oh, look. It's not an old article. It's in an issue that came out . . . today."

"Really? Can I read it?" I tried to peer over Anne's shoulder to see what she was reading. But the display was cracked and the text garbled in several places.

"Sorry, Tru." Anne sounded as if she meant it. "LIFU will need a complete overhaul before anyone can see anything more than bits and pieces on this screen again. I could pull it up on a computer for you and print it out, if you'd like." She twisted around to look up at me.

"Thank you, I appreciate the offer. But I'm sure I'll be able to find it for myself the next time I'm at one of the library's computers."

"Are you sure?" She raised a disbelieving brow.

"I'm sure. I did pay attention when you taught me how to use the new system. And I have been practicing with it as I teach our patrons the ins and outs of it."

"Okay. Holler if you need any help."

"Will do." I headed back to the front desk.

Mrs. Farnsworth had taken over working there. She waved me away when I approached, telling me that she'd handle the desk for the next hour or so.

Not one to question my good luck, I hurried toward the back stairs that led down to the secret bookroom in the basement. On my way I passed the rows of public computers that had replaced the reference section of the library. I stopped at one and typed Rebecca White's name in the search bar.

After wading through a few pages of results and finding nothing recent, I narrowed my search to only look for anything from the past month.

One result popped up on the screen.

I read it through.

My goodness.

According to the article, Rebecca White had been

hired for a supporting role in a new soap opera that was going to be filmed in Hollywood and aired on a cable channel. It sounded as if she was going to play a character like Delilah on *Desiring Hearts.*

Was Sissy mistaken when she told me that Rebecca's big news on the night of her death was that she planned to kick out the older society members? Was the news instead that Rebecca had landed a new job? Was she going to announce, in front of the documentary crew, that she was going to move back to Hollywood?

That would make more sense.

And who had gone searching for this article? Marigold? If she and Rebecca were truly as close as sisters, she would already know about Rebecca's return to acting.

Unless Rebecca hadn't told her . . .

And yet, if Marigold's sharp mind figured out that she was about to lose her idol . . .

That could be motive.

Chapter Seventeen

As soon as I'd passed through the heavy metal double doors leading into the secret bookroom, Dewey rushed over to greet me. He looked up at me with his bright, intelligent green eyes and gave a screeching meow.

Wait, that wasn't a greeting. That sounded more like a warning.

"What's up?" I asked him.

He glanced over his shoulder and then back up at me. *Crash!*

"It wasn't supposed to do that," Flossie exclaimed from somewhere on the far side of the bookroom.

"Watch it! You nearly took off the top of my head," Hubert Crawford cried at about the same time.

"Let me try again," she said.

"Let me get farther out of the way."

As I jogged through the stacks to find them, there was another crash.

"Peaches!" Flossie cried.

"Shh! This is a library." I was surprised how much I sounded like Mrs. Farnsworth. But really, the head librarian did have a point. Loud voices made thinking difficult. "What's going on over here?" I asked as I skidded to a stop.

"Look out!" Delanie warned.

Flossie's meteor hammer flew through the air and landed with a thump at my feet.

"It wasn't supposed to do that," Flossie complained, staring at the weapon. Gradually her gaze rose up and up until it landed on my unhappy face. "Sorry, Tru."

"Flossie, you know I love you, but someone is going to get hurt. You need to practice outside. And far away from people."

"I know, I know. It's just so wet and chilly outside."

"It is," Hubert agreed. He looked as if he had been having nearly as much fun as Flossie was. So did Delanie, who had been watching from a safe distance.

Hubert Crawford was the president of the Cypress Museum Board, a position he took seriously, dressing in tweed suits with matching waistcoats as if he lived in a different time. He shunned the use of technology, preferring to thumb through paper documents, which meant he had to travel extensively throughout the Southeast to research the history of Cypress and South Carolina and its residents.

He nudged his glasses up his nose. "Speaking of people getting hurt, I heard you are investigating Rebecca's death."

"I am asking some questions," I admitted. "I don't think Hazel is guilty."

"Really?" Delanie sounded surprised. "Everyone is saying the police have so much evidence against poor Hazel that even her lawyer is telling her to admit her guilt."

"I think the police are wrong." It really was as simple as that.

"*Really?*" Hubert smiled. "So, you've already uncovered something?"

"Not yet," I hated to admit.

"I'm sure you'll get all the answers to your questions, dear," Delanie said with a smile. "You're as clever as a raccoon trying to get into a chicken pen."

"Thank you, I think." The analogy made me sound like I was trying to go places where I didn't belong. "Did Rebecca say anything to you about bringing in more new members?" I asked Delanie.

"No." She glanced over at Flossie. "The society's membership is limited to ten members. And we have ten members. We'd been turning down applications solely because there simply wasn't room for new people."

"What about Hazel?" Flossie asked. "She told us that her membership was provisional."

"That's what Rebecca told Hazel. But the rest of us had already voted. Hazel is a member." Delanie frowned. "Rebecca saw Hazel as a rival. Hazel has always been known for being fashionable and throwing the best events. And Rebecca hated it when anyone got more attention than she did. I wish it hadn't been that way. Maybe then she would have let Hazel do what she knew how to do and plan the book club dinner without interference. Maybe then Hazel wouldn't have cracked and hit Rebecca over the head." She shifted uncomfortably from foot to foot. Clearly, she believed Hazel was guilty. "Oh, look at the time. I have a charity meeting to get to. Good luck with your investigation."

"Wait, I have another question about membership," I called to her, wanting to ask about Sissy's claim that she was soon going to be a member. I also wanted to talk to her about Marigold's relationship with Rebecca.

"Sorry! I really have to run," she called over her shoulder without pausing, her shoes click-clacking against the basement's concrete flooring as she raced across the bookroom toward the exit.

"Tru, I heard your daddy has gone missing—is that right?" Hubert said in the sudden silence after Delanie's departure.

"He is. I'm sick with worry over that too."

Hubert clicked his tongue. "I remember one time back shortly after you were born when your daddy left without telling anyone. Your mother had been certain that he'd crashed his car and died somewhere in a cotton field. She organized a spectacular wake and memorial service. And halfway through the memorial, in he walks and asks someone in the back of the church who died. When he heard he'd walked in on his own memorial, Ashley laughed so loud everyone turned to look. Your mother, on the other hand, didn't find anything about the timing of his reappearance at all funny."

I shook my head. It was true. My daddy did like to wander from time to time. I wondered why Mama Eddy was so upset about him leaving this time. It wasn't like they were married or even got along. "What's troubling me is that he's not been returning my texts. No matter where he goes, he has always kept in touch with me," I said.

"But Jace and his friends are searching, right? I'm sure you'll learn something by tonight." Flossie rolled toward me. "I'm sure your father is fine."

"In the meantime, we need to focus on helping Hazel, isn't that right?" Hubert said.

"Did you know Rebecca?" I asked him, hoping he could give me some startling piece of insight.

"Sadly, no. She never came to the Cypress Museum. I wish she had. I would have personally shown her around. Did you know that she wasn't the first retired actor to move to Cypress? Back in the 1950s, Button Monterrey, star of—"

"Have you heard of anyone who was Rebecca's friend?" I interrupted his lecture to ask. Hubert, while kind to a fault and super knowledgeable about the town's history, tended to wander into lengthy musings whenever anyone asked him a question. As a result, few ever dared to ask him anything.

I hated to cut this lecture short. I had never heard about this Button fellow, and I was curious about who he was (a clown, I guessed) and why he'd ended up in Cypress. But I didn't have time to find out about him right now. Mrs. Farnsworth would expect me back at the front desk when my lunch hour was up.

"Friends? Rebecca?" Hubert cleared his throat. "From what I've heard, our local starlet kept to herself. She was a recluse like Greta Garbo. Very glamorous."

"I think you must have heard wrong. Rebecca was president of the Arete Society." Flossie used a hushed voice as she said *Arete Society* as if she were talking about a religious experience instead of a book club.

"That silly group?" Hubert scoffed, as he pushed his glasses back up his nose again. They were constantly sliding down. "I heard it's nothing more than a bunch of gabble-grousers looking for an excuse to show off their latest recipes."

"What? What?" Flossie gasped several times before insisting, "The Arete Society is one of the oldest and most respected clubs in town. The members read the highest-quality literature and gather once a month to have thoughtful debates about what they learned from the book. A lady from a national news program had come all the way from Hollywood to attend this week's meeting because she wanted to film a documentary on them."

He made a rude noise with his lips. "That group of ladies is 'full of sound and fury, signifying nothing.'

Yes, the members of the club have convinced everyone that their 'society' is special, but it's nothing more than a bunch of snobs showing off how snobby they can be."

Dewey meowed sharply just as the hair on the back of his neck rose.

My muscles tensed. I moved toward Flossie, prepared to hold her back, in case she decided to swing her meteor hammer at Hubert for disparaging a local institution that seemed to mean so much to her.

Much to my surprise, Flossie tossed back her head and laughed. "Oh, Hubert, you are so nice to say that." She wiped her eyes with the back of her hand.

He smiled kindly at her. "Well, it's true. If they keep out great minds such as yours, I must question their worth. It sounds like a social club to me."

"He's right," I said.

"You know what? He is," Flossie agreed. The tension that she'd been carrying around with her seemed to slip away. "He *is* right." She clapped her hands. "I don't know what I've been thinking. It's a waste of time and energy to keep trying to please those ladies. I am who I am. I'm not changing for anyone. Who cares if they think I'm not good enough for their book club? I know they're wrong, and that's all that matters."

"Hear, hear," I cheered. "Thank you, Hubert."

His cheeks turned pink. He cleared his throat and nudged his glasses up his nose for a third time. "Don't thank me," he mumbled. "Thank Shakespeare."

"I've never been a big fan of *Macbeth*. Too much blood and death for my tastes," Flossie said. "But I do appreciate a man who can recite famous quotes at useful moments like this one."

"I live to serve." He gave a mock bow.

Flossie gave him a heated look.

Hubert returned it.

"Well, since that's settled, I'll just go get the returned books checked back in," I said, backing away. "Over there. On the other side of the room. At the desk. And let y'all finish this moment in private."

"Wait, Tru." Flossie touched my arm. "What's going on about Rebecca's death? And what can I do to help you?"

I told her about Marigold—*Goldie*—and the odd article about Rebecca that she may or may not have looked up. Did Marigold slam her hands against the robot's touch screen in grief and frustration until it glitched and came at her with a vengeance?

Had Marigold lashed out at her best friend in the same way when she'd first learned that Rebecca was leaving Cypress?

Was that the secret she was refusing to talk about?

Chapter Eighteen

————·————

Every murderer is probably somebody's old friend," Agatha Christie wrote in her debut novel, *The Mysterious Affair at Styles*. It's a brilliant truth that any good investigator should embrace.

Unfortunately, Detective Ellerbe refused to even listen to the quote, much less to my theory that Marigold and Rebecca might have suffered a falling-out that, sadly, led to murder. Instead, he rather rudely insisted I was chasing fairy tales. "Tru, you need to listen to yourself. Marigold wasn't in Hazel's house, which means she didn't have the opportunity to smash anyone over the head in a fit of anger," he told me when I called to tell him that he should go question Marigold.

"Details. Details. You wanted me to keep you in the loop," I reminded him.

"Yes, I did," he groaned into the phone. "But I didn't expect you to take your investigation into the pages of a fantasy novel. Facts, Tru. I need facts, not pie-in-the-sky theories."

"There's no pie," I insisted, but he'd hung up.

I don't know why he reacted that way. I didn't even mention the library's robot and its strange behavior after Marigold's interaction with it. If I had, he would have accused me of falling into a sci-fi novel instead of a fantasy.

I tapped my fingers on the old circulation desk that we'd set up in the basement. The more I thought about Marigold, the more I wanted to find out more about her relationship with Rebecca and her knowledge of computers (and possibly robots.)

I want to question Marigold, I texted Tori. Are you available?

Heck yeah, she texted back almost immediately. Hey! I know how to get us into her house without seeming like we're intruding.

How?

Two words. Joyce Fellows.

What? She couldn't be serious.

I'm serious.

When I didn't reply, she sent another text. Trust me.

I trusted Tori. But sometimes her well-meaning actions caused more trouble than I could handle.

"I haven't gone to lunch yet," I called to Flossie, who was still on the far side of the bookroom talking quietly with Hubert. "I need to have a chat with Tori. Do you want to go with me to Perks to pick up a salad?"

"Does she sell Cokes yet?" Flossie called back.

"I don't think so." This was a conversation we had

every time we went to Tori's coffee shop. Flossie thought every place that sold anything should sell soda.

"I was at the hardware store near the interstate the other day. You know what they were selling?" Flossie asked.

"Bottles of Coke?" I guessed.

"Bottles *and* cans. But I do prefer the bottles. A hardware store, Tru. It was selling Cokes. I can purchase the drink everywhere except at Tori's coffee shop. That girl is missing out on a world of business. I'm not the only one in town who isn't interested in drinking a hot coffee in the middle of a hot day."

"It's barely fifty degrees out," I reminded her as I rescued another historical romance from Dewey's jaws. "Naughty kitty. These books aren't for chewing."

"That's strange." Flossie had rolled over to the circulation desk. "I've never seen your kitty act like that before. He's usually so gentle with the books."

"I think it's all this chilly weather," I said. "He's ready for spring."

"Aren't we all?" Flossie reached down and scratched Dewey under the chin.

He looked up at her and meowed.

"Would you like me to pick anything up for you at Perks?" I asked her.

"No need. I'm coming with you."

"But what about the Coke situation?"

"I suppose I can survive with just water. I'm hoping we'll bump into some more Arete Society members. They all seemed gaga about drinking coffee two nights ago at Hazel's house. Poor Hazel was being accused of murder, and those women still expected to be served piping hot coffee. I was so appalled by that I didn't even think to ask the right questions about Rebecca."

"And I could ask them about Rebecca's biggest fan—Marigold," I said.

"Exactly! We all know there's a fine line between love and hate," Flossie said as she moved another historical romance out of Dewey's reach. He was systematically pulling them off the shelf near us. "Let's go," she said, as if my cat's behavior wasn't the oddest thing she'd ever seen.

"Why do you think he's doing that?" I frowned as he sniffed around, seemingly searching for his next victim.

"Who knows? He's a cat," Flossie said as she rolled toward the doors.

I paused and watched Dewey for a few more moments, wondering what had gotten into him, before chasing after my friend.

Perks was crowded that afternoon.

Tori was working behind the counter, filling orders as quickly as humanly possible. When she saw us, she held up a finger. "I'll be ready in a few. We're short-staffed, and . . ." She spread her arms to encompass the crowd. "Happens every time someone calls in sick. The world suddenly decides they need coffee."

As we headed to our regular spot, I spotted Emma Guerin sitting by herself at a table nearby. I tapped Flossie on the shoulder before heading over to Emma.

"I heard you were sick the other night. I hope you're feeling better now," I said.

About my age, Emma was one of the younger members of the Arete Society. She had recently started working as a travel agent and dressed as if she specialized in setting up lavish trips for the rich and famous instead of small weekend getaways for local residents, which I'd heard were the bulk of her business. Today, she had on a forest-green pantsuit with a silk scarf tied artfully around her neck. Her short blond hair looked freshly cut and was expertly styled with a cute wave that framed her oval face.

She looked startled to see us.

"Oh! I really was sick," she said. "Otherwise, I wouldn't have missed your presentation. Although"—she pressed a hand to her lips—"I suppose you didn't give your presentation, did you? Are they going to reschedule it? I'm still in shock about what happened. To Rebecca, I mean."

"It is troubling," I agreed. I then introduced her to Flossie and dropped a not-so-subtle hint that Flossie would like to be considered for membership in the Arete Society.

"There will be an opening now, won't there?" she said as her face fell and tears filled her eyes.

"Of course, it's still too soon to talk about that," Flossie said. "We're interested in finding out more about Rebecca so we can understand what happened and why."

Emma shook her head. "I owe Rebecca everything. A few years ago, she helped when I was out of work and on the verge of losing my home. And she helped me get into the Arete Society. She told me that the book club needed some younger members to keep the discussions from getting stale."

"This is why they keep turning me away?" Flossie grumbled. "Everyone thinks I'm too old?"

"No, that's not what I'm saying," Emma assured Flossie. "I have enjoyed the discussions. Having a range of ages in the group has been eye-opening. Some of the older members surprise me with how the books we read resonate so differently with them. It's sometimes like we've read different books. Rebecca knew how to keep things fresh by making sure the group remained a mix of ages and backgrounds."

"Did she say anything to you about bringing in even

more new members?" I asked her the same question I'd asked Delanie.

"No." She glanced over at Flossie. "The society's membership is limited to ten members. And we have ten members."

"How about for this month's meeting, did anyone warn you not to attend because Rebecca planned to announce that she was going to kick out some older members to make room for more younger members such as yourself?"

"What? That doesn't sound right. I honestly had a wicked stomach bug. As I said, I would have come if I could."

"You really haven't heard anything about membership changes?" Flossie pressed.

"No. But then everyone knows I'm not a gossip, so people don't come to me to dish." She leaned in close as if to spill a big secret. "Gossiping is not good for business."

"And yet only last week, you were in the library telling me how Mrs. Potts is cheating on her husband with Mr. Blandish," Flossie reminded her.

"That was news." Emma made the word *news* sound as if it had at least three syllables. "News isn't gossip. When is your next trip, Flossie? I could set up a package for you to somewhere warm and exotic and decadently luxurious."

"I'm sure you could, honey." In the South, sometimes we say things and mean the absolute opposite. I could tell by Flossie's lilting tone of voice that this was one of those times. "But I have decided to stick around and tend to my lake house."

"You can't work on a house all the time, Flossie. Come by my office and let me set you up with a weekend getaway. I'll get you a good deal." She sat back and smiled. "I don't know why the other members are so dead set against you joining the society. With your travel experiences, I'm sure you'd be a perfect addition to the group."

Flossie's shoulders visibly stiffened. She rolled closer to Emma. "Who is blocking my membership?"

Emma shrugged. "When Rebecca became president, she gave herself the ability to veto or approve any application without it having to go to the membership for a vote. I seem to remember yours was one of the applications she'd tossed."

"Why?" my friend growled. "What did she have against me?"

Emma shrugged, clearly not understanding just how upset Flossie was over this snub. "You'll have to ask some of the older members. When no one objected to tossing out your application, I assumed they all agreed with Rebecca's decision. But what do I know? Perhaps they were more interested in inviting Hazel. She is well-known for her gourmet spread whenever she's hosting an event at her house."

"Do you know how *you* managed to get an invitation?" Flossie asked.

"Rebecca befriended me," Emma said with pride.

"Why?" Flossie demanded.

"How did you get to know Rebecca?" I asked before Flossie let her emotions get control of her mouth. The tips of my friend's ears were turning red, which wasn't a good sign.

"I was visiting Goldie. She and her husband live in that old Victorian mansion at the far end of Main Street. Do you know the place? It's up on that little hill."

"I know where you're talking about," I said with a soft laugh. It just happened to be the only remaining Victorian mansion on Main Street.

"I was visiting Goldie," she repeated. "I wanted to see if she would be willing to let me rent the room above her garage. I'd just lost my job and couldn't pay the rent on my house. I was days from having to live out of my car! Well, Rebecca came up the walk while I was explaining my situation to Goldie. I was blown away by how generous Rebecca was. She introduced herself—as if she needed an introduction—and then asked about what kind of work I was looking for. When I explained how I wanted to work for myself—I was tired of depending on others—she asked how she could help. She asked *me* how *she* could help, and I was thinking, 'Are you kidding me?' Rebecca started brainstorming business ideas and Goldie joined in. They were the ones who came up with the idea that I should turn my desire to travel into a career. When they made the suggestion, it felt like everything just snapped into place. Honestly, I don't know how I didn't come up with the idea on my own. I was a secretary for many years. I already knew how to make reservations for others and how to follow up and make sure all the travel details were in place. As we were talking, the conversation turned to the book club. And next thing I knew, Rebecca was inviting me to join. I was surprised. I had never been part of a book club before. Never was interested in talking about the books I read."

"Why?" Flossie forced through clenched teeth. "If you don't love books enough to want to talk about them, why join the Arete Society?"

"Connections, of course. The best of the best in Cypress are members, aren't they? The name of the game in any business is networking, in this case networking to get clients who want high-end travel services. I have to network my way into getting my name out there as a travel agent who can get the job done. I can't do that by hanging around the Sunshine Diner. I need direct access to the people in this community who have influence or money. That's why I need the society. Those women have both."

Flossie pressed her lips together.

"There will be two openings now after what Hazel did," Emma said gently. "With Rebecca gone, you should put in another application, Flossie. I'll even put in a good word for you, maybe change a few of the other members' minds about you." She laughed. "Maybe we can even branch out and read something other than those depressing books Rebecca insisted would elevate us. I hated those books. I stopped reading the monthly pick after slogging through the novel where everyone died at the end. Why read five hundred pages just to have all the characters you were rooting for kick the can like that?"

"*Bucket*," Flossie murmured.

"What?" Emma asked.

"Nothing," Flossie said with a sigh. "The characters died at the end of the book, you said?"

Emma nodded. "I mean, what the heck? Worst. Book. Ever." She glanced over at Flossie. All the color drained from Emma's face. "Gracious, that isn't a book you wrote, is it? If it is, I didn't mean it. I mean, I suppose the writing may have been good."

"That's not my book," Flossie said tightly. "Tru, don't you need to get back to work?"

I glanced at my watch and saw that I had forty minutes left on my lunch break. But Flossie didn't give me a chance to answer. She was already moving toward the door.

"Do put in a good word for Flossie," I suggested before starting toward the door myself. "Joining the Arete Society has been something she's wanted for as long as I've known her."

"I will. And Tru," Emma said. "Be careful."

I chased after Flossie.

"Why are we running away?" I asked as soon as I caught up to her. We were both on the sidewalk outside Perks. A winter wind was blowing in from the north. I pulled my sweater tight around my body. "We came to find out what Tori had planned, remember?"

Flossie shook her head. She opened her mouth several times before saying, "I can't. Not right now."

She started to roll away. I'd never seen her so upset that she couldn't speak, and that worried me.

"Flossie! I can't let you leave like this. Please, talk to me. I'll take you to the hardware store. I'm sure they sell sodas. I'll buy you one."

She turned her wheelchair around and smiled at me. It wasn't a happy smile. "Thanks, Tru. But I need to be alone for a bit."

"Why? What did Emma say that upset you so? Don't tell me you wrote that book Emma was complaining about."

"No, it's not that. It's . . . I . . . I'll call you tomorrow." She turned back around and rolled away as fast as her arms would allow.

I knew from experience that when Flossie wanted to be alone, I should leave her alone. There'd be no budging her today. I stood at the corner and watched with concern as my friend turned off the sidewalk when she reached the library's parking lot.

What did Emma say? I wondered. But then I remembered how Emma had been so cavalier about her membership in the one book club that meant the world to Flossie. Despite Flossie's assurances that she no longer cared if she was invited to join the Arete Society or not, I figured that wasn't the complete truth. Hubert may have made her feel better about being excluded from the group for a while, but I imagined that exclusion still stuck like a burr in her toe. That had to be why she refused to stay and talk with Emma or to scheme with Tori.

I made a mental note to myself to give Flossie a call first thing tomorrow morning to make sure she was okay. In the meantime, I still had a murderer to find.

Chapter Nineteen

———··———

I marched back into Perks and headed over to the counter, where Tori was still struggling to keep up with the lunch rush. I slipped through the swinging half door that led behind the bar, grabbed a black "Perk Up Your Day!" apron that was hanging on a wooden peg, tied it on, and then washed my hands.

"What are you doing?" Tori demanded as she handed a rugged farmer a colorful unicorn mocha with a cherry on top.

"I'm going to help you, so you'll have time to help me."

"Do you know how to do this?" she asked.

"I know how to make the best coffee in the library," I said. "I think I can handle this."

"I hope so." She tossed me a stack of order sheets and then flipped through a stack of her own. "I don't have time to teach anyone the ropes."

For the next half hour, I struggled to help fill all the special orders that kept coming in. For such a small, rural town, the residents sure had a fussy sense of taste. I suppose I did too.

I stuffed a bag with an almond croissant and snapped the lid on a to-go cup of coffee.

"That's the last one," Tori said as she wiped her hands on her apron.

"How do you do this every day?" I asked, feeling bone-tired and like I'd just run a marathon.

Tori smiled. "I love the challenge. And I love seeing the smiles on my customers' faces. It's fun."

Her smiles had been coming faster and easier lately. I was glad for it. I suspected her relationship with a certain used bookstore owner contributed to her sunny outlook. Charlie was good for her.

"You said you had a plan?" I asked.

"I did. I do have a plan, I mean." She looked around. "What happened to Flossie?"

"We talked with Emma Guerin about Rebecca and the Arete Society." I nodded to the table where Emma was still sitting. She was sipping her coffee while gazing out the window. A smile creased her lips. "Flossie got all flustered after Emma admitted she didn't enjoy being a member of the book club. Apparently, she only joined so she could network to drum up business for her travel agency."

"So? Isn't that why anyone would join a book club? Well, I mean, besides the excuse to get together with your girlfriends and drink."

"No. Those aren't good reasons to join a book club."

"What?" Tori nudged me with her arm. "That's why I joined your mystery book club."

"I know." Tori rarely read the books. But because she was my best friend since forever, and I did enjoy her company, I didn't mind. "But Flossie has been trying for years to get into the Arete Society. It's more serious than our gathering of friends. The members read serious books and have serious discussions."

"Sounds like a yawn."

"Regardless, the Arete Society matters to Flossie. And she is upset. According to Emma, Rebecca played a big part in keeping Flossie out of the society. And I think it hurt Flossie to hear that Rebecca had invited members like Emma, who aren't in love with literature like we are, while tossing Flossie's application in the trash."

Tori gave me a thoughtful look. "Didn't you say that Flossie had been alone with . . . ?" Her voice trailed off, and she shook her head.

"Alone with what?" I asked.

"*Not what. Who*," Tori whispered. She shook her head again.

"She didn't do anything to Rebecca," I insisted.

"Not even in a fit of anger? You have to agree that Flossie does have a temper."

"She can be dramatic," I corrected. "But she wouldn't harm anyone. That's one thing I'm sure about."

"What about the boomerang incident? You aren't going to tell me that you believed her when she claimed her hand slipped?"

"That was different," I said.

"She smacked Delanie with a boomerang!" Tori pantomimed being hit in the head.

She had smacked Delanie in the head. And Rebecca had died from a blow to her head. I pinched the bridge of my nose. "That was different."

"If you say so." Tori poured two mugs of black coffee and handed me one.

I took a sip. Her coffee tasted heavenly. "So, what's

this plan you've hatched to get Marigold to tell us her secrets?" I asked, changing the subject.

"Oh! It's brilliant. And look, the key to my plan has just walked through the door."

"Trudy!" Joyce Fellows called out to me. "I'm so glad I finally caught up to you!"

Chapter Twenty

———•———

I love Tori. Ever since kindergarten, we've laughed and played together. We've cried together. I wouldn't trade her for the world.

But with that said, in that moment, I could have killed her with my bare hands!

"You didn't," I said as Joyce came toward us.

My friend smiled like an angel.

"You didn't tell her I wanted to be on her show," I cried as Joyce came even closer.

"Why not?" Tori looked truly pleased with herself. She spoke quickly since the talk show host and another woman who was slightly older were nearly upon us. Joyce Fellows was a tall woman with perfect mahogany-brown hair and perfect makeup and clothes that hung perfectly on her slender frame. Even her shiny high heels were perfect. I would have expected them to be scuffed after a long day chasing people around with that ridiculously large microphone of hers.

"You'll get national attention for all the hard work you've been doing for this town," Tori said, "and we get a brilliant excuse to get Goldie to talk about Rebecca." Her smile grew even larger. She turned to Joyce. "Tru was just telling me how excited she was to talk to you." Her voice boomed. Everyone in the café turned to gawp at us. "It's uncanny how you keep missing her."

"She ran from us," the woman accompanying Joyce grumbled. "More than once." She didn't look nearly as glamorous as the television star. Instead of a neatly pressed pantsuit, she had on jeans and a light blue T-shirt sporting the logo for Joyce's television show and a coffee stain. But she was wearing bright purple eyeglasses, which suggested she had a hidden fun streak. "Running from us doesn't scream excitement."

"She's shy, isn't that right, Tru?" Tori punched my arm and laughed. "I love your show, Ms. Fellows. I cannot believe I'm here talking with you. Right here, in our little town. I simply cannot imagine it. Can I offer you some coffee? I'm the owner here. I mean, this is my café. Perks. Let me pour you some coffee, or would you prefer tea?"

The other café patrons clustered around. Emma, I noticed, pushed her way to the front and was hastily applying fresh lipstick.

"I don't drink caffeine," Joyce said, not unkindly. But I cringed when she added, "It's poison, you know?"

"Have you been talking to a woman we all lovingly call Mama Eddy?" Tori asked, not at all bothered that someone she admired had just called her coffee poison. "Um, never mind . . . I do have decaf, if you—"

"I'll take a large coffee, black," the woman with Joyce said, interrupting Tori. She then held out her hand as she waited for Tori to pour the coffee into one of her tall mugs. The dark rings under her eyes were a sharp contrast to Joyce's perky, well-rested look. "I'm Gail Tremper, producer for *Ideal Life*."

"Oh!" Tori exclaimed. "You're the one who decides on the topics for the show." She elbowed me in the side. "What an exciting career."

"It's a laugh a minute," Gail said dryly. She then turned to me. "Joyce would like to interview you for her show. On camera, of course. She'd like to talk to you about what you saw the night Hazel Bailey killed our beloved Rebecca." The LIFU robot's voice had more emotion than this woman's. "You'll need makeup, of course."

"Hazel didn't kill—" I started to say.

"She'd love to!" Tori said, nudging me with her elbow again. "Plus, don't you think it would be fabulous if the interview included other members of the Arete Society? Marigold Brantley, for instance, was Rebecca's dearest friend in town."

"Rebecca had friends?" Gail said, her brows furrowing.

"Of course she had friends," Joyce said with a nervous laugh. "Rebecca White was a beloved small-screen star. Everyone wanted to be her friend."

"Yes, we all loved her!" Tori gushed.

"I was her friend!" Emma called from the crowd.

"So was I," someone else said with a chuckle.

"Me too!" another woman cried.

"Put me on TV," yet another woman called out.

Others started joining in, laughing, clearly excited at the thought of being interviewed for national television.

"How well did you know Rebecca?" Joyce asked Tori. "You didn't happen to be there when Hazel killed Rebecca, did you?" The talk show host then turned to her producer. "This one has a lovely stage presence even though she runs a coffee shop. I think we should find a way to get her some screen time."

"Sadly, I wasn't on scene—isn't that what they call it in the television world?—I wasn't on scene when Rebecca was killed . . . *not* by Hazel, by the way." Tori quickly added that last part after I nudged *her* in the side with *my* elbow.

"Did either of you know Rebecca well?" I asked Joyce and Gail. If Marigold wasn't the one who had killed Rebecca, perhaps one of them had reason to want the former actress dead.

"Only heard stories from other producers," Gail said, and then added, "Horror stories."

"She's kidding. She's kidding." Joyce laughed. It was a nervous kind of twitter.

Gail hadn't looked like she was kidding.

"Everyone loved Rebecca," Joyce repeated.

"Did you know her well?" I pressed.

"I, um, she and I didn't have the closest relationship," Joyce stammered, "but we knew each other profession- ally. When she invited me to this, um, quaint town to film her little book club, I was flattered."

"Tru thinks Rebecca lied to you when she invited you here to film the book club," Tori said.

"Why did she invite us, then?" Joyce asked me with a patronizing smile.

"I saw an article—it just came out today—announcing Rebecca's return to television," I said. "I suspect she had been planning on making that announcement to the book club and wanted it televised."

"That would have been a ratings bonanza," Gail said, her stony expression still unchanged.

"Covering her murder investigation will be a huge ratings draw as well," Joyce said brightly. "Bigger than an announcement about her grasping onto some bit part in a show nobody has ever heard of."

"I thought you loved her," I said.

"Professionally," Joyce clarified. "Let's get you ready for your interview."

"I . . . um . . ." I really didn't want to talk to anyone on camera about finding Rebecca's body. For one thing, Mama Eddy would never forgive me. According to her, good Southern ladies didn't talk about such unpleasant things like murder, especially not on television. The only appropriate reasons for appearing on television were beauty pageants and charity fundraisers. Everything else was, in Mama Eddy's estimation, vulgar.

"Marigold Brantley is the one you really need to talk to," I insisted, trying to get us back on track with Tori's plan to encourage Marigold to open up. "She and Rebecca shared all their little secrets. I wonder if one of those secrets isn't the key to finding Rebecca's killer."

"I thought the police already knew who killed our star?" Joyce said.

"They do," Gail said in that flat, tired voice of hers. "Can I have another coffee? This is one of the best brews I've ever tasted."

"Thank you," Tori said. "I roast the beans here in the shop. They're organic and fair trade. I sell them if you'd like to take a bag home with you."

"After we're done filming the documentary about Rebecca's last days, I'd like to schedule a session with you and your coffee shop. That is, if we still have a show."

"What does that mean?" I asked.

"That would be awesome," Tori said at the same time. "You could film my roasting process. It's a technique I learned from an old Mayan man I met when I was on my honeymoon with Number Three."

"Number Three?" Gail asked.

"She numbers her ex-husbands," I explained. "And the police haven't arrested the right person. Hazel didn't kill anyone. I'm sure of it. Why are you worried about your show?"

"Ah, the mousy one has a personality after all," Gail

said. "I'll get a makeup team over here. Joyce, you'll have to keep reminding Trudy that the police think they've already arrested Rebecca's killer. That'll keep the stakes high and the viewer interested."

"My name isn't Trudy." Hadn't I told them that already? I was pretty sure I had. "It's Trudell."

"I like that name. Got a Southern twang to it," Gail said. She pointed to our regular table, which happened to be underneath an antique metal feed and seed sign with a large rooster on it. "We can set up over there."

"Shouldn't we go over to Marigold's house?" I asked, my gaze locked on Tori. She'd gotten me into this. "Plus, my lunch hour is just about up. I need to get back to the library. And y'all heard Mrs. Farnsworth this morning. She doesn't allow cameras in the library."

"I could get my husband to make an exception." Annabelle had pushed her way to the front of the crowd. She was holding her phone high in the air. "I wouldn't want you to miss your chance to get the recognition you deserve, dear."

Although getting interviewed for the TV show was the last thing I wanted to do, I was surrounded by friends and neighbors who were trying their hardest to help me. I flip-flopped between feeling dismayed and touched by their kindness.

"Who are you?" Joyce asked Annabelle.

Annabelle explained how her husband was mayor of Cypress.

"She's also a member of the Arete Society," I was quick to say. "Have you interviewed her yet?"

"Oh! Tru, how kind of you to think of me!" Annabelle cried. "I wish I had worn a different dress. Does this blue look good on me?"

"You look awesome," I said, giving her a nudge toward Gail. "And Emma." I waved for the younger member of the society to come over. "Emma has some stories about Rebecca that might be of interest to your viewers. She's also a member of the Arete Society. Aren't you, Emma? She also creates unique vacation packages for adventurous travelers."

"What are you doing?" Tori whispered to me.

"Getting out of here," I whispered back.

"But, Tru, this could be your *moment."*

"I don't want a moment. Not like this. All I want to do is help Hazel. And this isn't helping her."

The eager women in the café crowded around Joyce and Gail while I edged my way toward the exit. As I slipped out the door, I heard Gail wonder aloud, "Hey! Where did that mousy girl go?"

Chapter Twenty-One

———·———

On the way back to the library, I passed Charlie's used bookstore, the Deckle Edge. The classic brick, two-story storefront was on Main Street in the center of town. Through the large plate-glass window, I spotted Keven Verner having what looked like an argument with Marigold. What could that be about? From the way she was talking earlier, I had gotten the impression that the two of them didn't know each other.

Unable to pass by without seeing for myself what was going on, I stepped inside the store.

"Tru!" Charlie greeted me with a booming voice that was most unlike him. His eyes danced between me and the unhappy pair, who had wedged themselves between the sci-fi and self-help aisles. "Can I help you find a book?"

"Just browsing," I said. I moved toward the self-help section. The first thing I noticed was that someone had pulled out Isaac Asimov's short story collection *I, Robot* and left it sitting on top of a shelf of how-to books geared toward confidence building. Had Marigold or Keven pulled that book from the shelf?

It had to have been one of them. Charlie was meticulous when it came to keeping his bookshelves in order. I imagined he was itching to get over there and put the book back where it belonged—I know I sure wanted to place it back on its proper shelf—but he couldn't do that until Marigold and Keven moved out of the way.

"Marigold," I said, plastering on a huge smile. "Just the person I was looking for."

"*You're not going to get away with this*," Marigold hissed to Keven through her teeth, before turning toward me. "Oh, hi, Tru," she said, looking suddenly all sweet and innocent. "What's going on?"

"Is everything okay between you and Keven?" I asked.

"Yeah. I was just telling him how his robot came at me like it was out of control. He needs to fix that. What's up?"

"The *Ideal Life* film crew is down the street at Perks. They're interested in interviewing local residents who knew Rebecca. I told them they really needed to talk to you."

"Me?" She blushed a bit. "On TV?"

I nodded. "You'd do great."

"Oh, I don't know." She took a step toward me.

Keven looked like he might follow her. His mouth was set in a firm line, and his jaw trembled with tension. But he glanced over at Charlie and quickly backed away. He glanced at the books in the sci-fi section before grabbing a book and carrying it to the checkout counter. Charlie gave the book a sideways glance before ringing it up.

"We could practice the interview," I said to Marigold. "You could tell me the things you know about Rebecca.

Then together we could sort through what might have TV appeal. How does that sound?"

Marigold shook her head as if still unconvinced. "Before that awful robot came at me, I spent some time looking up that Joyce Fellows lady and her TV show. According to the article I read, the show is on the verge of being canceled. Apparently, its ratings are rapidly falling due to repetitive content. I have a feeling that awful Joyce Fellows will try to exploit Rebecca's tragic demise and twist things around just to save her show." Tears filled her eyes. "I don't want to be a part of that. Rebecca once told me that certain talk shows even go as far as to create drama in order to boost their ratings. Can you imagine?"

"You don't think Joyce killed Rebecca so she'd have a murder to cover for her show, do you?" That sounded a little far-fetched.

"I wouldn't put it past her. I mean, if we didn't already know Hazel was guilty. Rebecca once told me that Joyce liked fame better than anything. She did not trust her. Did you know they were on *Desiring Hearts* together?"

"No, I didn't. What part did Joyce play?"

"I'm not surprised you don't remember her. No one remembers her from the show. She had some bit part. But she made an impression with the cast. Rebecca told me that Joyce was jealous of Rebecca's instant fame and kept trying to sabotage her career. Can you imagine? Rebecca is a natural talent. Anyone who spends even a moment with her can recognize that."

"If Joyce is like that, why would Rebecca contact her and ask to be on her show?"

"In show biz," Marigold said, as if imparting a great truth, "you do business with your enemies if they have something you need."

"And what did Rebecca need?" I asked.

"Publicity."

"Because she was taking that new acting job? She wanted to get back into the public eye?"

"Um . . . uh-huh," Marigold murmured.

"You did know about Rebecca's return to acting before looking it up on LIFU's computer, didn't you?" I asked.

Marigold opened and closed her mouth.

"The article about it was the last thing on LIFU's screen. I assumed you were the one who had pulled it up. Am I wrong?"

"No. Not wrong." Her shoulders dropped. "Rebecca had been acting cagey these past couple of weeks. She'd walk out of the room when taking phone calls. Plus, she'd been packing up boxes of her belongings. When I asked her about it, she tut-tutted and told me that I'd find out about it along with everyone else." Tears sprang to her eyes. And she sobbed, "Me! She had started treating me like I was just like *everyone else*."

"But you must have suspected what she was planning if you were looking up articles in the library's database today," I said.

"I wasn't looking for that! I was looking for a Hollywood-style obituary. But there wasn't one." She sniffled, while dabbing at her eyes. "I don't understand it. She deserves more than a passing mention in the papers, more than a shout-out that a has-been actress was murdered. That's what they were calling her, a 'has-been.' She would have hated that." She clenched her fists as she spoke.

"I should think so," I agreed. Marigold's arms looked mighty powerful, powerful enough to kill someone with a casserole dish. I took a step back to put some space between us. "It sounds as if she was getting ready to move back to the West Coast, which means that even if she were still alive, Cypress would have still lost her."

In my mind's eye, I pictured Marigold attacking LIFU after reading about the new acting gig, because she was furious that her "best friend" had kept this secret from her, furious that Rebecca would dare leave Cypress and those who worshipped her.

Or perhaps Marigold had found out that Rebecca was leaving Cypress before the book club meeting and, in a panic, killed her. And maybe she had only later learned that the reason Rebecca was moving away was that she was returning to acting. That was why she had attacked LIFU. She realized she'd killed her best friend's dream of going back to a career she had loved. She had killed her friend, but it had been a mistake.

It was all very violent . . . and dramatic.

Sheesh, I must have read about too many of *Desiring Hearts*'s ridiculous plotlines. They were rotting my brain. That theory was just as unbelievable and outlandish as any story on the soap opera.

Marigold looked down at her shoes. "Rebecca didn't tell me about her TV deal. I wish she had. I would have been so pleased for her. She missed the attention. I would have supported her. Instead, I was worried that I was losing a friend, you know?"

"Why do you think she kept it from you?" I asked as gently as I knew how.

"Obviously, she didn't want to upset me," she said to her shoes. They were sensible shoes, very similar to the ones I had on my feet. "Now, if you'd excuse me, I have to go. I'm meeting with Annabelle to plan a memorial for Rebecca."

"Wait," I said before she could move. "Please tell me the secret Rebecca had shared with you. I promise it'll remain between the two of us."

Marigold seemed to consider it. But then she shook her head. "It has nothing to do with her death."

She started to walk out of the store.

I couldn't let her get away from me that easily. I still needed answers from her, answers that would help me prove Hazel's innocence. I jogged to keep up with her long legs.

"Wait! Please," I called after her, desperate for her to tell me something, anything. "Who else might have been angry about Rebecca's leaving?"

Again, she shook her head. "I . . . Everyone. No one. We all loved her. She's going to be missed. I know it's hard for you to accept, but Hazel snapped. She couldn't admit that she needed help hosting the meeting."

"Did Rebecca ever mention to you that she was going to kick out some of the members in order to make room for younger readers?" I called just as she reached the door.

She was halfway out the door when she turned to me. "She wouldn't do that. The Arete Society is a serious book club. The membership represents the best of Cypress. Rebecca knew that."

With that, she let the bookstore door swing closed behind her.

Charlie smiled ruefully after Marigold's dramatic exit. "Do you think she was taking acting lessons from her unfortunate friend? That was quite the 'exit stage left' maneuver."

"I don't know what is going on. No one will give me a straight answer, especially when I ask about the Arete Society and Rebecca. It's as if Rebecca is still poised to punish anyone who speaks up against either the book club or her."

"That sounds like a clue to me," Charlie said.

"What do you mean?"

Charlie rarely gave straight answers, so I was surprised when he said after a long pause, "I think you need to focus on the book club and the books for a motive. Rebecca was killed at Hazel's house on the night of the book club for a reason." He shrugged. "At least, that's what I think."

"You might be on to something there," I said, remembering that the police had found pages from a mass market paperback book at the crime scene. The book club picks were always hardcover books.

"I am usually right." He put his hand to his heart, like it pained him. "It can be a curse sometimes."

I chuckled. While the book angle was something I needed to pursue, I still suspected that the motive for murder had to be linked to Rebecca's return to acting and not to the book club. Book clubs were groups of like-minded people (often women) engaging in lively conversations about books—not exactly a life-and-death situation.

Bottom line, people didn't *die* because of a book or a book club.

But fame?

Well, fame *and* power seemed to make people crazy.

"Can you tell me what book Keven Verner bought just now? Or is there some kind of bookseller–book buyer confidentiality clause that keeps you from talking?"

"I don't usually like to gossip about these things," he admitted. "But since we are all trying to track down a killer because the police are sitting on their hands, I think it's okay to talk." His eyebrows dipped down toward his deep brown eyes. "His purchase was odd. It was a space opera involving unicorns and space princesses that was clearly geared toward preteen girls."

"Was he buying the book as a gift?"

"That's what I thought. I asked him if I could gift wrap it for him, but he declined. He refused the bag too, which makes good environmental sense. But he pushed a twenty across the counter and ran off before I could give him his change."

"And he'd been arguing with Marigold? Who started that?"

"Keven had come in first. He had a book in his hand and looked ready to check out when Goldie came marching in. She grumbled a hello in my direction before heading directly over to Keven. She shook her finger at him, grabbed the book he was holding, and tapped at the cover while whispering angry words." As he spoke, Charlie moved to the bookshelf and picked up the book that had been left haphazardly tossed on top of the shelf. "I tried to intervene, but neither would pay any attention to me."

"Is she the one who set that book down in the self-help section?" I pointed to the book he was putting back into its proper place.

"That's right," Charlie said.

"That's interesting."

"It is," Charlie said. "And that's what I'm saying. We need to follow the books."

I chewed my bottom lip as I studied the cover of the book in question. "But how can a robotics expert's interest in *I, Robot*, a book detailing the three laws of robotics, be at all related to Rebecca White and her return to the small screen?"

"If you can figure that out, maybe you'll find out who really killed Rebecca."

"I don't know . . . Was there even a connection between Rebecca and Keven?"

"Follow the books," Charlie said with a shrug.

He was right, and I needed to get back to the library

since my lunch break had ended about fifteen minutes ago. I was moving toward the exit when I noticed Tori's hard-sided suitcase leaning against the wall by the door to Charlie's office. It really was unmistakable. Hers was the only suitcase I had ever seen with giant daisies on the sides.

"Are y'all going somewhere?" I asked him.

He followed my gaze to the suitcase. "No, no. Tori was just bringing some things over for upstairs." Charlie lived in the apartment above the bookstore. Tori had once told me that it was surprisingly luxurious. "I have every confidence that you'll be able to figure things out, Tru."

"For Hazel's sake, I hope you're right."

Chapter Twenty-Two

——— · ———

Follow the books.

After a busy hour working with library patrons up-stairs, I was finally able to head to the basement to check on Dewey and my secret bookroom patrons . . . and to spend some time with the books. I walked through the thick double doors, stopped, closed my eyes, and inhaled deeply.

Ah. There's a peace that washes over a person when surrounded by so many words. Laughter, tears, and wisdom are there for the taking. The air felt lighter down here in my secret library. Fresher.

Hubert was in the local documents section with a map spread out on the table in front of him. Frank Cal-houn, another member of the local museum board, stood by his side, nodding. They both smiled and waved when they noticed me watching them but went back to their work.

Dewey ran over to me and nudged my leg with his head.

"Hey, little guy." I reached down and scratched him

under his chin. He purred loudly and stood up on his hind legs so I could continue petting him. His purrs grew louder. "Staying out of trouble, I hope?"

His green eyes flashed. His purring motor went silent. And he dropped back down onto all fours. With a flick of his tail, he turned away from me and sauntered away into the stacks in his "I don't care for your accusing tone" manner.

"I'll take that to mean you've been making more trouble." I went off in search of the mess he'd made this time.

It didn't take long to find it. He'd wandered down the fiction aisle, pulling historical romance novels from the shelves. He'd torn a few pages in one of the books.

"Oh, Dewey. Why are you doing this?" I looked up to find my naughty kitty watching me with his large owl eyes. Why just the historical romances?

It was almost as if he could read.

Which was ridiculous. Cats can't read.

I shook my head and started scooping the books up off the floor. Someone must have sprayed a perfume on the historical romance novels that Dewey could smell.

It had happened before. My dad's neighbor, Mrs. Carsdale, used to spray the library books with perfume to cover up the smell of her cigarette smoke. But that was years ago. And I don't remember her ever checking out historical romances. She tended to stick to gardening books and sci-fi.

I sniffed one of the books Dewey had taken from the shelf.

Like before, I smelled nothing.

Hmm . . .

I carried an armful of the displaced historical romance novels to the desk. Perhaps it wasn't a perfume. Perhaps Dewey was detecting the scent of another cat on them, or even a dog, which made me wonder if the same person had checked out all the books Dewey had been attacking.

I had started looking up who had recently borrowed the books when Emma came stomping into the secret bookroom.

"They wouldn't interview me," she complained. Her gaze landed on the stack of historical romances on the desk in front of me. "Someone likes their bodice rippers," she said with a sardonic laugh.

"We don't call them that anymore." That term always felt disparaging toward the entire romance genre.

"Well, whatever they are, don't you think that's an excessive number of books for someone to check out all at once? Doesn't the library have a limit on the number of books a patron can check out?"

"We don't. But most people only take out a few books at a time," I said.

"Clearly, not everyone." Emma pointed to the pile of books.

"These weren't checked out." I explained Dewey's strange behavior with these books. "Maybe there's a scent on them. I've just started looking up who has had these books out recently to see if there's a connection with the books that would make Dewey go after them."

She chuckled. "I love that cat of yours. He has the best personality. Good luck with your search. And if you hear of anyone who is looking to rush off to the tropics to get away from this cold weather, please send them to me. Some great deals have recently come in." She started to walk away, but then she stopped. "Actually, if you have a moment, I could use some help. I'd like to find something fun to read. Now that Rebecca is no longer around to dictate our reading habits, I plan to go wild and read something decadently entertaining."

"Some of the patrons have donated mass market paperback books that were published this year. Delanie even brought in a few uncorrected proofs that had been sent to the local newspaper for them to review." I led her over to where the books could be found. "I've shelved them over here on this bookshelf. I've not had a chance to get a sign up yet, but I'm going to make this area our New Books section."

"Fantastic! Are there any books here that you'd recommend?" she asked.

As I was showing her some of the more popular new books, Delanie came breezing into the secret bookroom. She was in a cheery lemon dress with white polka dots and matching yellow high heels that clacked against the basement's concrete floor.

"My, look at that stack of historical romances," she said. "Did someone go on a reading spree?"

"No," I said, and explained to her about Dewey and that I was planning to see if the same person had checked out these books.

She nodded absently. "Anyhow, did you see Perks café?" she asked, putting great emphasis on each word. "It's like when the first shipment of fresh collard greens arrives at the Piggly Wiggly. What a crush!"

"Yes, I was in the middle of it." I still felt lucky to have made such a clever escape. I left Emma to her browsing and returned to the circulation desk.

"That TV crew certainly has everyone stirred up." Delanie fluffed her hair and checked her makeup in a small mirror compact she'd pulled from her purse. "Everybody is suddenly Rebecca's dearest friend. Such shameless behavior. Oh, hi, Emma. I didn't see you over there. I wasn't talking about you, dear. You actually knew Rebecca. Anyhow, I slipped the producer my card and told her to call me when they're ready to talk with someone who was Rebecca's friend. Which is my best side? This one or this one?" She turned this way and that, while making faces into her tiny mirror.

"Not you too," I said.

"What's the harm in wanting to be on television? It's exciting. And besides which, I deserve a little payoff for putting up with Rebecca's constant preening about how she had been a star, which made her think she was better than the rest of us." She leaned against the old circulation desk where I was working and tapped her finger on the stack of historical romance novels. "Speaking of which, how is the investigation going?"

"Slow." I pushed the romances aside. Dewey's odd behavior would have to be a mystery for another day. "But I think you can help me with something. When you got to Hazel's house that night, was anyone already there?"

"Hmm. Let's see. I wasn't the first to arrive. And Lida rode with me since Hazel lives so far from the center of town. It's like driving to the next town over to get to her house. Who else came up that long sidewalk with us? Let's see, I believe Annabelle and Gretchen. That's about it."

Not Marigold?

My shoulders dropped with disappointment. Did that mean Marigold didn't sneak in the back door to kill Rebecca in an attempt to keep the star from leaving Cypress?

Ah, well . . . I supposed it was back to the suspect board for me.

"Oh!" Delanie jutted up her neatly manicured finger. "And Goldie was there."

"Do you know who arrived first?" I asked, feeling my heart rate speed up again.

"I don't, Tru. You'll have to ask the others. Why is that important?"

I waved my hand in the air in a dismissive gesture. "It's not. Just thinking about who might have had opportunity to sneak in Hazel's back door."

Delanie leaned closer to the desk and whispered, "And you think it might have been Annabelle, Gretchen, or Goldie?" She whistled. "If you say one of them is guilty, then I believe you. But, honey, tread with care, you hear? Those are powerful women in the community. Until you have solid proof, don't let on that you have any of them on your suspect list."

"You can trust me. I won't."

"Mind, you can talk to me about your suspicions," Delanie said. "I won't repeat what you say to the television crew." She checked her phone. "Why hasn't the show called yet? I really would like to be on TV."

"What's so great about being on TV?" I asked with a laugh.

"It's for the recognition, dear. Anyhow, if anyone deserves to be interviewed, it's you. After all, you're the one who's going to figure out what happened to Rebecca . . . and who is responsible."

"Thank you. I appreciate your vote of confidence. You know, you're one of the few Arete Society members who doesn't blame Hazel for Rebecca's death. Why is that?"

"Two reasons. First, I believe in you. And don't you dare tell me I shouldn't. Second, Hazel is such a sweet soul. I have a hard time picturing her hurting a fly, much less striking down a guest in her home. She's too smart and too well-mannered to do that. Speaking of smarts, how is Jace holding up?" she asked. "It's got to be killing him that he can't be out here investigating the murder."

"He's frustrated," I admitted. "But he's staying busy. He's been searching for my father while also babysitting his own father to make sure Beau doesn't go and do something that will make things worse for Hazel."

"I wish Jace luck with the last one. Beau does tend to have a short fuse." She leaned in closer. "But what's going on with your dad?"

I explained to her how Mama Eddy had found mail piled up on Daddy's porch and how he hadn't answered any of the hundreds of texts that I'd sent him. "I'm starting to worry that something truly awful has happened," I said.

"Heavens." Delanie frowned. "You must be beside yourself."

"I am!" I cried. Mama Eddy hadn't called or texted for an update since early this morning. That, too, worried me. A silent Mama Eddy was nearly as concerning as an intrusive one. "I've been told that my daddy used to run off like this without a word to anyone. But that was ages ago. And recently he's always kept his phone on for me."

"Your daddy sure put Mama Eddy through some trying times." Delanie seemed to laugh at a memory but then quickly sobered. "I'm sure there's a reasonable explanation, dear. Have you tried asking that Tech Bros fellow? Did you know they're building robots? Of course you do," she said before I could answer. "I heard one of their robots has been filling in at the library. There's another that has been standing guard in the community gardens, not that he needs to. Nothing is growing this time of—"

Anne burst through the doors, interrupting everyone.

The canary-yellow IT tech's eyes were wide. "Tru!" She stood in the doorway and waved frantically at me.

"You need to get upstairs. There's someone from the police who is insisting on talking to you. And"—she gulped a breath—"Mrs. Farnsworth is heading down here to search for you."

"Oh dear." I jogged out of the secret bookroom. Anne jogged alongside me.

"I'll come too," Delanie said, as she hurried to catch up to us. "If I need to, I can distract Lida from wondering too much about why you weren't where she expected you to be."

"I'm coming too," Emma said with a little laugh. "There might be a news crew out there."

I doubted it. But I let them follow along behind me.

"Thank you for coming to get me," I said to Anne as I matched her long stride. "Who's here? Is it Detective Ellerbe?"

Anne shook her head. "Never saw the woman before. But she isn't in a good mood."

"I wonder if this is about my dad." My heart stopped for a moment, and then when it started again, it pumped double time to make up for lost beats. "I hope he hasn't run into some kind of trouble."

By the time I reached the library's front desk I was in a full panic, complete with shortness of breath and a trembly pulse.

"No news crew or cameras," Emma said with a disappointed sniff.

"Ms. Becket, where have you been?" Mrs. Farnsworth demanded.

"She was organizing the supply closet in the basement," Anne said. And thank goodness she had answered for me. I needed time to catch my breath. Plus, I wasn't good at coming up with believable lies when my mind was clouded with visions of my dad floating dead in the lake. "Tru!" Anne snapped her fingers to get my attention, which I'm sure she could see had wandered deeper into panic territory. "You really need to let someone know where you're going before you disappear like that."

"Yes. I . . . um . . . I . . ." I managed to wheeze.

"This lady from the state police says she has some questions to ask you," Mrs. Farnsworth said. "It was most distressing when we couldn't locate you. I was worried that you had somehow gotten yourself stuck in a heating duct again."

"*Again?*" Anne snorted.

"That happened thirteen years ago!" I said, but Anne only started laughing harder. "I'm not the one who is dyed yellow."

"Not fair! I blocked the powder from going all over you."

"Excuse me," said the tall, dark-haired woman standing next to Mrs. Farnsworth. I recognized her from Hazel's house. She had been part of Detective Ellerbe's team of crime scene technicians, the one who had intimidated the usually unflappable Ellerbe. "I hate to interrupt your fun, but I urgently need to speak with Ms. Becket."

Urgently?

"Is this about—?" I couldn't finish that question. I couldn't ask if this was about my father.

I felt like I was going to throw up. And the last thing I wanted to do was throw up all over the library's terrazzo floor, especially considering how I was the one tasked with cleaning up such messes.

I breathed in a slow, steady breath and prayed that the contents of my stomach remained in there.

"I'm Dr. Lacy Daufuskie." She jutted out her hand.

I looked at it a moment before shaking it. "Trudell Becket."

"Is there some place we can talk?" Her gaze flicked to the other women around me. "In private?"

"You can use one of the recording studios," Anne suggested.

I gave a nod. "This way."

The recording studios were in the part of the library where the periodicals used to be shelved. I missed flipping through the magazines when they arrived every month and feeling overwhelmed by the sweet-scented perfume ads.

Now a series of small, soundproofed rooms lined that wall.

I led Dr. Daufuskie to the end room, flipped on the bright fluorescent lights, and then stepped aside so she could go in first.

This room, which doubled as a meeting space, had a green screen on the far wall, several roller chairs, a small conference table, microphones, special lighting, speakers, dedicated audio recording equipment, and a state-of-the-art computer setup.

"Impressive," Dr. Daufuskie said as she looked around. "I'd been told to be sure to take a library tour. Now I see why. If only I'd had a place like this when I was a child. I would have loved to play in here."

"Wh-what did you need to tell me?" I stammered, wondering why she was going on and on about this room when my father's life might be hanging in the balance. Was she building up the courage to tell me that they'd dredged my dad from the bottom of the lake?

My heart started to race again.

The air in the recording studio seemed to shift when she closed the door. I knew it was an illusion from the fact that the rooms were soundproofed so our patrons could make clean recordings, but still, I shivered.

I moved toward one of the chairs, but Dr. Daufuskie remained standing and crossed her arms over her chest. If she wasn't going to sit, then I decided to stand as well.

"Please tell me what's going on," I begged.

She took a few deep breaths. "You. That's what."

"Me?" *Not my dad?*

"I want you to know that I've been working in the field of forensics for more than fifteen years. Do you understand how hard it is to gain respect as a woman in this field, especially in the South? It's close to impossible. I have more degrees than most. I work longer hours. I pay close attention to the details. You know why?"

I shook my head.

"Because I have to. Because that's the only way I managed to earn anyone's respect. It's taken over a decade to get to a point in my career where others say, 'If Lacy Daufuskie said it's so, it's so.' And then *you* come along. How long have you been working in law enforcement?"

"I don't work in law enforcement. I'm a librarian." I was taken aback by her temper.

"A librarian?" she said sarcastically.

I nodded.

"Not a forensic scientist? Not a PhD?"

"You already know who I am and my credentials. So please, stop taunting me. Just spit out why you're here."

"I'm standing here instead of doing my job, because despite all the evidence I have carefully scrutinized over the past several days, I'm being told to go back and look at everything again thanks to an assistant librarian who has declared that the police have arrested the wrong person."

"Hazel didn't kill Rebecca White," I said, defending myself.

Dr. Daufuskie clapped her hands. "Brilliant. I'll just toss out all those pesky evidence bags. They're meaningless. I simply needed to ask the librarian in town to tell me what's what."

"Please, I'm sorry if I've caused you trouble." I truly was. I knew what it was like to have to fight to have my voice heard. And yet, at the same time, it pleased me to know that Detective Ellerbe *had* been listening to me even if he had acted uninterested. "Look. I know I don't have the experience or training you have. And I am sorry people are second-guessing your findings. I get how frustrating that must be. But I was there in Hazel's house when Rebecca was murdered. Plus, I know the members of the book club. And I think you might be overlooking something."

"What?" she snapped. "What am I overlooking?"

The books. But what about the books? I didn't know . . . yet.

So, instead of telling her that Rebecca's death might be somehow book-related, I said, "I suspect one of the book club members came in the back door while Hazel was taking out the trash and killed Rebecca. I think that person then came around to the front door and pretended she'd just arrived."

Lacy stared at me for nearly a minute.

"Impossible," she finally said.

"No," I countered. "That's what happened." The more I thought about it, the more certain I felt that it was true.

The rumor about someone getting kicked out of the book club to make room for younger members may have upset someone, upset her so much so that she felt she needed to kill Rebecca before the meeting. Or perhaps Marigold, upset that her idol was saying goodbye to

Cypress, attacked her in a twisted way to stop her from leaving.

Dr. Daufuskie and I had another staring contest. This one lasted even longer than the first one.

"Impossible," she said again. "And I have proof on my side."

I tilted my head and smiled a bit. "Do you care to share that proof?"

Chapter Twenty-Three

———·———

A steady, cold northern wind came off the lake and whipped through the tall cypress trees, making the Spanish moss hanging from their branches sway and wave. It looked almost as though they were frantically trying to warn us away.

Dr. Lacy Daufuskie had driven her government-issued white sedan to Hazel's house. I'd followed in my old Camry.

"I called and received permission from the property owner to be out here," she said when we met up at the street.

"I called too," I said.

"It's good to call first," she said. "Don't need to get shot for trespassing."

"They wouldn't do that, but it is good manners."

Dr. Daufuskie made a *harrumph* sound in her throat. "Let's go, then."

I had been surprised that Mrs. Farnsworth had been so accommodating, letting me go on this little excursion. In fact, the head librarian had nearly pushed me out the door while Delanie, Anne, and Emma wished us good luck.

I had hoped Dr. Daufuskie was planning to share the evidence that she and her team had collected, but she'd said she didn't have authorization to do that. She could, however, show me her process, what she examined at the crime scene—aka Hazel's house—and explain why I couldn't possibly be right.

In turn, I planned to explain to her why I was totally right.

As we neared the house, Jace stepped out onto the porch.

He smiled when he saw us, but it was clear the stress of the situation was wearing on him. Everything about his expression looked tense and tired. He introduced himself to Dr. Daufuskie.

"It's good to meet you, Detective," she said. "I've heard good things about the work you've been doing here in town."

"Please, call me Jace. I'm off duty. Perhaps forever."

"Okay, Jace. I am sorry about all this. You can call me Lacy."

He gave a stiff nod. "Very well, Lacy. If the two of you need to come inside, my parents and the lawyer have given their permission." He turned to me and brushed a quick kiss on my cheek. "Hey," he murmured. His expression softened. "I'm working a new lead that might help us find your daddy. It seems promising."

"And you think Daddy is okay?" My heart still hadn't settled down from jumping to the worst conclusion about why Lacy had come to the library.

"I think so." Jace gave my hand a squeeze.

I nodded toward the front door. "How are your parents holding up?"

"My mom is cleaning and baking and pretending

nothing is wrong. My dad exploded after the third batch of cookies came out of the oven. He went out for a long walk and hasn't come back yet. The lawyer just keeps making phone calls. I told him to leave, because we won't be able to pay his fee if he stays here around the clock like this. But he told me now wasn't the time to worry about money. I was glad Dad wasn't in the room to hear that."

"Well, your lawyer is right," I said. "Defending your mother ought to be our focus right now."

"Then let's get going," Lacy said. She took long strides toward the back of the house.

I ran to catch up to her. "Should I call you Lacy as well?" It still stung that Marigold had apparently invited everyone except me to call her Goldie.

Lacy looked me up and down before mumbling, "I think Dr. Daufuskie would be more appropriate."

Ouch.

The cold wind picked up. The Spanish moss looked even more frantic by the time the three of us reached the back door.

Lacy—*excuse me*—Dr. Daufuskie explained in precise detail how she examined the door and the doorknob and searched for footprints, and she pointed out that there was no path leading to the front of the house. Anyone wanting to get to the front of the house from the back would have to either walk through the house or squeeze through the space between the house and the thick hedges, a muddy route that would have left a clear trail of footprints in the wet weather. I looked. I nodded. I made the appropriate noises to indicate I was giving her the benefit of the doubt.

And yet "You're wrong" were the first two words that came out of my mouth.

No wonder she doesn't want me to call her by her first name.

Lacy started to argue with me about how I didn't have the training to understand why I shouldn't question her findings.

"With all due respect," Jace said in that calm, Zen-like voice of his, "I understand how things might look. But I do have the appropriate training to understand what you've told us. And I agree with Tru. My mom didn't kill anyone."

Lacy didn't say anything for quite a long time. What could she say?

"I understand, Jace," she said kindly. "No one wants to think the worst of their own mother. But the facts—"

"The facts are that whoever came through that back door didn't take the muddy path to the front door," I interrupted. "I get that."

"There is no other way to get to the front door. I checked," she said. "And there were no fresh footprints in the mud."

"Then whoever killed Rebecca must have gone that way." I pointed toward the shadowy cypress forest.

At the same moment, something zinged between me and Lacy.

The next thing I knew, Jace tackled the two of us. We all fell onto the muddy ground next to the high hedges.

"What?" I wheezed.

"Gunshot," Jace said. "Stay down."

"Are you armed?" Lacy asked.

"Not today." Jace sounded sick about it. "Are you?"

"I'm a forensic scientist. I'm never armed," she cried.

"Could it be a hunter?" I asked.

"Could be," Jace said.

"Don't lie to her. It's not," Lacy said. "That was a bullet from a handgun."

We all stayed on the ground, holding our breath, listening as the wind continued to rustle the needles in the trees.

"What are y'all doing wallowing in the mud like that?" Beau Bailey, Jace's dad, walked out of the shadowy cypress forest and toward the house, unaware of the danger lurking behind him in the woods. "Get up, boy. You're going to ruin your clothes. And we don't need your mother fretting over that."

"Wait. Wait! WAIT!" Fisher shouted over the noise of everyone speaking at the same time in Hazel's living room. "All y'all need to simmer down. I only want one person to talk at a time. Understand?"

Beau grumbled angrily to himself about how he'd never wanted his wife to join that stupid book club in the first place and then stormed out of the room.

"You can talk later," Hazel said. "The children need to get out of these wet clothes." Just as Jace's father had predicted, she'd been fussing about needing to wash our clothes ever since we came into her home with mud-smeared shirts and pants. If she had her way, we'd be in our underwear and wrapped in the oversized burgundy towels she had brought out and draped over our muddy shoulders.

"We're fine, ma'am," Lacy said. "And thank you for the chocolate chip cookies. They were delicious."

Hazel beamed with joy. "I'll pack you a box of them to take with you, Dr. Daufuskie."

"Please, ma'am, call me Lacy." Lacy looked over at me and smiled as she said that.

"Only if you call me Hazel. You're a sweet girl. How in the world did you get yourself mixed up in this kind of nasty work?"

"It's always been a—" Lacy started to say.

"What I want to know is what in the world you are doing back at this house, Lacy. And more importantly, what in blazes are you doing here with Trudell?" Detective Ellerbe snapped. He'd been standing near the front entryway, his jaw muscles jumping.

"With all due respect, sir," Lacy said. "I'm here because you questioned my findings due to the fact that this . . . this stubborn librarian says I am wrong."

"She promised to straighten me out on that," I said.

"And did she?" Ellerbe asked.

"What do you think?" I smiled.

He rolled his eyes.

"My wife is being unfairly persecuted," Beau said as he came back into the room with a crystal glass filled with an amber liquid. The ice in the glass clinked. "Now, if you don't mind, I think y'all should go and leave us in peace."

"Cooperating with the authorities after there was a shooting on your property is a show of good faith," the lawyer, Mr. Redi-Finch, said quietly. "That's why I suggested you invite them inside."

"I don't like it." Beau took a deep sip of his drink.

"Honey, please," Hazel said, sounding a little desperate.

"Dad." Jace took his father by the arm and tried to lead him out of the room. "Don't you think you've had enough of those?"

"Don't you go running off on me, Jace," Police Chief Fisher said from the armchair that he was using like a royal throne. "You have some explaining to do as well. I told you to not interfere with my investigation. And yet here you are, in the center of everything."

"Sir, I'm at my parents' house," Jace said.

"With the lead forensic scientist and that nosy girlfriend of yours. That looks like investigating to me," Fisher said.

"Boy, are you getting yourself in trouble again?" Beau slurred his words a bit. "I put my reputation on the line when I pulled all those strings to get you a position in this town after you mucked things up so badly in New York City."

"You did, sir. And for the record I haven't done anything other than stay with you and Mom, pacing and eating cookies," Jace said.

"He has been such a help to us, dear," Hazel said. "He worked hard to get word to you about my little troubles. And I'm grateful for that. He's been the perfect son."

"But—" Beau looked over at his wife and then shook his head. "You're right, Hazel. He has been helpful around here. It's just . . ." He took another sip of his drink.

And then everyone started talking again.

Everyone except for me. I sat on the sofa that Rebecca had made me move all over the room. I clutched the burgundy towel that was still wrapped around me like a cloak. And I chewed my bottom lip while wondering why someone would shoot at us.

Had it been a warning shot? Had it been someone trying to scare us? Or was the shooter trying to kill someone?

Why shoot at us there? Why at that back door?

And gracious, it was hard to think with everyone talking all at once.

"I thought I told everyone to simmer down!" Fisher hollered.

The room fell silent.

"Good," he said, and hitched his thumbs into his belt. "Good. Now then. While my men scour the woods for our perpetrator, I want to hear exactly what happened. And I want to hear it from you." He pointed to Jace.

After listening to Jace's description of the events, Fisher then had Lacy recount what she saw. He finally glanced over at me and scowled.

"Well then," he said as he rose from the armchair. "Someone standing in the woods shooting at you with a handgun would be lucky to hit the side of the house at that distance. I hazard to guess that whoever pulled the trigger isn't an expert sharpshooter. If I wanted to shoot one of you, for instance, I'd bring a rifle."

"Why come back to the house at all?" I asked. "Rebecca is dead. The best forensic scientist in the state has already combed through this area. There's nothing more to find. So why risk returning? Why risk getting caught by taking wild shots at us? It doesn't make sense."

"It doesn't have to make sense," Fisher said. "Criminals make bad decisions all the time, starting with killing someone." He looked over at Hazel when he said that last part.

I supposed he had a point. But, still, like those books Dewey kept pulling off the shelves in the library, something outside Hazel's back door felt out of place.

Fisher stood up. "Mr. and Mrs. Bailey, I'll let you know if my officers find anything in the woods that you need to be concerned about. Detective Bailey, you keep your nose out of this investigation . . . and that includes reining in your girlfriend, you hear?"

Jace glanced over at his father before answering. "Um . . . yes, sir."

Fisher didn't have the authority to stop me from asking questions. And he had no right to hold Jace's job security over my head.

I wanted to tell him that. I wanted to wag my finger at him while I told him that. Jace must have sensed I was about to say something that would get us all in trouble. He locked eyes with me and shook his head.

I had to bite my tongue to keep it from moving.

"Tru," Ellerbe said, as he rose as well. "Can I have a word with you out back?"

"Sure." I was glad for the excuse to get out of the room. Fisher and I always seemed to rub each other the wrong way.

"Lacy, I think you should join us," Ellerbe called over his shoulder.

She smirked. "Yes, sir."

"Stop!" Hazel jumped up and shouted. "No one can leave until I pack up the cookies."

Chapter Twenty-Four

Tru, I'm worried. First, someone tried to poison you. And now someone is taking potshots at you," Ellerbe said as he touched the scarred doorframe where a member of the state's forensics team (not Lacy) had dug out the bullet.

As Lacy had predicted, the bullet had been fired by a handgun. The officer standing watch at this new crime scene had told us the kind of handgun they thought had been used. But that information was pretty much useless to me.

Books, not guns, had always been my primary interest.

Why would someone shoot at me? Why here?

No matter how many times I let those questions tumble around in my mind, I couldn't come up with a reasonable answer.

Yes, I'd solved crimes in the past. But those cases had links to the library. This one had nothing to do with the library. The only reason I was involved at all was because of Jace's mom.

"Hazel didn't do this," I said aloud. "She didn't poison me." *No one did.* "She didn't shoot at us. And she didn't kill Rebecca."

"Yes, we know that's what you think." Ellerbe sounded tired.

"I showed your librarian friend why her absurd theories about someone sneaking into the house were wrong," Lacy said. "That's why I was here. To convince her."

Ellerbe nodded.

"No one could have broken into the house, killed the victim, and then walked around to the front door to attend the party. If that was what had happened, the ground would have told me. But it didn't. I showed her that," Lacy said.

Ellerbe nodded again.

I looked at the ground. The back door opened onto a large river stone patio. At its periphery was a shed where the Baileys kept their garbage cans. So, no muddy footprints in that direction. A large wooden pergola covered with winter-bare muscadine vines created an inviting outdoor dining space. Next to the pergola was an outdoor kitchen that was larger than my house's *indoor* kitchen. A gravel trail at the far end of the patio led through the grassy backyard and into the shadowy cypress forest. And yes, there were no neat pathways leading to the front of the house. The sides of the house had planting beds and thick hedges. The only way to get through, as Lacy had already pointed out, was to take a muddy path right next to the house.

And if that were the case, no one coming to the book club could have killed Rebecca.

"Tru, you do realize that if you manage to prove Hazel truly didn't act out against Rebecca in a fit of anger, the only other suspect is your friend Flossie," Ellerbe said.

"Flossie is in a wheelchair," I reminded him.

"That doesn't mean your friend is not strong and capable and passionate. She might have struck out in a moment of blind anger."

"But-but there's no—" Lacy started to sputter.

"She was in the room alone with the victim," Ellerbe cut in. "Hazel insists that Rebecca was alive when she left the kitchen. If we believe Hazel . . ." He held out his hands.

I curled mine into fists.

"What about the book pages you found in the kitchen? I heard that forensics found pages from a paperback novel," I said, because even though Flossie was acting strangely, I knew in my heart she'd never lose her temper and kill anyone.

"You know we cannot discuss that," Ellerbe said.

"How do you know about those pages?" Lacy said at the same time.

"If it's from a book, I'm a book expert. Maybe I can help figure out where the book—that isn't a cookbook— came from and what it was doing in the kitchen." *And why I didn't notice it*, I left unsaid.

"The pages were ripped out of a—" Lacy started to say.

Ellerbe cleared his throat and gave the crackerjack forensic scientist a look.

"Which we cannot talk about," she amended.

Since the two of them were proving to be no help, I turned away from them and looked at the yard again. Hazel had been in the shed. My gaze traveled to the outdoor kitchen, then the outside dining area, and the yard, and finally toward the forest beyond where a shooter had hidden less than an hour ago. The police had scoured the area and found no evidence that anyone had been out there. But we knew the bullet that had scarred the doorframe was proof that someone had been in those woods.

According to Lacy, the ground, like a book, could tell a tale. But could the ground also hide the story?

"You're not usually this quiet, Tru," Ellerbe said. "Are you okay?"

I turned around and found them watching me. I hadn't realized I'd wandered so far from the back door.

"I'm often this quiet," I told him. "Of course, it's usually when I have a good book in my hands."

He smiled at that. "And that's what you're going to do? Keep busy with your books?"

"Um . . ." What was I going to do? "I'm going to take a walk through the woods and see where that leads me."

And with that, I set out down the gravel trail that led through the Baileys' backyard and into the foreboding cypress forest, hoping to uncover some of its secrets.

"I'm not done saying what I need to say to you!" Detective Ellerbe called after me.

But I kept walking.

I hadn't gotten far into the forest when I heard the pounding of someone running behind me.

"Do you mind if I come with you?" Jace said as he ran up alongside me.

"Only if you don't mind following another one of my half-baked theories." Lacy's assessment of my ideas might have stung a bit.

"Are you kidding me? Those are my favorite kinds. Cookie?" He held out one of his mother's chocolate chip cookies.

"Thanks." Hazel added both semisweet and milk chocolate chips to the cookies. They really were good.

"Why are we heading down this path?" he asked.

"Because I want to see where it leads." The trail wound around some impressively big cypress trees and down to a stream. "Is this all your parents' land?"

"No," he said. "Their property ended where the grass ended. The forest belongs to the state, save for a few properties here and there. Why the sudden interest in Cypress's hiking trails?"

"Because if the killer didn't go around the side of your parents' house to ring the front doorbell, then she must have made her escape this way."

"She?" Jace lifted a brow.

I nodded. "I think so."

"Do you have a name to go with your half-baked theory?" he asked.

"Not yet." I looked up and down the streambed. The trail seemed to continue onto the other side. There were a few large, flat rocks in the shallow stream that anyone could use as stepping-stones. "Do you have any ideas?"

"It's your theory," he said as he walked across the stream. "I'm glad my parents didn't own this house when I was in high school. I would have hated living so far away from my friends."

"You might have spent more time with your school-books instead of getting into trouble."

He smiled at me. "And where's the fun in that?"

I just shook my head and jumped over the stream in one long leap.

He pulled another one of his mother's cookies out of his jacket pocket and took a bite. "So, Rebecca's killer hiked through the forest, waited in the shadows for a chance to strike. How would our perp know that Rebecca was alone in the kitchen?"

"There is that big window on the kitchen door. And another window over the sink. It was getting dark. The lights were on in the kitchen. Anyone in the forest could look in."

"But why would someone even think to strike at my mom's house? It feels like a long shot."

"It does." He was right. I was grasping for a motive. "That's why this theory of mine is half-baked. But I like it better than any of the others."

"If it means my mother is proven innocent—half-baked or not—I'm all in," he agreed.

We'd walked in silence for about a mile when we emerged from the forest. What I saw there surprised me.

"This is where the trail ends?" I said, because as unbelievable as it seemed, I was looking at my father's lake house.

Chapter Twenty-Five

Mama said that Daddy's mail was piled up on his front porch, which means he left days before Rebecca's death," I said aloud, more to assure myself that his disappearance had nothing to do with the murder than to tell Jace something he already knew. "It's just a coincidence that we ended up here. We could have turned anywhere in the woods and ended up at any number of other places."

Jace simply listened while I blathered on.

"I mean, it's not as if my daddy and Rebecca even knew each other."

Jace walked toward my father's ramshackle cottage. I followed. Someone had picked up the mail. Mama Eddy, if I had to guess.

"Daddy didn't kill Rebecca." I refused to point the finger of blame in his direction, even if it meant helping Hazel.

"Never suggested he did. But we do need to find him. My friend in Charlotte, North Carolina, has been following a lead. Let me check in with him."

I paced my father's yard while Jace chatted with his friend.

"What? What? What did he say?" I demanded as soon as he ended the call.

"He's checking flights out of Charlotte. But he doesn't have anything yet. I am sorry, Tru."

Jace looked bothered by something, but he still didn't say anything. And his silence made me feel itchy. It felt like I was standing in a library where all the books had been jumbled up. My father was missing. Tori hadn't told me about that packed bag she'd taken over to Charlie's, making me wonder what else she was keeping from me. Flossie was acting cagey about what she had been doing in Hazel's kitchen before I got in there. Dewey kept pulling those historical romances off the shelves. And no matter what clue I followed with Rebecca's death, none of them seemed to lead me anywhere.

And Jace had been keeping silent. He was silent about what was worrying him right now, silent about what the lawyer had been telling him about the case against his mother, and silent about his late-night whereabouts these past couple of months. "*Jace is growing restless,*" Sissy had mocked.

It was all . . . all too much.

I admit it. I needed order in my life. I needed answers.

"Are you cheating on me?" I blurted, because he was standing right next to me and the memory of Sissy's taunting voice had suddenly become the loudest.

Jace snapped his head back as if I'd hit him. "What? Where did this come from?"

How could he not know? I stared at him, searching for signs of deception. He looked . . . well, he looked confused. "For the past several months, you've refused to tell me what you've been doing all hours of the night.

You've been canceling dates at the last minute for no good reason. I've not even met your dog yet." I curled my fingers into a fist and propped it on my hip to hide how trembly and nervous I felt. Not that it mattered since my voice warbled and grew high-pitched as I said, "And then Sissy warned me that you were growing restless and that you'd started to stray."

His eyes opened wider. "Sissy? When did you start listening to anything Sissy says?"

"She also told me that she'd been warned not to come to the book club meeting. And you still haven't answered my question."

He drew in a long, slow breath. "I didn't tell you because I didn't want you to get angry."

"Tell me what?" Gracious, he *had* found someone else. Well, maybe he should let *her* help prove his mom's innocence. He should let *her* get poisoned and shot at, even though I was fairly certain no one had poisoned me. Why hadn't Dr. Lewis called with the test results yet?

"You're going to get angry," he warned.

"I'm already angry."

"So you are." He kicked a smooth lake rock lying in the winter-brown grass. "I haven't been around lately because Fisher has been assigning me extra shifts—rookie grunt work—as a punishment for getting involved with you."

I stamped my feet on the hard, muddy ground. "Ohhhh, that does make me mad!"

"I told you that you'd get angry. The police chief sure has a huge chip on his shoulder against you. What did you do to him?"

"I didn't do anything! He's simply upset that I'm doing his job."

Jace didn't look convinced. "I think it's something else. I think—"

"Just you wait. The next time I see him, I'm going to give him an earful. I'll tell him to grow up and to leave you alone."

"Please, don't."

"But he can't—!"

"He can. And he can also fire me. Heck, he might already kick me out of the department for what happened today. And if that happens, I don't know what I'm going to do." He touched my cheek. "I like living in Cypress again. That's something I never thought I'd find myself saying, but I do." He stepped closer to me. "I'm sorry I made you worry. I'll take you to meet Bonnie if that's what you really want. And I should have been honest about what's happening with my job from the get-go. But please, don't make a fuss. I can handle it. What I can't handle right now is having to think about moving away."

My heart softened.

"I should never listen to Sissy," I said ruefully.

"You probably shouldn't," he agreed. "She's awfully jealous of you and the attention the town's been giving you. She wants to see you fail. I wouldn't trust anything she says to you."

I chewed my bottom lip. "You're right. I shouldn't. And yet I've been basing much of this investigation on what she told me. But what if she was lying about that too?"

"About what?" he asked.

"About Rebecca's plan to kick out some of the older members of the book club to make room for her and others like her."

"You were thinking that someone like Goldie killed Rebecca before she could make major changes to the Arete Society's membership?"

"Yes." My brows crinkled. "But not Goldie. She

would never get kicked out, she's Rebecca's biggest fan."
My mind kept spinning. "But what if she did something
in an attempt to keep Rebecca from leaving Cypress?"

"A superfan turned dangerous? That's happened before."

"But it can't be her. She would have had to run
through the mud in order to get to the door by the time I
opened it. And no one had run through the mud."

"Which takes us back to my mom."

And Flossie. But I refused to let my suspicions stray
in that direction. "There's this trail between the lake and
your parents' house. With all those hedges, no one
standing in your parents' front yard would be able to see
what was going on in the back or in the woods. And
there is also my missing father to think about." I looked
around. My goodness, there was another person missing
from this scene. "Have you noticed?"

"Noticed what?"

"Marianne Carsdale isn't out here asking us what
we're doing. Whenever I visit my daddy, she's out of her
house and talking to me before I ever get to his front
door." I looked around again. "So, where is she?"

Jace peered in the direction of Marianne's house.
"Look, your father's house blocks her view of this path.
We can't see her house from here, and she can't see us. We
could walk down to the lake, hop in your father's boat,
and she wouldn't notice until we were past that point over
there." He pointed to the narrow strip of heavily forested
land that jutted out into the lake between my father's
house and Marianne's.

"Maybe this is how the killer got to your parents'
house. She took a boat to my daddy's landing and walked
through the woods, all without Marianne seeing her.
And then she waited for an opening. Perhaps she didn't

even know if an opening would come. But all of this would hinge on my daddy being gone, wouldn't it?"

"I don't have a good feeling about this." When he turned to me, I could see the worry in his eyes. "We need to find your father."

Since searching for my daddy (seemingly) had nothing to do with Rebecca's murder, Police Chief Fisher finally let Jace utilize department resources. News quickly spread throughout the town that Ashley Becket had gone missing and that a full-on search for him was now under way.

Mama Eddy was the first person to contact me while I was working the front desk at the library. "That man is going to be the death of me," she yelled into the phone. "I'm mortified that our family is at the center of such a hubbub. Mor-ti-fied. I wanted to keep this all quiet. What will the parents of the children in my cotillion class say? I'm supposed to be a model of exemplary behavior and Ashley has run off without a word to anyone and you are getting shot at? You are too much like your father. Too much. And I haven't forgotten about getting over to your house for an intervention. You need to start treating your body like a temple and stop eating all that junk food."

"Uh-huh . . ." I muttered as I tried to chew Hazel's delicious chocolate chip cookie as quietly as possible. But Mama had ears like a fox.

"You're eating junk right now, aren't you?"

I had to swallow before I could answer. "Hazel assures me that all her food is completely healthy. I'm going over to her house tonight for dinner."

After the shooting, Jace insisted on acting as my shadow. He had driven me back to the library and planned to pick me up after the library closed so we could drive over to his parents' house together.

"I'm not sure you should be spending time with that family, what with the murder charge and all. And I never liked that you were dating someone in law enforcement. It's best to cut ties with them despite how well Hazel sets a table. She's an artist when it comes to that, you know. But people are saying that not even you will be able to prove Hazel's innocence, not with all the evidence the police have. The woman snapped. Plain and simple. Just like I'm going to snap when I see your father."

"Yes, Mama," I said, because I'd learned long ago that once her mind was made up, there was never anything I could say to change it. "I'll call as soon as I hear anything. I promise."

"Good. And for heaven's sake, go drink some water."

I disconnected the call and dutifully went to fill my water bottle. The water fountain was over near the bathrooms, tucked away past the 3D printers and the hacker space. As I was filling the bottle, I heard the whirl of wheels. And then a soft beep.

I turned around to find LIFU coming toward me. Keven must have worked quickly, getting it repaired and returned to the library.

"Enter your request," it said in that flat metallic voice as it rolled toward me. I frowned at it for a moment before deciding to put the robot to work.

Find Ashley Becket, I typed into its search bar.

My father's name appeared on the screen along with his birthday, his address, and a list of accomplishments including "Senior Engineer at Tech Bros."

I wished he had told me that he'd been helping Keven and Trey build this mechanical behemoth that was trying to replace me.

"Thank you," I said, disappointed that it hadn't provided me with GPS coordinates of my father's current whereabouts. But I did understand the technology well enough to know that the robot wasn't magic.

LIFU simply stood there and stared at me with its unblinking electronic eyes.

Creepy.

"You may go now." I made a shooing motion for it to get out of my way.

It refused to move.

I huffed.

It stared.

Well, since it seemed to be waiting for me to do something else, I decided to ask it another question. I typed, *Give me the list of projects Keven Verner is working on.*

RESTRICTED. The bright red word flashed onto the screen.

"Okay." I held up my hands in surrender, just in case LIFU decided to spray yellow powder at me. "I just wanted to know what Marigold Brantley has against your maker."

The robot's screen went blank for a second before scrolling all sorts of information on Marigold Brantley. Her birthday, her age, her educational background.

"Voice commands?" I didn't know that the robot could respond to voice commands. It never seemed to react when I tried to talk to it before.

According to the scrolling data, Marigold had a bachelor of science in electrical engineering and computer science from a top college in the Northeast.

"So she would know computers and robots," I said.

I half expected LIFU to say "Affirmative" in its tinny voice. But it didn't. What it did do was continue to scroll information about Marigold Brantley's life across its screen.

After college she moved back to Cypress and married Sherwood Brantley. His family owned the feed and seed store, and that became her life . . . until they passed the store on to their son, who didn't want to run it. Once he had ownership, he promptly sold the store to Tori, which caused all sorts of bad feelings between Tori and the Brantley family. They accused Tori of seducing Junior into selling. That was nonsense, of course. But they continued to make trouble for Tori.

"Oh," I said to myself as a lightbulb flashed over my head. "That explains why Marigold has never invited me to call her Goldie. I'm Tori's best friend and, by association, Marigold's enemy."

Marigold tended to hold on to grudges like a hungry alligator clamped down onto its prey. I wondered if—

"Tru!" Emma ran toward me. "Tru! Thank goodness I found you." She skidded to a stop and put her hands on her knees. "I was downstairs looking at some books when I heard that the police are searching for your father." She paused to catch her breath. "If I'd known you thought he was missing, I would have told you sooner. He's—he took a last-minute deal on a Caribbean cruise. I set it up for him."

"He went on a cruise?" I asked. "By himself?"

"Not by himself." Emma grimaced. "With someone he's been working with. A woman. I'm sorry to be the one to tell you. Please, don't hate me for it."

I don't know what hurt more: learning that Daddy had gone on vacation without telling me or that he was in a relationship and hadn't told me. In all the years after the divorce, he had never dated.

That I knew of!

Mama Eddy had gone through a string of relationships, with dramatic breakups. But not Daddy. He kept busy with his work. Traveled a bit. But never dated.

That I knew of!

"I can give you the number for the ship," Emma offered.

"Yes, thank you. But why hasn't he returned my texts?" I asked, still feeling worried that something terrible had happened to him. He always answers my texts.

"This cruise ship is known for charging high fees for add-ons like Wi-Fi and cell service. That's why the base tickets are so cheap. Your father may have opted not to pay for the service."

My shoulders relaxed a bit. "That does sound like him."

"Let me get you the ship's number." Emma flipped through her phone and then jotted what she found there onto the back of a receipt she'd dug out of her purse. "Call this number and give the operator the ship's name." She tapped where she'd written it on the receipt. "You'll then be connected to the ship's operator. If you give her your father's name and his cabin number"—she tapped the receipt where she'd written that number—"she'll be able to connect you to his room. I hope that helps."

A lump in my throat prevented me from thanking her properly.

"Let me know how it goes and if you need anything else," she said. "I am sorry y'all have been so worried."

"No. No. Thank you for letting me know. I appreciate it."

"I see the robot is back up and running. I've heard how it's been giving everyone fits lately."

"It seems better." I glanced over at the screen. It was no longer showing information about Marigold. Well, not precisely. It was now showing her library search history. Keven really shouldn't let LIFU show people that. But since the information was scrolling across the screen, I stood there and read it. Emma did too.

"Although I don't cotton to gossip, I do love reading celebrity articles like these. They're one of my guilty pleasures," Emma said as she peered over my shoulder.

As Marigold had mentioned, she'd looked up Joyce Fellows and her television show *Ideal Life*. Nothing in those articles was news to me, until I came across an article about Gail Tremper, the producer for the show. According to this article, the cranky producer was willing to go to any length to keep the show from being canceled.

"Wow, that sounds suspicious," Emma whispered.

"It's . . . interesting," I agreed.

"You're smiling," Emma said.

"I am," I said. "Thanks to you, I'm smiling."

She patted my arm. "I'm simply glad I could help."

My smile remained in place as I watched her go.

"LIFU, I take back all the bad things I've said about you," I told the sweet, clever metal powerhouse. "You've been very helpful."

As if shocked by my compliment, LIFU sparked. Hiccuped. And toppled over.

Chapter Twenty-Six

⸻•⸻

After telling Anne that LIFU was on the floor again (and not because of anything I did!), I sent a quick text to Jace. I found my father! He's on a cruise.

While Anne and I waited for Keven to come rescue our fallen metal librarian, I called the ship's number Emma had given me and followed her instructions. It took a few tries, but I finally was able to hear my father's voice. Daddy apologized once he heard how worried we all were. He had indeed opted not to pay the ship's Wi-Fi fee and had been without cell reception for most of the cruise. He promised to explain more when he got home, which would be in two days.

Tears of relief filled my eyes as I disconnected the call. I texted Jace again. Got off the phone with my daddy. He's definitely on that cruise. With a date!

I still couldn't believe that last part.

"Why do you hate technology, Tru?" Keven cried as he followed Anne to where the robotic librarian had fallen. He was dressed in a colorful Hawaiian shirt with a long-sleeved white T-shirt underneath, khaki pants, sandals, and that porkpie hat that seemed to be his signature look.

He happened to be at the library because he'd just set the newly repaired LIFU loose not twenty minutes before the robot came searching me out like a needy puppy.

"I don't hate technology," I said. "And actually, I was finding LIFU helpful until she glurped."

"Glurped?" Anne asked.

"That's the sound she made before she fell over," I explained.

"She?" Keven asked.

"Oh, she's definitely a girl robot," I said.

Anne rolled her eyes.

"You Beckets are a thorn in my side," Keven grumbled.

"Yeah, I heard that my father is working for you."

"Working for me!" Keven made an ugly growling sound. "He and my secretary, a lovely woman who is the only one who knows where the papers are filed and if the bills have been paid, are both gone. They both came in last week and told me that they were taking their vacation time. Immediately."

So that's who he was secretly dating?

"Who is your secretary?"

"Lucinda Farley. The most competent secretary to have ever walked the earth."

I'd never heard of her. "Is she new in town?"

"Yes. She came with me. And I need her back."

"And they didn't tell you where they went?"

"No! If they had, I'd be there right now, begging them to come back. What with LIFU glitching for no good reason and trying to figure out the filing system, I need them both here and working. None of this"—he gestured at the fallen LIFU—"would be happening if they were here. I've had to research robotics protocols—not my area of expertise—because your father is gone. Poof!"

Keven struggled to lift LIFU. "The second day they were gone, Lucinda finally answered my texts. She told me to stop texting her and blocked my number. Well, I'm going to have to take LIFU back to the barn to see if we can't figure out what's going on with her. When I test her out there, nothing goes wrong. It doesn't make sense. Next time you talk with your father, tell him to get back to work."

Anne and Keven started to push the heavy robot toward the elevator.

"Wait," I called out to them.

They paused and turned to me.

"Mrs. Farnsworth said you'd installed safeguards on LIFU so the robot couldn't harm anyone. She had recited the three laws of robotics. Are those laws part of the programming?" I asked, thinking back on Keven's run-in with Marigold, and Marigold's technological background.

Plus, Charlie had recommended that I needed to follow the books, which I was trying to do.

"I'm a computer programmer," Keven admitted, "not a robotics expert. That's why I hired your father. He was supposed to be helping with the robotics side of things."

"He's an engineer." Surely Keven knew that. "He's a fantastic tinkerer, but he's not a robotics expert."

"If he was here, he could help me figure out how to solve these problems," Keven insisted, looking even more stressed than before.

"Is that why you were trying to buy Isaac Asimov's *I, Robot* when you were at the bookshop earlier today?" I asked.

"Yes! I told Mrs. Farnsworth that LIFU had safeguards. And it does! Somewhat. But she assumed I knew all about the three laws of robotics. I didn't, not until I Googled them. Then I wanted to read about them from the source. I ended up downloading the anthology in ebook form after my run-in with that unpleasant woman at the bookstore."

"Why are you building robots if you're not an expert?" I asked.

"I can program anything," he said. "And robots are the future. I thought I'd hired a reliable engineer to help with the technical end of things. A CEO isn't expected to know everything." He huffed.

"Making a robot follow the three rules of robotics is a programming problem, not an engineering one," Anne muttered.

Keven grimaced. "As I said, a CEO isn't expected to know everything. And I need to get this back to the barn if I'm ever going to figure out how to make it work right."

I stood there, sipping on my water for a few minutes after they left, thinking everything over. I sipped on my water a bit more while gathering up all my courage. Then I pulled out my cell phone and gave Mama Eddy a call.

She deserved to know what my daddy had been up to these past several days.

"I knew it!" Mama Eddy raged, after I'd told her everything. "That man never considers others. He left us without warning. Here we were worrying and worrying about him, needlessly." She paused only a moment to catch her breath. "When is he getting back? I want to be there on his doorstep to give him an earful."

"Um, perhaps don't do that right away," I said.

"Why? Because he'll be tired from his vacation?" She laughed. "That man never gets tired. That's why he gets himself into all kinds of mischief. It's that relentless energy of his."

"Yes, I understand," I said. I sank into the nearest chair, which happened to be a comfortable gamer's chair set up in the hacker space. "But he, um, he didn't go alone on the cruise. He went with a . . ." *Courage, Tru.* "With a woman."

"Oh! So he's dating?" Her voice grew louder.

I held my breath and moved the phone away from my ear, expecting her to explode with more drama than I could handle.

"Finally," Mama Eddy said after a span of silence. "Good for him." She actually sounded . . . happy. Seriously. She sounded happy. "Do you know her?"

"I don't," I admitted. "He didn't tell me anything."

"Silly man. I bet he didn't want to upset you. But here we are. You're upset."

"I'm not upset." But my heart felt like someone was squeezing it.

"Oh, honey," she crooned softly. Knowingly. "Your father and I both love you. Even in the toughest of times, that's the one thing we've always agreed on."

"I know. I know." I sniffled. "And I've got to get back to work. I simply wanted you to know as soon as I did that we found him. And that he's okay."

"Thank you, Tru. You're a good daughter."

I disconnected the call and stared at the phone. When I finally looked up, I noticed that Mrs. Farnsworth had come to the back of the library and was standing with her arms crossed, watching me.

"I'll-I'll get back to work," I said, still feeling shaken by . . . well, by everything.

She shook her head. "Ms. Becket." She cleared her throat. "Tru." She'd softened her voice. "Go home."

"They found my father. He wasn't missing. He'd gone on a cruise."

She gave a curt nod. "Go home," she repeated. "I'll cover for you. Go home and figure everything out. Figure out how to save Hazel. Figure out how to save the Arete Society."

"But the police—"

"The police have already made up their minds, haven't they?" she said.

I tilted my head. "What was going on with the book club?"

"What do you mean?"

"Everyone I talk to gives me a different story. Rebecca was looking to kick out the older members to make room for the younger ones. Hazel only had a provisional membership. If you were caught reading the wrong sort of books, Rebecca would make sure all the members would ostracize you. Rebecca only let Emma stay in the club because of her superior icebox cake. Rebecca had invited Joyce Fellows to come film the meeting because she planned to announce her return to television." I drew a breath. "I don't know which story to believe."

She looked at me hard. "I think you do."

As always, Mrs. Farnsworth was right. I did know.

I rose from the ultracomfortable chair and started toward the basement steps to go get Dewey.

"Oh, and Tru," Mrs. Farnsworth said sternly as I passed her. "Be sure you don't shatter the glass front doors when you leave."

The last time that had happened was fourteen years ago. Fourteen years! I smiled at her. "No, ma'am. I won't."

Chapter Twenty-Seven

Dewey greeted me at the heavy door leading into the secret bookroom with a shrieking meow, the loud, startling kind of meow that he'd give when he was feeling especially playful. A paperback historical romance was under his front paw. I recognized it as one of the ones I'd placed on the circulation table a few hours earlier.

"You're a scamp," I said as I scooped the book from the floor and carried it back to the table. Along the way, I came across three more books that Dewey had mistaken for kitty toys. I put them all back onto the pile of books I'd made.

Since I had some time before Jace was scheduled to come and pick me up, I decided to take a moment to discover the connection between the books Dewey kept pulling from the shelves.

I found my trusty notebook and set it on the table, and then I opened the front flap of the top book in search of the book slip that was supposed to be there.

When we opened this secret bookroom, we returned

to the low-tech way of loaning out our collection. I had only experienced this way of keeping track of library loans as a child. When a patron wanted to take out a book, they'd write their name on the card found in the front pocket. This card—often called a circulation card—would then be filed behind the patron's name in a borrower's file drawer in the circulation desk. I could pull out the drawer and see what books a particular patron had currently checked out. When the book was returned, the card was put back into the book's pocket. On it was the list of names of everyone who had checked out the book.

Because the circulation desk does not always have someone available to help patrons check out the books, I'd taped step-by-step instructions on how to self–check out the books onto the circulation desk. We'd successfully implemented electronic self-checkout kiosks upstairs several years ago, so I felt comfortable letting the patrons take control of their book borrowing down here.

But unlike the computerized system upstairs, where I could pull up a book and review its circulation history with only a couple keystrokes, I needed to pull the cards from the fronts of the books Dewey had been playing with and search the names on the circulation cards to see if one name appeared again and again on the cards for all these books.

But when I went to pull the card from the first book, I discovered that the pocket was . . . empty.

I flipped to the front cover to check the pocket of the next book in the stack . . . also empty.

And the next one . . . empty.

And the next . . . empty.

Someone had pulled the circulation cards from all the books that Dewey had removed from the shelves.

I sat back in the squeaky chair and looked at the pile.

Why would someone do that?

Why would someone want to hide that they had checked out these books?

"Hey, sexy, what are you concentrating on so hard there?" Jace asked, startling me. "Did that sound okay? I thought I'd play around with this whole 'we're dating and not trying to hide it' thing we have going on. But at the same time, I don't want to be . . . creepy. Was that creepy? Calling you sexy, I mean? Is it okay to call a librarian sexy, or is that cliché and offensive?"

I chuckled. Jace was cute when he got flustered. "Hey, boyfriend," I said, and leaned over the desk to give him a quick kiss. "I don't really think of myself as sexy, but I suppose I don't mind you calling me that. Well, perhaps not all the time. Just some of the time."

"Gotcha. Are you ready?" he asked.

"I have to get Dewey," I said, pushing the books aside. Figuring out what happened to the circulation cards could be a mystery for another time.

"I hate that your first dinner with my parents is happening under these circumstances," he said. "Hello there, Dewey." He picked up my little tabby cat and scratched him under the chin before carefully lowering him into the tote bag I used as a cat carrier.

"Are you sure your mom and dad will be okay with me bringing Dewey to their house? He might get cat fur on your mother's furniture." According to Mama Eddy, it was the height of rudeness to bring a pet into someone else's home. Mama Eddy also didn't believe animals belonged in houses. Her bias against our furry friends was one reason Dewey was my first pet.

"They'll love him."

"Are you sure?" While I didn't agree with Mama Eddy on many things, this was one point of etiquette where I thought she might be right. "Have you brought

Bonnie to their house?" I asked, pretty sure I knew the answer.

"What? Of course not! Bonnie has no manners at all. She would chew the legs on their priceless antique dinner table."

"That settles it. We should take Dewey to my house before driving to your parents'," I said.

Dewey meowed, as if in protest.

"I'm sorry, Dewey. But you haven't been on your best behavior lately." I gave a nod at the pile of books on the desk beside me.

Dewey gave another protest meow and then turned to plead his case with Jace, using his irresistible cute face.

"Aw, he wants to come with us. I'm sure he'll be fine." Jace was a sucker for Dewey's big green-eyed stare.

"No." I had to be the meanie. "It's worrying enough sitting down to dinner with your parents for the first time. Plus, there's the stress of your mother's . . . um . . . troubles. Let's not add to all that by having to wonder if Dewey mistakenly thinks your mother's doll collection are cat toys. Your mother is a wonderful cook. I'd rather sit down and enjoy it instead of chasing after my sweet, adorable—but naughty—kitty."

"Sorry, buddy," Jace said to Dewey, who was batting at Jace's arm. "She makes a good point there. Mom would cry if anything happened to one of her creepy dolls."

After taking Dewey home and leaving him with some extra treats as well as his dinner and a new toy Jace just happened to have for him in his Jeep, Jace set out toward his parents' house. On the way, he drove past my father's lake house, past the barn where Tech Bros had set up operation, and down a bumpy country road where the cypress trees grew tall and the shadows loomed deep.

A police cruiser was parked on the street next to the driveway that led to Jace's parents' house. The officer waved as Jace pulled in.

Jace didn't wave back.

I'd learned from reading fiction that some lies can reveal unexpected truths. Sissy, I figured, had lied to me because she had wanted to make me look bad in front of the town by sending me on a wild-goose chase. There really wasn't any deeper truth to be found there. But who else was lying about their relationship with Rebecca? And more importantly, what could I learn about those lies?

"I think I know what happened," I said to Jace.

"You do?" he asked. Even though we hadn't been talking about Rebecca or his mother or the need to catch a killer, those thoughts had clearly been heavy on both our minds. He knew exactly what I was talking about.

"Everyone loved Rebecca, or so everyone I talked with claimed," I said. "But Annabelle and Rebecca had clashed over the changes being made to the library. Delanie and Mrs. Farnsworth were tired of Rebecca's constant need to stir up drama. And Joyce Fellows had lied about being friends with Rebecca."

"But those women were all at the front door that night," he reminded me. "And the killer, if she'd—" He paused and flicked a questioning glance in my direction. "You still think the killer is a she?" he asked.

I nodded.

"If the killer left by the back door, she couldn't have circled around to the front without leaving evidence for Lacy to find," he said, finishing the thought.

"That's true."

"And what about Charlie's gut feeling that Rebecca's

murder is about the books? Do you think he's right about that?" Jace asked.

"Maybe. But none of what I think matters if I can't prove it." I sighed. "I've felt as if I've been running around in circles for the past few days without learning anything important that can actually help your mother, and I hate coming to her house for dinner empty-handed. For one thing, it's rude to show up without a gift for the hostess."

Jace listened thoughtfully as I complained. He then turned off the Jeep's ignition before he turned to me. "If you were running around in circles, no one would be taking crazy potshots at you."

"Our villain could have been shooting at you . . . or Lacy," I said.

He raised one eyebrow. "Do you believe that? And please, don't make me remind you about being poisoned."

"I wasn't poisoned."

That handsome eyebrow of his remained raised. "What did Dr. Lewis say?"

"She hasn't called with the lab results."

"You know, you could call her," he pointed out.

He was right. I whipped out my phone and dialed the urgent care center. After waiting on hold for a while, the receptionist came back on to tell me that the doctor was busy with a patient, but she'd call as soon as she got a chance.

He frowned at that. "They're going to close in less than a half hour. I hope she doesn't wait until tomorrow."

"I wasn't poisoned. I was overly tired, so I'm not really that concerned that someone is trying to get to me," I lied. After being shot at, I admit I'd started feeling jumpy about my safety. "Let's go see what your mother has for us to eat. And I suppose I'll grovel about coming to her dinner without anything to offer."

"If you brought anything, it'd only go to waste. My mom has cooked enough food to feed half the state tonight," Jace said.

Hazel greeted us at the door. This time, she beamed a huge smile. She kissed first her son's cheek and then mine. "Come in. Come in. Beau is fixing drinks in the living room. Get in there and tell him what you'd like."

"It smells amazing in here," I said as my stomach growled. I put my hand on my middle and prayed that I'd actually get to eat some of her delicious food this time.

"I hope you don't mind, dears," Hazel said as she herded us like a couple of sheep into the house. "I invited a few others to the party."

We walked into the living room to find Tori and Charlie standing near the bar while Beau seemed to dance with an icy cocktail shaker tin.

"Tori!" I exclaimed. "Charlie! Why didn't you tell me you were coming?"

Tori spun around and propped her hands on her hips. "Why didn't you tell me, your bestie, that someone was shooting at you today?"

"I'm sorry!" I explained how busy I had been all day. But the truth was, after being consoled by Jace, I didn't feel a burning need to call Tori and pour out my feelings to her. "What are y'all doing here?"

"Tru, I can't believe you have to ask," Tori said. "We're here to figure out who killed Rebecca."

Beau made a rude sound at the mention of Rebecca's name and then went back to concentrating on tending the bar.

"What a splendid idea." A council of war was exactly what we needed.

"Don't start hashing out ideas until after you eat," Hazel called from the kitchen. "Dinner will be ready in fifteen minutes."

"We need to wait for Flossie, anyhow," I said.

"She can't make it," Hazel sang as she happily hurried back into the kitchen.

"She can't?" Tori asked.

"She told me she was busy watering her plants," Hazel said.

No sooner had she said that when the doorbell rang.

"Who else did she invite?" I asked Jace while worrying why Flossie was keeping away. "Fisher or Ellerbe?"

"Neither," Hazel sang as she swept out of the kitchen and nearly floated toward the front door. "Delanie, so good to see you. Everybody is already in the living room enjoying themselves."

Delanie? I mouthed to Jace.

He shrugged.

"It sounds like she's invited our small-town version of the Scooby gang," Tori said. "It feels odd doing this without Flossie, though. You said she was upset earlier?"

I nodded. "Emma had said something about the Arete Society that upset her, but I can't figure out what exactly."

"I heard she dotes on her plants," Hazel said. "They belonged to her late husband, you know. I'm sure she's fine. Beau, please fix Delanie her usual."

Delanie came in and brushed kisses on everyone's cheeks. She had changed into a winter-white suit dress. "Watering plants, my foot. What is up with Flossie lately? She wasn't at the library this afternoon. We were supposed to meet up and talk about a literacy program I'm trying to bring to our town. She stood me up."

"I don't know," I said. "I'll check on her on my way home tonight."

"We'll check on her," Jace said. "On the way to your house."

"Son, everyone in town has been talking about how

you've practically moved in with Ms. Becket," Beau scolded. "I don't want you besmirching the young lady's reputation without intentions of doing something about it."

Besmirching? Tori mouthed to me.

I chuckled.

"Sir, you may recall that someone shot at Tru today. I'm not going to leave her unprotected at her house. And I only stayed over at her house last night because someone poisoned her."

"I wasn't poisoned," I objected.

"Such a romantic," Tori said, rolling her eyes.

"I was protecting her," Jace said.

"Regardless, people are talking. You need to—" Beau started, but Hazel interrupted him with her elegant voice letting us know that "Dinner is ready."

Dinner was . . . I don't know how to describe the food that she served. Calling the meal delicious seems like an insult. Hazel is a culinary artist. How she blended spices, textures, flavors—my taste buds had fallen on a fainting couch with an arm slung over their eyes, and that was where they'd spent dinner sighing with joy. We all left the table and returned to the living room feeling sated, relaxed, and happy. Hazel would not listen to any of our offers to help with the dishes.

"Tru, I heard your daddy was found," Beau said as he lowered himself into an armchair. "I'm sorry he put you through that kind of worry."

"Thank you. I am relieved. Emma let me know that she'd booked him a last-minute cruise. He hasn't been answering the texts I'd sent him because he didn't pay the cruise line's fee for connecting to their Wi-Fi."

"That's Ashley for you," Beau said with a chuckle.

"Emma is a good travel agent," Hazel said as she entered the room, carrying a tray of coffee. "She booked Beau's Florida fishing trip."

Beau jumped up from his chair and took the tray from her. "Yeah, she suggested that it would be best for everyone if I wasn't underfoot while Hazel and Rebecca prepared for that awful book club," he grumbled. "She's working with the rental agency to see if I can get a partial refund for the time I didn't use the fishing cabin."

"Emma's been spending quite a bit of time at our house. I've been teaching her how to sew and how to cook," Hazel said as she handed out mugs of coffee. "She's quite dreadful with a needle and thread, but she's a natural in the kitchen. She was here one day last week so I could help her on a project—she wants to sew a small quilt for her mother—and she saw the trouble Rebecca was causing. She pulled Beau aside and suggested he go away fishing. I was thankful for that. Did you know that she—?"

"Mom, you're stalling," Jace said softly. "I know the criminal case against you is something you don't want to talk about, but let me remind you that bringing everyone here for dinner was your idea. We need to hash out what happened the night of the book club or else . . ." He spread his hands out and frowned.

"You're right, Jace," she said as she spooned an incredible amount of sugar into her coffee. "It's just that it's so unsettling to think about. A killer in my house?" A splash of her hot drink sloshed over the rim of her cup and dropped onto the muted colors of her Oriental rug. "Oh dear. That's going to stain. I need to go get a wet rag."

"Leave that to me, Hazel. I can get a stain out of anything," Charlie said as he headed toward the kitchen.

"But—" she started to protest.

"Stay. Help everyone brainstorm. I'll be right back with the right ingredients for making that coffee disappear."

Hazel started to follow Charlie into the kitchen but stopped before reaching the swinging door. She turned back toward us and put on a brave face. "Well, then." Her fingers trembled as she smoothed out a wrinkle on her skirt. "Where do we start?"

For several moments, no one spoke.

Finally, I said, "Well, I think we all agree that the police are wrong. There's no way you lost your temper and killed Rebecca. But someone wanted it to look like that's what happened."

Everyone in the room nodded.

Beau grumbled something profane. Hazel scolded him for it.

"Yes, we all know it wasn't Hazel. But how would someone know when to go into the house? How would that person know that they'd even get a chance to act against Rebecca?" Tori asked.

I turned to Hazel. "Why did you decide to take the garbage out right before the guests arrived?"

She shook her head. "I-I had to. Oh, it's so embarrassing, really. I must have made a mistake when I turned on the oven. I'd thought I'd set the temperature to 375, but a few minutes into baking my quickie red velvet cake, I smelled that it was burning. In my haste to make that last-minute dessert, I must have accidentally set the stove to broil"—she shook her head—"although, for the life of me, I don't remember doing that. But I must have. Anyhow, I knew I had to get that burnt smell out of the kitchen right away or else the overwhelming acrid scent would seep into the rest of my dishes. The burnt cake had to go out. It's common knowledge."

I'd never heard that you had to get burnt food away from your other dishes, but I nodded anyhow. "So, you were outside. Did you see anyone?"

Hazel shook her head. "No. I carried the trash out to the shed where we keep the garbage cans. I wasn't gone for more than a minute or so."

"What about your friend?" Beau asked me. "I heard she was alone with that bitter actress."

"Flossie would never—" I started to say.

"Dad, we've already been over this. Flossie uses a wheelchair and can't stand up. She couldn't hit anyone over the head," Jace said.

"Well . . ." Beau drew out the word.

Charlie came into the room holding a stack of clean white cloths and a bottle of seltzer water. He'd tied an apron around his waist. It made him look quite dapper. "I hope I didn't miss much. But, like the tides and time, stains wait for no one." He knelt next to the stain and got to work, dabbing at the liquid with the cloth. As soon as his dabbing efforts produced a dry cloth, he poured the seltzer on the coffee stain. Like magic, the bubbly liquid flushed the stain right out of the rug. He blotted the area dry with the remaining cloths in his stack.

"I think Flossie could kill someone," Tori said in the silence that followed Charlie's entrance. "If she was angry enough."

"Flossie isn't a suspect," I insisted.

"That's because the police think they've already closed the case," Beau complained. "It's infuriating."

I held up my hand. "I'm with you one hundred percent. The experts seem to be reading the evidence wrong. And it's up to us to change their minds by figuring out the who, how, and why for them."

Charlie held up the last cloth. "It's all dry," he said. "And no sign of the stain."

"Heavens, you did a fantastic job," Hazel declared. "Where did you learn to do that?"

"In Vegas. That town produces more messes than I could handle some days on the job," Charlie said with a wink.

"What did you do there?" Beau asked.

"Security," Charlie offered. "But I was tasked with cleanup on a regular basis." He smiled as he seemed to be remembering something. "Anyhow, back to Hazel's troubles. I've been listening. Who might have had access to the kitchen's back door?"

"Anyone," Hazel said. "It's never locked."

"Oh, you should change that," Charlie said, suddenly all serious.

"Very few people lock their doors around here," I pointed out. "This is Cypress."

"People are people everywhere, which is why we're here having this conversation," Charlie said, giving us all a hard look. "Lock your doors."

"How would anyone know that they could come in and kill Rebecca without being caught?" Delanie asked.

I had a ready answer to that question. "I noticed the large window over the sink looking out into the woods in the kitchen, and there's also a window on the door," I said. "Anyone could have hidden in the shadows of the forest, waiting for an opportunity."

"An opportunity that may have never come," Tori pointed out.

"True. But the burnt cake created that opportunity, didn't it?" I closed my eyes, remembering that night. "Hazel, you put the cake in the oven and then came into the living room. You were in there with us watching Rebecca redecorate when you noticed the cake was burning, isn't that right?"

"That's how I remember it," Hazel said thoughtfully. "My red velvet cake burned almost immediately because the broiler was on. What a goopy, stinky mess that was. I've never made a mistake like that before, setting the oven to broil instead of bake."

"You did that because Rebecca had you so flustered, dear?" Delanie asked.

"No," I said. "The cake burned because someone was watching the kitchen and saw the opportunity to change the oven setting to broil."

Hazel was nodding. "I suppose that is what could have happened. That rude person who came into my house uninvited must know her way around the kitchen, because she knew I'd take that smelly disaster of a burnt cake out to the garbage right away."

Again, I didn't know that was a thing. But then again, I didn't kill Rebecca. And the more I thought about it, the more I liked this theory.

With a little more talking like this, I was sure we'd have our culprit figured out before we finished our coffees.

Chapter Twenty-Eight

———·———

Two hours later, the coffee cups had been emptied and refilled and emptied again. Hazel had brought out two kinds of cakes (classic chocolate and raspberry creme) and three plates of assorted homemade cookies. Most of the cookies and half of both cakes were now gone. I'd described how the trail behind the Baileys' house led to my father's cabin and then shared what Lacy had told me about finding no evidence in the muddy ground that led from the back to the front of the house.

"Well, that settles it. We know who it wasn't." Delanie set her coffee cup onto its saucer. It made a delicate clatter. "No one in the book club could have been responsible, which is a relief, really. I hate looking at my friends and wondering if one of them is secretly a monster."

"Secretly?" Beau muttered. "Those harpies don't keep anything about their natures secret."

But that wasn't quite true, was it? Marigold hid her technological prowess. Annabelle hid her temper. And

who knew what else might lurk under the polished ve-
neers of the ladies I hadn't questioned.

I was glad I didn't need to find out. Mama Eddy
would have never forgiven me if I'd angered any one of
those pillars of Cypress society by prying too hard.

Tori leaned over toward me. "You know who did it,"
she whispered.

I tried to keep my expression neutral as I shrugged.

"I knew it!" she exclaimed.

"Knew what?" Charlie asked.

"I knew that our girl Tru has been holding back
on us."

Everyone turned and stared at me.

"Not holding back," I said, holding up my hands.
"Just not spouting off wild hunches without having proof
to back them up."

Jace smiled at me in a way that made my heart melt a
bit. "And how do we get this elusive proof?"

"Y'all remember Gail?" I asked.

Delanie groaned at the mention of *Ideal Life*'s producer. "She won't return my phone calls."

"So rude," Tori said with a twinkle in her eye.

"She'll return my phone call," I said. "She's desperate
to keep her show on the air. And will do anything to get
a big story."

"Anything?" Delanie said. "As in—?" She gasped.
"She wasn't with the rest of the film crew that came with
Joyce Fellows that night."

"She wasn't," I agreed.

I was about to say more when my cell phone chimed.
I checked the screen. Dr. Lewis was finally calling.

"I need to take this," I said as I hurried into the
kitchen.

Jace followed me.

"There must be a stomach bug going through the

elementary school," Dr. Lewis said after apologizing for calling so late. "I've been busy all day with kids with upset tummies. I haven't had a chance to catch my breath, much less make any calls. But I do have your blood results right here, and I knew you wanted to hear back as soon as possible." Paper rustled. "Are you sure you didn't take caffeine pills that morning?" she asked.

"No. I had a few cups of coffee, that's all. Why? What do the results say?"

"The lab results are clear, Tru. You overdosed on caffeine. And this isn't the kind of overdose a few cups of coffee would cause. I'm talking about megadoses of caffeine."

"I only had four cups of coffee that morning." And I'd spilled most of one of them all over the desk.

"It had to come from somewhere," Dr. Lewis said. "Did anyone give you a drink? Or something to eat that morning? Perhaps someone slipped you something, trying to poison you."

"No" came my automatic answer. "I brewed the coffee that I drank that morning."

But then I remembered that wasn't exactly right.

Flossie had brought me a coffee.

I looked at Jace.

He looked concerned.

"We should go talk with Flossie," I said.

"Tonight?"

"Tonight."

Flossie's house sat on the shore of Lake Marion. It had been owned for generations by her husband's family. After Truman had inherited it, he'd installed a ramp around the side of the porch for Flossie's wheelchair. He'd also made several modifications to the house's interior that allowed Flossie to live independently. A woman from town came in twice a week to help with cleaning, laundry, and any projects Flossie might need handled. A lawn service kept the lawn neatly mowed and the flower garden, which had been Truman's pride and joy, in pristine condition.

Moonlight seemed to make the pearly white moon-flowers glow as Jace pulled up to the house.

"You can't seriously believe she'd do anything to hurt you." Tori had leaned forward from the Jeep's back bench and stuck her head in the space between the two front seats.

"Of course I don't," I said.

"People do all sorts of unbelievable acts when they find themselves in a difficult situation. She might have killed Rebecca in a fit of anger and then realized that her best friends would figure out the truth without any trouble," Jace said. "That's why she didn't come tonight."

"This is Flossie we're talking about," Tori argued.

After Jace and I had said our hasty goodbyes at Hazel's house and left, Tori had jumped into Jace's back seat and demanded to be told what was going on.

"Flossie might have a temper," Tori continued, "and she might threaten anyone who dares disturb her writing time, and she lives a secretive life that she fiercely protects."

"You're only making my point," Jace said. "And don't forget that this is the same woman who chased the plumber down the street with a broadsword."

"That was completely justified," Tori said. "I've worked with Marvin, and he's totally unreliable."

"She chased him with a broadsword," Jace reiterated.

"He was five hours late and had interrupted her when she was writing a crucial scene," I said.

Jace turned off his Jeep's motor and turned to me. "If

she's so innocent, why did we just run out of my parents' house moments after hearing from Dr. Lewis that you were poisoned, which may I remind you, I've been saying all along?"

I held up my finger and smiled. "Because she is holding on to a piece of vital evidence."

"Why would she do that?" Tori cried from the back seat.

"Because she doesn't think it is vital, and she's embarrassed about it," I said.

"Oh!" Tori's eyes grew wide. She jumped out of the Jeep with the prowess of an Olympic pole vaulter. "This is going to be good!"

"We're not here to embarrass her," I cautioned as I climbed out of the Jeep.

"I still don't have a good feeling about this," Jace said. "Didn't you say that Flossie brought you a coffee to drink that morning you were poisoned, and that no one else had given you anything?"

"Well, I did." The poisoning scenario still didn't sit right with me. But I didn't say anything, since Jace now had Dr. Lewis to back up his theory that someone was out to stop me from solving Rebecca's murder. "Let's just go talk with Flossie and see what she says."

"Yes, let's," Tori said, tugging on my arm and sounding far too eager.

"I sincerely hope she's not in the middle of writing a crucial scene," Jace muttered.

I chuckled as we approached our friend's front door.

The wooden door was stained red. "It's a bloodred," Flossie had once told me while contemplating painting it a friendlier color.

A soft breeze blew in from the dark, winter-silent lake that reminded me of a gaping hole beyond her house.

"I don't have a weapon," Jace whispered just before I knocked.

I gave his arm a nudge. "This is Flossie we're talking about. She's a pussycat."

One of Jace's eyebrows rose. "A sword-wielding, boomerang-throwing, meteor-hammer-swinging pussycat?"

The bloodred door swung open. Flossie, dressed in a somber black dress, was on the other side of the door. She wasn't smiling.

"Flossie," I said softly.

"Girl, it's time you come clean with us," Tori blurted before I had a chance to say anything else.

Flossie looked at me, and then at Tori, and finally at Jace before bursting into loud ugly tears.

"Now, now," I said, and handed her a tissue from one of the many gaudy tissue boxes scattered around the large wood-paneled living room. Truman's cousin Gracie liked to crochet tissue box covers and give them as gifts to her relatives, which was lovely in theory. The problem was that Gracie was color-blind, so the colors of her creations often clashed in a way that strained the eye. And Flossie was one of Gracie's few remaining living relatives (if only by marriage), which meant Flossie received a crocheted tissue box cover every year for Christmas and Easter and Thanksgiving and Valentine's Day and even the Fourth of July.

Flossie didn't have the heart not to use them. That was why there were nearly twenty color-clashing crocheted-covered tissue boxes . . . in the living room alone.

"I knew"—*sniff*—"as soon as I saw it at Hazel's"—*sniff*—"you'd"—*sniff*—"find me out." She blew her nose loudly in the tissue I'd handed her. "And . . . and then that nasty Gail woman with the *Ideal Life* show started poking around in my business. She's desperate for a huge story, you know?"

"I've heard," I said.

"Wait?" Tori said. "Are you confessing?"

Jace stood a bit taller. I didn't blame him for getting that excited look in his eyes, like a predator getting ready to pounce. After all, his mother's freedom was on the line, and he saw Flossie's confession as the solution to his troubles.

Flossie sighed. She spun her wheelchair toward a doorway that I knew led into her office, a room she rarely used for writing and never allowed anyone to enter. "Follow me." She sounded defeated, flattened. "It'd be easier if I just showed you."

"Flossie, you don't have to worry," I told her. "We're your friends. You can trust us with your secrets."

"I'm also an officer of the law," Jace reminded us as he stepped into Flossie's inner sanctum. "I cannot help cover up a crime, especially not a crime my mother is being accused of committing."

Flossie looked over her shoulder. "A crime?" She seemed to think about that for a moment and then sighed again. "I suppose it was a crime."

"Do you want him to leave?" I asked her.

He looked at me as if I'd just offered to help Flossie push him off a cliff.

Again, Flossie took a moment of thoughtful consideration before answering. "No, I don't suppose I do."

I nodded.

Flossie's office was lined from floor to ceiling with bookshelves absolutely packed with books. Even above the doorframe and above the windows looking out onto the lake, someone had covered every bit of the walls with bookshelves. If I had to guess, this was Truman's handiwork.

Also, tucked in here and there, I spotted several writing awards, plaques, statues, and framed certificates. All naming various well-known authors.

In the middle of the room was a large wooden desk, its top neatly organized. A bin holding bills sat on the left side of the desk. A second bin with what looked like outgoing mail sat on the right side. There was no desk chair since Flossie wouldn't need one. There were also no other chairs in the room, suggesting that she never invited anyone, perhaps not even her husband when he was still alive, into this room.

"Tell us what you want to tell us already, the suspense is killing me," Tori complained.

I pointed to the library book that had been placed at the center of the desk. It was one of the new mass market paperback books that Delanie had donated to the secret bookroom. To be more precise, it was one of the uncorrected proofs that Delanie had donated.

"You didn't want anyone to see that," I said. "You took it from Hazel's kitchen."

"Obviously she was trying to protect the secret bookroom." Tori jumped between Flossie and Jace. "You can't arrest her for that!"

"No one is getting arrested," I said.

"Yet," Jace muttered. He still looked unhappy. And I still didn't blame him. His focus was (as it should have been) on protecting his mother.

I turned to Flossie. "You didn't take the book because it belonged in the library," I said, guessing at the truth. "You took it because you wrote it, and you didn't want Rebecca to see it."

Flossie sniffled.

"That doesn't make sense. Rebecca was dead," Tori

said, shaking her head. "She couldn't see anything. And even if she could, her deadness would make it so she wouldn't care."

My gaze remained on Flossie, who was fidgeting with her hands. "When you went into the kitchen, you didn't know Rebecca was dead, isn't that right, Flossie?" I remembered how my friend was just as surprised as I was when I found Rebecca on the other side of Hazel's kitchen island.

Flossie nodded. "I saw the book and made a grab for it before anyone else came into the room. I guess I ripped out a few pages when I'd rolled over them in my haste to get it off the floor. I rammed my wheelchair into the counter as I reached for it, which had to be that second crash you'd heard. The book had been sitting there, splayed open, the pages crumpled and swimming in the spilled tuna casserole. And all I could think was that Rebecca might walk in and see it and somehow know it was mine. Foolish, I know, but all night she'd been seesawing between ignoring me and outright telling me that I wasn't Arete Society worthy. It was maddening." She looked over at Jace. "Not murderous maddening, mind you," she told him. "It wasn't as if she'd interrupted me when I was writing the all-important ending of a book. But maddening because it made me think that she somehow knew about the kinds of books I wrote and that was the reason she thought I couldn't be part of the book club."

"That's why you were so upset after we talked with Emma, isn't it?" Oh, why hadn't I seen it sooner? "Emma said that no one had objected to Rebecca tossing out your membership application. And then she had badmouthed one of the books the book club had read, and she apologized, worried that you had written it."

Flossie was shaking her head sadly from side to side.

"The reason you couldn't get into the Arete Society wasn't because of the types of books you've written," I said. "They just don't want to accidentally insult you by talking about one of your books in front of you."

"I hadn't realized that was the reason until Emma said it," Flossie said tearfully. "I should have seen it. Others have made the same comments, even you, Tru. But I didn't get it. I didn't understand that my writing was creating a wedge between me and my friends. I hate that."

"Wait. Hold up." Tori lunged across the desk and scooped up the library book Flossie had taken from the crime scene. The muscular man on the cover was standing on the side of a craggy mountain wearing a red-and-green tartan . . . and nothing else. Tori shook the book. "You wrote this?"

Flossie nodded.

"This is what you write?" Tori asked, shaking the book some more.

"I can't control what the publisher puts on the cover," she said. "My editor tells me that whenever they use that particular model, sales go through the roof. It's a good story, though."

"A good story?" Tori sounded incredulous.

"It is!" Flossie insisted, sounding more like her old self again.

"It's not merely good. It's smoking," Tori nearly shouted. "Charlie and I have been reading a copy to each other at night." She waggled her perfectly arched eyebrows in a suggestive way. "Plus, Charlie can't keep them in stock in his store. Everyone is reading this book."

"Oh . . ." Flossie blushed. "Thank you."

I recognized the author's name on the cover. She was

one of our patrons' most requested historical romance novelists. I took the book from Tori and flipped it over to look at the back cover. The photo, which I recognized from previous books by that author, was of a young, stylish woman wearing a slinky red dress and making a pouting face as she leaned against a brick wall.

"No," I said. This couldn't be right. "I know her. I saw her talk about her books at a book signing in Charlotte last year."

"Yeah." Flossie rolled over to the office door and closed it. She lowered her voice. "What I'm going to say right now cannot leave this room."

"I can't make that promise," Jace said rather stubbornly.

"Then leave," Tori snapped. "I want to hear her dish."

"I do too," I agreed.

"It's not anything illegal nor does it involve Rebecca's murder," Flossie said, and made a cross over her heart. "I swear."

Jace took several deep breaths before saying, "Flossie, I consider you a friend. That's what makes this even harder. My mother . . ." He shook his head. "She could go to jail. If you had information that would have helped the police look for suspects other than my mother, you would have saved my family a world of heartache by handing it over. It's hard enough for my mom to accept that someone was murdered in her house. It's even worse that she's being blamed for the death."

Flossie nodded. "I understand. And I know I shouldn't have taken the book. And after Tru discovered Rebecca's body, I really should have returned it, but by then my fingerprints were all over it and it's a book from the secret bookroom, and . . . none of that matters because this is your mother we're talking about." She drew a deep breath. "I am sorry, Jace. But please, don't make what I'm going to tell you right now public unless you feel you have no other choice."

"I can do that," he said.

"Thank you," I said, and gave his hand a squeeze.

"Very well," Flossie said. "Here's my secret. I'm a ghost."

Chapter Twenty-Nine

—·—

"Oh, come on. Stop teasing us." Tori poked Flossie's shoulder. "Flesh and blood, just like the rest of us."

"No. It's true," Flossie said. "I'm a ghost."

"She means she writes books for other authors," I explained. "She writes the books and someone else takes the credit."

"That's not fair," Tori cried. "Why would you do something stupid like that? Why would you avoid becoming famous?"

Flossie shrugged. "For a couple of reasons."

"Which are?" Tori pressed.

Flossie looked down at her wheelchair. "I'm older, and not exactly in the best shape. In the publishing business, image matters."

"That's nonsense, and you know it," Tori said. "Look at you. You're unique!"

Flossie smiled at that. "Thank you, dear. But it's not only image. Readers expect an author to write the same kinds of books over and over and nothing else. I would get too bored if I had to do that. I love the challenge of stretching my talents and seeing if I can pull off some-thing completely different. Plus, I write fast and I'm good at following the directions given to me by the au-thors I'm ghosting for. Publishers like that. So I write books professionals don't know how to write, or books famous authors don't have the time to write. Not all the best sellers do it. But a few use writers like me. It gives them time to go on extended book tours and television shows and have a life. I don't have the patience for any-thing that takes away from my writing time. Really, it's a win-win for all involved."

I turned around and looked at the books crowding her shelves. "How long have you been doing this?" I asked her.

"Oh, I don't know. Twenty years or more?"

"And these books . . ." Gracious. There were nearly as many books crammed into these bookshelves as there were in the secret bookroom. There were romances, thrillers, mysteries, nonfiction, and even a few literary works. "*All* these books? You wrote them?"

"There are some here that were written by friends. And a few reference books," Flossie said, as if it were nothing.

I shook my head, still not quite able to believe it.

"Now, Tru, don't be disillusioned by what I've told you. Most authors write their own books. Most authors work quite hard at writing *and* marketing. I can only imagine what a balancing act it must be for them."

I opened and closed my mouth, not sure what to say. I wasn't disillusioned. I was in awe. I couldn't take my eyes off the walls of books.

"It's not that I didn't want to share this secret with you. The truth is that I couldn't tell you," Flossie said, sounding worried now. "I am contractually obligated to not tell a soul that I've written these books. No one can know that those authors didn't actually write their own books."

"Your secret is safe with us," I said, with a querying glance in Jace's direction.

He nodded. "Is that . . . ?" He pointed to a blockbuster novel on the shelf that everyone in town had raved about. "Did you write . . . ?"

Flossie's impish smile returned. "I did. And what a grand time I had writing that one too. The action spanned three continents. The author and I texted back and forth about the action scenes for weeks to make them as accurate as possible. He sold weapons to foreign countries before retiring and starting this second career as a thriller writer. I work with him to fictionalize his past experiences and"—she winked—"I embellish his stories a bit too."

Wow, Tori mouthed.

Jace wandered around a bit before shaking himself out of the amazement we all seemed to be feeling. "Tru, I'm confused about why you rushed us over here. I thought we came here because Dr. Lewis had confirmed that you'd been poisoned with excessive amounts of caffeine and Flossie was the only person who gave you anything to drink that morning."

"You were poisoned?" Flossie covered her mouth with her hands.

"I . . . um . . ." I still didn't feel comfortable with Dr. Lewis's diagnosis. "Maybe?"

"Who?" Flossie demanded. "Who did this to you?"

"That's the thing," I said. "I don't know how it could have happened."

Jace squared his shoulders. "Tru told us that you brought her a coffee. And that's the only thing she had that morning that she did not make herself. So, I'm wondering, where did that coffee come from, Flossie?"

Flossie shook her head. "It came from Perks, of course."

"Could someone have tampered with it?" he asked.

"No. No one could have tampered with it. I carried it from the café and came directly to the library to place it on Tru's desk," Flossie said.

Jace still had that grave look. "And you didn't—?"

"We're not here because of anything Dr. Lewis said," I interrupted. "We're here because I needed to get my hands on this book." I picked up the stained historical romance from Flossie's desk and held it like a warrior returning from a quest with a mystical treasure. "I needed *this*."

"What?" Jace stared at me as if I'd lost my mind. "Why?"

"Because Dewey has been pulling all the historical romance novels off the library shelves, and I think he's trying to tell me something. Oh, don't look at me as if I'd lost my mind. Certainly y'all must find it interesting that the book Flossie picked up at the crime scene is also a historical romance novel from the secret bookroom? Dewey wanted me to pay attention to something. He wanted to help us solve Rebecca's murder."

Now Tori and Flossie were also looking at me with squinty eyes and wrinkled noses, as if trying to figure out if I was serious.

"Well, anyway," I said. "Someone stole the cards out of the historical romance novels that Dewey has been pulling from the shelves. The cards had been removed before I could check to see if the same person had checked them all out." I waved the book in the air again. "Don't you see?" Clearly, none of them were picturing in their mind's eye the pieces of the puzzle falling into place like I was. "This book is the key to catching our killer."

Chapter Thirty

———·———

Yes, I admit it. I could have been wrong.

Jace and Tori were both convinced that there was no way in the world that a romance novel could be the cause of all this trouble. (I was equally convinced they were wrong.)

The one thing we all agreed on was that our next move needed to be done carefully.

Someone had shot at us simply because I had been talking with Lacy. At least, that was the only explanation for the shooting that made any sense to me. Whoever had killed Rebecca must have realized that I was getting close to figuring out the truth and panicked.

Why else would someone steal the circulation cards from the historical romances Dewey had so helpfully pulled from the library shelves?

"Maybe she did it because she was embarrassed that she'd read all of those books and is worried that you'd tell everyone about her reading habits," Jace suggested as he drove me home after dropping Tori off at Charlie's shop.

"It's possible," I agreed. But that didn't mean I wasn't going to follow the clues to where they seemed to be leading me.

When we got home, Dewey hopped up onto the kitchen table to nuzzle the paperback novel I'd taken home from Flossie's house. He rolled around, purring loudly, as if he agreed that I was on the right track here. Or perhaps he was pleased that I'd finally figured out what he'd been trying to tell me all along.

I rubbed my kitty behind his ears. "You are a clever thing, aren't you?"

Jace and I stayed up late again that night as we set out our plan and then made a few phone calls to make sure we had enough cheese in our trap to catch Rebecca's killer. Once the pieces were all in place, I was sure our scheme would work . . . well, only if my suspicions were correct.

My suspicions *had to be right*. Hazel's freedom depended on it.

When I arrived at the library the next morning, I was tired. Dewey insisted on riding in the tote bag with the book Flossie had found and was purring loudly as I made my way—yawning—toward the basement.

"Ms. Becket, I need to talk with you in my office." I tried to pretend I hadn't heard Mrs. Farnsworth, but she was standing right in front of me, blocking my path to the back stairs.

"Can I go put my things down?" I asked her. Dewey was wiggling around in the tote bag. I really needed to get him to the bookroom.

"This won't take long," she said, and gestured toward her open office door.

My heart beat double time. This could not be happening. Not today.

"Um . . ." I said rather stupidly.

"Let me take that," Anne said as she whisked the tote bag off my arm and hurried away.

Thank you, Anne.

With my head lowered, I followed Mrs. Farnsworth into her office.

She closed the door and told me to sit. She then took her time as she rounded her desk and sat in her office chair. Its springs squeaked as she leaned back.

"Do you really think I don't know what's going on in my library?" Mrs. Farnsworth asked in a way that made the pit of my belly shiver.

"I . . . um . . . No, ma'am." I stared at my shoes. Sure, it made sense that she would discover what I was doing in the basement, but I had hoped that she hadn't been curious enough to go looking.

Mrs. Farnsworth made a sound in the back of her throat.

"Ma'am?" If she was going to fire me, I needed her to do it now and get it over with. It didn't matter if I was jobless or not. The plan's schedule had to go forward or else we'd miss our best chance to catch the killer.

"Ms. Becket, you have an annoying habit of not looking at me when I'm speaking to you," Mrs. Farnsworth said.

I looked up at her. "You intimidate me," I admitted.

"Good." She let that one word hang in the air between us for a while. "When we couldn't find you yesterday there was one place I could have looked for you, but I didn't. Do you understand that?"

I nodded. Slowly.

"Very well. Keep doing what you're doing and get out of here," she said.

"Yes, ma'am." I rushed out of her office and hurried toward the basement. I felt as if I were floating. It was such a relief to know that she knew. Her knowing about the secret bookroom meant I no longer had to go to work every single day dreading that this might be the day Mrs. Farnsworth fired me for creating the space.

When I glanced over my shoulder, I saw that the old woman was standing at her office door watching me . . . and smiling.

Dewey greeted me as soon as I entered the basement bookroom. I scratched him under the chin and told him that he was a good boy before getting to work. Now that I knew the title of the book that the killer had left at the crime scene, it was an easy thing to look up who had checked it out of the secret bookroom.

When a patron checks out a book, they write their name on the first empty line on the card. A due date is then stamped next to the name. That card is filed under the patron's name while a due date book slip to remind the patron of when they need to return the book is then placed in the pocket at the front of the book.

It's a simple and efficient process.

Except for when a patron removes all the cards.

With a computerized system, it would be harder to erase who checked out the books, but secret bookrooms didn't have the budget for computers and software.

I thumbed through the names in the file drawer until I came upon the card that belonged to Flossie's romance novel.

The name I read on the card didn't surprise me. Actually, it was the name I'd expected to find written there.

Hazel Bailey.

I slid the card back into the book's front pocket. The book was damaged and couldn't be returned to circulation. Besides, it was now evidence. If things didn't go as planned today, I would need to give the book to Detective Ellerbe to help him build his case.

I sighed.

I really didn't want to give the book to the detective.

"What are you doing?" Emma asked as she leaned over my shoulder. "You look so serious."

I set the book aside. "Just dealing with a damaged book. I'm lucky that most of our patrons take such good care of our books. But sometimes accidents happen." I glanced at the clock above the double doors. It was barely after ten o'clock, our opening time. "What are you doing here so early on a Friday morning?"

"I'm supposed to meet Flossie here. She wants to talk about booking a trip to—"

Before she could tell me where Flossie was planning to jet off to on her newest adventure, the heavy double doors swung open as if hit by a hurricane-force wind. Delanie—looking less than perfect with her hair not quite combed, her dress misbuttoned, and a red chunky-heeled pump on her left foot and a navy strappy sandal on her right—rushed into the secret bookroom.

"Tru!" she cried. "Tru!"

"Shh!" I jumped up from my chair. Everyone in the library upstairs would come down to the basement to investigate if she kept shouting like that. "Whatever it is, you need to talk quieter."

Her eyes were wild. She shook her head. "Tru." At least she'd softened her voice. "Tru. I have a confession to make. *It was me. I poisoned you.*"

"You did?" I drew a quick, sharp breath. That was not what I was expecting. "*You?*"

Had Delanie killed Rebecca and then tried to kill me?

She was nodding furiously. "I'm sick with grief about it."

I should think so. I thought she was my friend.

She started hobbling toward me. "I-I'm so sorry."

I backed up. "You need to turn yourself in to the police."

She seemed surprised by that. "The police?"

"Yes. You need to go to the police and tell them what you've done." I had never even suspected Delanie. Not even for a moment. None of the clues pointed in her direction. And not only that, Delanie was my friend. How could she poison me like that? "Did you also shoot at me?" I demanded as I backed farther away from her.

She rushed toward me and grabbed my arm. "Shoot you? Gracious, dear, why would you think I'd do that?"

I stared at her hand that was squeezing my arm with a strength that startled me. "I don't know why you'd poison me. Or why you'd kill Rebecca. And you're scaring me."

She threw her arms in the air. "Oh! Oh!" She backed away from me, which made me feel somewhat better. "I rushed over as soon as I realized what had happened. Everyone has been talking about how you were poisoned. And then last night, Dr. Lewis said you'd suffered from an overdose of caffeine."

"Caffeine can kill you?" Emma asked.

"According to Dr. Lewis, it can be pretty serious," I said.

"I didn't realize what that meant last night," Delanie said. "It wasn't until this morning when I was putting on my makeup that I realized what had happened. I got dressed as fast as I could manage and hurried over here. I'm so sorry. I never meant for you to get hurt."

"I don't understand," I said.

"I don't either," Emma said.

"Oh! Of course you don't. I'm not explaining myself very well." She started digging around in her purse. I started to dive under the nearest table.

"You-you don't have a gun in there, do you?" I asked.

"A gun?" Delanie asked. "Goodness, no. Lida would never allow me to carry my gun into her library. She posted those notices all over the front door that guns weren't allowed." She pulled a makeup compact out of her bag. "This is what I wanted to show you. It's that cover-up. Remember, I loaned you some? I didn't realize it contained caffeine. High levels of the stuff, apparently. That's the magic ingredient that makes the puffiness go away. But, see here." She pointed to the ingredient list on the compact. "Caffeine is the first ingredient, and it does say it should be used sparingly. At least, I think that's what it says. My French is rusty. Remember I told you that I had the stuff flown in from Paris?"

"Oh, right!" I clapped my hands together, feeling vindicated. "I knew I wasn't poisoned. Can I borrow this? I'd like to show it to Jace and Detective Ellerbe."

"Of course, dear." Delanie handed it to me. "I am sorry. I never expected that my special cover-up would nearly put you in the hospital."

"That is a surprise," Emma agreed.

And a relief. I had worried for a moment that our carefully constructed trap would fall apart with Delanie's revelation. We not only needed to provide the police the name of Rebecca's killer. We also needed to hand them irrefutable proof.

"Now that you're here," I said to Delanie. She had a role to play in springing the trap. "I hope you haven't forgotten that you'd promised to—"

"Oh, good heavens, look at me," Delanie cried before I could finish what I was saying. "I am a mess. I need to get home and make myself presentable for the day. Goodbye! Goodbye!"

She ran from the bookroom without a backward glance.

Emma and I stared at one another. "That was . . ." I started to say. My heart was still pounding.

"Eye-opening," Emma finished.

I turned the makeup compact over in my hand and nodded. "Indeed."

Although I needed to follow up on this revelation and let everyone know that I wasn't poisoned—at least, not on purpose—I also had a murderer to catch and a trap to set. And I had to do it without Delanie's help because apparently, in her frantic state, she'd forgotten that she'd promised to play a role today. Oh well, with or without her assistance, the plan still needed to go forward.

I looked over at Emma and smiled.

"How would you like to help me catch Rebecca's killer?" I asked her.

Chapter Thirty-One

The first thing I did after heading upstairs was ask Mrs. Farnsworth for permission to take the morning off. The head librarian was remarkably accommodating. I figured her desire to save her beloved book club from all this drama had made her more agreeable than usual. She even went as far as wishing me luck.

So, after briefly explaining the plan to Emma, I drove to Cypress's Waterfront Park, located on the shore of Lake Marion. Emma followed in her own car.

In the center of the park was a large pavilion where concerts were held on warm summer nights. Today, the wooden structure looked lonely and desolate with the gray winter backdrop of the lake and sky.

I hugged myself against the crisp morning breeze as Emma and I made our way toward the prearranged meeting spot. Flossie and Tori were already there waiting for us at the base of the pavilion. Tori had a tray of steaming coffees. She handed Emma and me one each.

"Here comes Marigold," Flossie said, after taking a sip of the coffee she had cupped in her hands.

"That's everyone," I said with a nod.

"Where's Delanie?" Tori asked. "Wasn't she supposed to help with this?"

"She was," I said, and then explained how frazzled she'd been this morning. "She wouldn't be in the right mindset to help out even if she had remembered to meet us here."

"I'm filling in for her," Emma said. She looked around. "Isn't Gail Tremper supposed to be here, too?"

"She texted to let me know she's on her way," Tori said. "That woman is pushy. She wants to feature Perks on her show and has been bugging me with questions half the night and all morning too."

"We all know why that is," Emma said knowingly.

"It's because she's desperate to save that silly show of hers," Marigold added as she walked up to the group. Tori handed her a coffee.

As Tori had predicted, we didn't have to wait long for Gail's arrival. Like the other day, she was dressed casually in jeans and a warm puffy jacket. A red knit scarf was wrapped artfully around her neck.

"What's the big story you have for me?" Gail asked Tori.

She seemed surprised to be met by such a large crowd.

Tori handed her a coffee. "We're going to prove who killed Rebecca White," she said with a bubble of excitement.

"The police already did that," Gail said in that flat bored tone of hers.

I shook my head. "Nope. They're wrong. They hate it when I tell them that, but they'll change their minds after we gather the proof we need to show that Hazel was cleverly framed."

"Oh." Gail took a long sip of her coffee. She seemed unimpressed. "How long is this going to take?"

"Hopefully, not too long," I said. "We just need to ask a few questions."

Gail looked around. "Could have picked somewhere with chairs."

We stayed at the base of the pavilion even though the plan had been to stand inside. But the wind was whipping around the open-sided shelter, and none of us wanted to stand up there and shiver.

I started out by explaining what I saw and heard the night of Rebecca's murder. I left out any information about Flossie picking up the library book. I then told Gail about how, according to Lacy Daufuskie, no one at the meeting could have raced from the back door to the front door, since there were no paths at the house to allow for that.

"No one attending the meeting could have killed Rebecca," I said.

"Which clears all the members of the Arete Society," Emma added. She moved closer to the producer. "That also provides alibis for Joyce Fellows and your film crew. But not you, Gail. You weren't at Hazel's house the night Rebecca died. Why was that? Isn't it your job to be there?"

Gail looked around somewhat nervously, but then rolled her eyes. "I couldn't make it." She took a sip of Tori's coffee and seemed to relax. "I thought we were here to discuss interviews for the show. I wanted to talk about the piece I want to do featuring your coffee shop, Tori. But since you invited half the town here, let's talk about our Rebecca retrospective. I'd like to do a series of short bursts, where each one of you says something about how Rebecca pushed Hazel toward murder. Any and all dirt welcome."

"I'm not doing that." Marigold set her hands on her hips and stared daggers at the producer. "Rebecca was kind and generous and that's what everyone should be hearing."

"Stories like that don't make good TV," Gail coolly explained. "Conflict. That's what the viewer wants to watch."

"We read in the gossip mags how you make up stories just to get better ratings," Emma said.

"I may have used creative editing a time or two." Gail shrugged. "Everyone does it."

Marigold shook her finger at the producer. "I don't want you going around making up lies about Rebecca."

"Oh, when it comes to Rebecca, I don't have to make up anything," Gail said dryly. "Her life is literally a gold mine of drama."

"*Figuratively*," Flossie whispered.

Gail didn't hear her. "You do know that Rebecca didn't leave *Desiring Hearts* willingly?"

"Stop." Marigold gritted her teeth.

"No," Gail continued. "The truth is that Rebecca was kicked off the show after one season, because she was so difficult to work with. And while we know she told everyone that she quit acting because there were no roles that matched her talent"—Gail chuckled—"that was a lie too."

"No. Don't." Marigold started breathing hard.

"She couldn't get work because her reputation for being a diva caused her to be blacklisted by all the studios. She had to leave acting because no director in their right mind would hire her," Gail said. "And I'm sure she tormented the townspeople just as relentlessly as she did the cast and crew of that soap opera of hers."

"She's not like that!" Marigold exploded. "Not anymore!"

"Is that the secret you were keeping for Rebecca?" I asked Marigold. "You knew that she was fired from the show?"

"Yes, I knew. She shared everything with me."

"Not everything," Flossie said. "You didn't know that she'd taken an acting job."

Marigold dropped her head into her hands and started to cry. "You're right. I didn't know that."

"Oh, don't be too upset," Gail said. "That tiny cable role was a short-term gig. She would have been back to your little town before the end of summer."

Marigold looked up. "Really?" she croaked.

Gail nodded. She even gave Marigold a kind smile. "It's true. Your friend wasn't leaving Cypress. Not forever."

This only seemed to make Marigold cry harder.

I patted Marigold on the back. "I know this is hard. I am sorry. But we do have to admit that Rebecca liked to make a big splash. She liked to be in control. Isn't that right?"

Marigold looked at me for a long while before nodding. "That was her only failing."

Gail rolled her eyes but did so out of view of Marigold.

"Sometimes she also lied to the newer members of the Arete Society," I said.

"You mean like how she told Hazel that she would be kicked out if the food at the meeting wasn't perfect, even though there was zero chance that would happen?" Emma said.

"Ouch," Gail said. "That sounds like motive for murder to me."

"It sure does," Emma agreed. "I'm sorry, Tru. But Rebecca also told Sissy Philips that she wanted younger members and was looking to kick out some of the older members from the society."

"She wouldn't have told Sissy that," Marigold snapped.

"She couldn't kick anyone out of the society without a membership vote."

"But she did like to kick up a fuss and make drama," Emma said to Gail. "I'll be happy to give you more examples of Rebecca playing these kinds of mind games on camera."

"Great. What's your name again?" Gail took out a small notebook and started writing furiously in it.

"I have no interest in being part of this," Marigold said. "I thought we were here to catch a killer."

"Yes, that is why we're here," I said. "Although some of us might also be interested in getting on TV." I nodded toward Tori. "And that's a bonus, right?"

"I don't understand," Emma said. "Why are we setting up interviews with the person you're trying to prove killed Rebecca?"

"You think I killed Rebecca?" Gail tossed back her head and laughed. "Oh, I'm so out of here."

"No. Wait—" I started to say.

"You're going to want to be here for this," Flossie called as Gail headed toward her car.

It was time to spring the trap.

Tori turned to Marigold. "You don't really believe Hazel killed Rebecca, do you?"

"I don't know." Marigold started to back away from us. "Everyone is saying how Hazel snapped under the pressure of putting together the perfect event. She even sent her husband away, because she couldn't handle taking care of him and trying to get everything together for the book club meeting."

Flossie rolled up beside Marigold. "Emma was the one who'd suggested Beau go on vacation. She set up the trip, just like she sent Tru's dad on a last-minute cruise."

"That's right. I was helping out," Emma said with a

puffed-up tone. "I'm good at what I do. There is an Amazon cruise coming up next summer. I could get you a good deal, Flossie."

Flossie smiled. "How kind of you."

Emma handed Flossie a business card. "This has been fun and all, but I need to get to my office. I'm sorry, Tru. I know you wanted to trick Gail into confessing, but I think the police have arrested the right person. All the evidence points to Hazel. She killed Rebecca."

I nodded. "I have to admit I was stumped by everything until I started to wonder why Dewey kept pulling those historical romance novels off the shelves."

"That cat of yours certainly has a nose for mysteries," Flossie said.

"You think your cat is solving the murder for you? Oh, you are desperate," Emma said with a laugh. "I'm leaving now."

"I know Rebecca didn't tell Sissy that she was going to kick out the older members," I called after her. "I wonder how long it would take for the police to determine where those texts Sissy received really came from. The state forensics teams could probably give Detective Ellerbe a name within the hour."

Emma turned around and stared at me as if I'd lost my marbles. "You think I—?" She laughed. "And what do you expect me to do now? Do you want me to break down and confess?" She laughed again. "This isn't one of Gail's fake docudramas. This is real life."

"I don't need your confession," I said. "I'm simply distracting you while Detective Ellerbe and his team search your home and office for the gun you used to shoot at me and Jace and Ellerbe's top forensic scientist." I tsked. "I'm nobody. But taking potshots at officers of the law is a pretty big deal, don't you think?"

"Oh my goodness. You couldn't be more wrong. They won't find anything," Emma said.

"Why?" Flossie asked. "Is the handgun in your purse?"

"Why would I shoot at you?" Emma demanded. "I wasn't even at the stupid book club meeting that night. I was home with a stomach bug, remember?"

"That's what you wanted everyone to think," I said.

"Wait. Wait," Gail said, as she jogged back over to us. She hadn't really gotten very far away in the first place, as slowly as she'd been walking. She must have been listening to everything that was being said. "I have to get some cameras down here. You're all going to have to wait."

No one paid the producer any attention. Emma walked toward the water, where the town had recently built a sandy beach. We all followed.

"Why would I want to hurt Rebecca? She got me into the Arete Society. Because of her, I started my travel business and it's now booming." Her steps were stiff and quick. "And you said it yourself, Rebecca lied whenever she told people she was going to kick them out of the book club. She lied and lied and lied. It was ridiculous, really."

"There was one thing she never lied about," I said. "And I think you knew it."

Emma propped her hand on her hip. "I don't know what you're talking about."

"A few years ago Rebecca spotted Ginger Faraday reading a paperback romance," I said.

Marigold stepped forward. "Rebecca said we had to maintain high standards," she said. "Ginger was reading trashy romance novels instead of the books the club picked out for our meetings. She wasn't contributing to our discussions, so she had to go."

"But y'all didn't just kick her out of the Arete Society,

isn't that right?" I asked Marigold. "Rebecca led a campaign against her. Wasn't it true that no one in your club would attend a party if she had been invited?"

Marigold shook her head. "Our interests weren't the same."

"No, it went even deeper than that." I turned back to Emma. "Rebecca's influence went further than the Arete Society, didn't it? Ginger had been the only travel agent in town. But after Rebecca's campaign against her, Ginger's business completely dried up, so she moved to Charlotte and started working for a large company. And around the same time someone new started her own travel agency, one that Rebecca helped get off the ground. Emma, you owed your success to Rebecca."

"So?" Emma said, angrily. "I never made that a secret. Yes, I was grateful to Rebecca for her help. Very grateful. Why would I want to hurt her?"

"Because she discovered that you were just like Ginger," Flossie said.

"No, I'm not. That's an ugly thing to say."

"And you were afraid that she would ruin you like she ruined Ginger," Flossie continued.

"You don't know anything, old woman," Emma spat.

"We have proof that you were borrowing historical romances from the secret bookroom," I said.

"No, you don't," Emma snapped.

"Okay, you're right, I don't have proof because you pulled the cards from all the books you'd checked out," I said. "But I do have records of the books you borrowed before the library's conversion to an electronic collection. Those records are still on our computers. And I looked up your borrowing history after the circulation cards went missing from all the historical romances that Dewey had pulled off the shelves. And guess what I found?"

"No!" Emma shouted. "No!"

"When Annabelle claimed Rebecca had texted her, saying that we needed to talk about your membership at the next meeting, I thought Annabelle was lying to make herself sound important," Marigold said. "But she wasn't lying, Emma, was she? Rebecca had texted Annabelle, hadn't she? She texted her to say that we were going to vote on your membership?"

"Why would Rebecca text Annabelle and no one else?" Emma scoffed.

"Because she's the society secretary and makes printouts of the meeting agenda," Marigold said.

"The police could easily check out Annabelle's claim," I added. "They're already checking Rebecca's phone for her texting history."

"No!" Emma shouted. "No!"

"And just recently, you started taking sewing lessons from Hazel. That was part of your plan, wasn't it? You were scoping out Hazel's house so you could figure out how to stop Rebecca . . . permanently. The night of the book club meeting, you faked being sick. But you weren't home. You boated to my daddy's house, walked along the trail that leads to Hazel's house."

"No!" Emma shouted. "No!"

"Oh my goodness!" Marigold exclaimed. "Everyone has been talking about how you booked Ashley Becket on a last-minute cruise. You did that to get him out of town?"

"I believe she did," I said. "And she also snuck into Hazel's house, changed the oven setting from bake to broil to make sure her dessert burned. And she did this because she taught you that you have to get burnt food out of the house immediately or else the acrid scent would taint all the rest of the food."

"And that was her opening? When Hazel left to take

out the garbage?" Gail asked, finally off the phone and listening as I unraveled what had truly happened that fateful night.

"It was," I said. "And don't forget that Emma was the one who had suggested Beau go out of town and had arranged his trip. I don't think she expected that Flossie and I would arrive at Hazel's so early. She thought it would be just Hazel and Rebecca at the house."

"But you were there," Gail said to Flossie and me. "Can you wait until the cameras get here before you say anything else?"

"We stayed out of the kitchen," Flossie said, ignoring Gail. "Well, until . . ."

I nodded.

Marigold made a low keening sound.

"No," Emma moaned.

"It's too late, Emma," I said. "We know. We know how you set it all up. Where did Rebecca see you reading books that the club had deemed unworthy? When did she threaten to kick you out of the club?"

"Why would you—?" Emma demanded.

"You left a library book at the crime scene, a historical romance novel much like the ones you've been checking out lately."

"That wasn't my library book! Hazel is the one who had checked it out," Emma cried. "Look for yourself. You'll see. That was Hazel's book."

"I did check. And while Hazel's name is on the card, I recognized your handwriting," I said. "You left the book as yet another way to frame Hazel for your crime."

Flossie tsked. "Rebecca was wrong to judge you or try to ostracize you. Heck, I'd back you up one hundred and ten percent that you should be allowed to read what you want to read. But murder?"

"But . . . but . . ." Emma stammered.

"No. We cannot support that," Flossie said firmly. "That's not how booklovers should act."

"No. No. No." Marigold was still shaking her head. "We expect our members to read only elevated literature. To flout that rule is cause for immediate expulsion."

"How did Rebecca find out you were reading romances?" I asked Emma, choosing not to argue with Marigold.

"She-she . . ." Emma stammered. She closed her eyes for a moment and then sighed. When she spoke again, her voice was a low, guttural growl. "I'm not going to go to jail for this."

She opened her eyes. The wild look she gave us made me instinctively shrink back. In her hand was a small gun.

"There it is," I said, sounding braver than I felt. "Our proof."

Out of the corner of my eye I spotted Jace and Detective Ellerbe running across the field toward us. They were shouting something I couldn't hear.

But they didn't reach us in time. Marigold, with a shout of her own, tackled Emma like a defensive end would take down a quarterback.

"You killed my best friend!" Marigold screamed just as the detective and Jace arrived. It took both of them to pull her off the much smaller woman.

"Prove it!" Emma shouted.

I was fairly certain that ballistics tests would prove that the gun Detective Ellerbe pried from her hand was the same one used to shoot at Lacy, Jace, and me. From there, Lacy would be able to build a case against Emma, proving she'd killed Rebecca.

"Why in the world did you tell her that we were searching her home and office? We didn't have an ounce of evidence against her," Detective Ellerbe said after handing Emma off to one of the waiting officers. Jace and the detective had heard everything that had been said through Jace's phone. "Even if I'd wanted to get search warrants, no judge would have given me one. You were lucky Jace was able to convince me to be on hand today for this fishing expedition."

"I knew you needed more than a hunch in order to get a search warrant, but Emma didn't know that," I said. "Were you able to record everything?" I asked Jace. We'd planned this all out in advance, the open phone line and getting Detective Ellerbe to come out and wait with Jace.

He patted his jacket pocket. "Our plan worked perfectly."

Ellerbe shook his head. "I still don't understand how you figured out Emma was the mastermind behind the murder."

"She worked hard to make sure the evidence pointed to poor Hazel," I said. "But there were bits and pieces that simply didn't make any sense to me. And then when I learned Hazel had recently started to teach Emma how to sew, that cinched it for me."

"Really?" he asked.

"Remember the night of the murder? You picked up a piece of material that was torn apart, as if it had been sloppily sewn and then inexpertly taken apart. It was quite out of place in an otherwise neat craft room. That was the first clue. Then, I started thinking about Annabelle. She said that Rebecca had contacted her to say that they needed to discuss Emma's membership. I had dismissed this clue because not that long afterward Sissy told me that Rebecca had been texting her about removing the older members to make room for younger, more fashionable members."

"She wouldn't do that," Marigold said as adamantly as before.

"No, she wouldn't," I agreed. "But Sissy's piece of misinformation threw me off course until someone"—I glanced over at Jace and smiled—"reminded me that I really shouldn't listen to anything Sissy said to me. She and I have a . . . a history . . . and she sometimes makes up lies just to get me riled. And that's what I thought she'd done. But later I started to wonder, what if she was telling me the truth?"

"She was," Detective Ellerbe said, looking even more confused than before. "I interviewed Sissy. She showed me the note she'd gotten, telling her to stay away from the meeting. And she showed me the texts about membership she exchanged with Rebecca."

"You mean the texts that claimed to be from Rebecca," I said. "Dig a little deeper, and I think you'll find that she never actually talked with Rebecca in person about the Arete Society. I believe the discussion about getting her into the book club only happened over text messages."

"That's not so unusual in this day and age," Ellerbe said, clearly still not satisfied.

"Trace those texts, and you will find they were sent from a phone Emma was using. Emma not only had to cover her tracks for the police, but she also realized she had to keep me from figuring out what she'd done. And she—like everyone else in town—knew that the best way to get under my skin and distract me was to involve Sissy." I shook my head ruefully. "I shouldn't let that woman upset me, but I do. I always do."

Detective Ellerbe was rubbing his chin. "But the books? How did you know that Rebecca had caught Emma reading books that would get her kicked out of the book club?"

"That goes back to Annabelle telling us that Rebecca had texted her about Emma's membership. That text was real. While Rebecca liked to tell the newer members that they could get kicked out for this or that, I learned that only two things could truly get a member kicked out of the club. First, not showing up to the meetings. If you're not participating, the members will pick someone to take your place. And second, a member would be kicked out if caught reading what the other members considered 'trash' books. I hate that term. It only happened once before, isn't that right, Marigold?"

She nodded.

"After y'all kicked that poor woman out of your book club. Rebecca then took it a step further and convinced the other members to ostracize her. It was all very dramatic and shades of Rebecca's old soap opera, wasn't it?"

"I'm ashamed to say, we did all go along with Rebecca," Marigold said.

"Emma was a new member at the time, and witnessed all this happening?" I asked.

"She was," Marigold said.

"So it would be easy for Emma to imagine that the same would happen to her after Rebecca spied her reading a romance novel."

"And if not for you, she would have gotten away with it." Jace put his arm over my shoulder. "Even though all of y'all were wearing bulletproof vests, my heart nearly stopped when she pulled out that gun." His voice shook a bit. "She could have shot you in the head or the leg or anywhere vital."

"But she didn't shoot anyone," I said.

"And it's over now," Flossie added.

"Thank you." He sighed. "Thank you. I knew if anyone could figure this out, it would be you, Tru. And you did it. You saved my mother. You saved my family. Thank you."

Gail's long-requested cameras arrived just in time to record the police driving away with Emma in the back seat.

I hurried to my car before she could turn those cameras on me.

Chapter Thirty-Two

————·————

T he truth does not change according to our ability to stomach it," the Southern novelist Flannery
O'Connor once wrote in a letter that was later published
and became quite famous. This truth squawked—like a
noisy peacock—in my head as I entered Perks the next
morning.

The Saturday crowd all wanted to shake my hand and
congratulate me for solving yet another crime. While I
should have been pleased to get the attention without
having to contend with television cameras, my mind
wouldn't let go of a truth that made my stomach quiver
with dread.

Tori waved me over to the bar where she was working. "Girlfriend, don't frown so hard. It causes wrinkles.
Besides which, you should be smiling. You're the hero
of the hour. And, after the scintillating interviews
Flossie, Goldie, and I gave to Joyce Fellows, the whole
crew hightailed it back to Hollywood or wherever they
came from to get the show ready for air."

I sank down on a barstool. "My father came to visit me last night."

"How'd that go?" she asked as she made me a chai latte. The milk frother hissed.

"He's getting married." It still felt strange saying it aloud.

Something ached in my chest. I felt like I was losing something, like I was losing him. Which was silly. He'd been divorced from my mother since I was a teen.

"He is?" Her perfectly plucked brows shot up. "I didn't even know he was dating."

"Apparently, he kept things quiet because he didn't want to upset Mama Eddy."

Tori puffed out her cheeks. "She's not going to like being blindsided by a marriage announcement."

"No. I suppose not." I stared at the shiny bar top as if I might find all the answers to my problems there. "But maybe she won't be terrible about the wedding. When I told her that Daddy had run off to go on a cruise with Lucinda Farley, she seemed oddly calm about it . . . like she was happy for him."

"Who is this Lucinda Farley he ran off with? I don't know her."

"She's new to town. She's Keven's assistant at Tech Bros. Daddy met her at their shop since he now works there building robots to replace librarians."

Tori picked up a bottle of chocolate sauce and swirled the deep, dark elixir into my tea. "You're going to need this." She slid the large cup over to me.

"My father deserves to find someone he likes." I took a sip of the spicy, chocolaty tea. My friend was right. The drink hit all the right spots that needed hitting. "He says he's happy, so I'm happy for him."

"No, you're not. And it's okay that you're not happy

right now. Feel your feelings. That's the only way you're going to work your way through them."

"I do feel kind of . . . ill about it," I admitted. "And guilty. He does seem happy. I volunteered to help with the wedding planning."

"You didn't."

"It seemed like the thing to do. Can I have your latest issue of *Brides Today*?"

"Um." Tori turned away as she busily wiped down the counter.

"What?" I asked.

"I canceled the subscription."

"Really?" That surprised me. She'd kept her subscription to the magazine after her marriage to Number Three, saying that it was simply easier to keep up with bridal trends than having to scramble and do tons of research whenever she wanted to remarry. "Why?"

She still refused to look at me.

"Tori?"

"I didn't want to upset you."

"Upset me?" My voice squeaked. I thought I'd had enough upset in the past several days to last me for a lifetime.

"Charlie, he has been wonderful and . . ." She looked away and smiled.

"And?"

"And I've moved in with him. Please, don't get upset. I wanted to tell you, but so much has been going on with Rebecca's murder and Hazel's troubles and the tension between you and Jace. And it just didn't feel right to share all my happiness with you when you've been so stressed."

"You canceled your subscription to *Brides Today*?" That pain in my chest grew tighter.

She nodded. "I'm going to sell my house."

"But are the two of you getting married?" Certainly she was going to plan another big wedding.

"Tru, for the first time ever, this relationship feels like the real thing. I feel like this is going to last forever. I don't want to mess with that by planning another over-the-top wedding. I just want to be with him."

Tori finally looked up at me. Worry tightened the skin around her eyes. She'd been married and divorced four times now. She pretended her failed marriages didn't bother her, but I knew my friend well enough to know that they'd left her deeply hurt.

"Oh my goodness, Tori! I'm so happy for you." I threw myself across the counter, spilling my chai tea, to pull my best friend in to a tight hug. "I'm so happy for you." Tears sprang to my eyes. Happy tears. Sad tears. They were all there in the mix. "You deserve this. You deserve to be happy with Charlie. And you're right. You don't need another wedding to be happy. Just be happy."

It was nice to arrive at the library and not have to worry that I might be ambushed by a film crew. But local reporter Betty Crawley was there on the steps leading up to the front doors. She shouted a few questions that I ignored. It didn't matter whether I said anything to her or not, she was going to publish whatever she thought would make good copy, using quotes that she wanted people to say instead of actual quotes. I waved to her and called, "Good morning! I'm sorry you weren't able to get hired by the *Ideal Life* crew."

"I wouldn't have wanted to work for them anyhow," Betty shouted back. "I'm a serious journalist."

"Good for you!" I called back. "Good for you."

Inside the library, everyone seemed cheery that morning, like a weight had been lifted off their shoulders. Mrs. Farnsworth congratulated me on clearing up the troubles that had been plaguing the Arete Society.

"You could thank me by inviting Flossie to join," I told her. "She's been wanting to be part of your society for years."

"We were planning to invite you," Mrs. Farnsworth said as Dewey wiggled impatiently in his tote bag. "Are you sure you don't want that honor?"

"I think Flossie would get more out of it than I would," I said. "But before inviting her you're going to have to relax that 'no reading books the society deems unworthy' rule. Everyone should have the freedom to read whatever they want as long as they are also reading the monthly book club pick, don't you think?"

Mrs. Farnsworth nodded. "I never was comfortable with that rule. With Rebecca gone, I'm sure we can get it changed."

I reached into my tote bag (not the one with Dewey, but the one with the books) and pulled out my personal copy of Flossie's latest book. The romance novel with the sexy, shirtless Scotsman on the cover. I handed the book to Mrs. Farnsworth. "Maybe the Arete Society should consider reading this book," I said.

Mrs. Farnsworth handed the book back to me. "That book isn't book club quality."

I felt disappointed for Flossie's sake.

But then Mrs. Farnsworth surprised me when she added, "We've read that one already. That series has long been popular with Arete Society members—albeit in secret, of course. Despite those silly covers, the books are all quite well researched and written."

"Is that so?" I smiled. Flossie would be thrilled to hear that.

My smile only grew bigger as I continued to make my

way toward the basement and the books waiting for me in the secret bookroom. On the way, I nodded to Anne, who was having a discussion with the robot. Anne's yellow tint was no longer as bright as it had been. And someone had taped a cheerleader bow to LIFU's metal head. Annabelle was right. The bow did make it look friendlier.

And for the first time in a long time, I felt like everything was going to work out for the best. All was right in my hometown, my favorite town, Cypress.

Acknowledgments

———·———

There are always so many invisible hands at work when it comes to putting together a book. Sure, you get to see and hear from the author. But if it stopped there, the book you've just read would have been completely different from the one that you (hopefully) enjoyed. It's impossible to acknowledge all those invisible hands, but let me try anyhow.

I cannot thank my Berkley team enough for being so understanding and awesome. This book wouldn't exist without any of them, especially my editor, Michelle Vega, who has a magical way of looking at a story and teasing out the best ways to make it better. I'm also grateful to Jennifer Snyder for keeping the publication process moving so smoothly and to Elisha Katz and Yazmine Hassan for helping let the world know about the series. Thank you for all that you do.

A big shout-out to Anne Wertheim, the cover artist, who took my idea and brought it visually to life in such a spectacular fashion.

Many thanks also to my agent, Jill Marsal with the Marsal Lyon Agency, for always being in my corner.

Let me also thank my librarian friends: Leslie Koller, branch manager at the Dorchester County Library; Frankie Lea Hannan, assistant branch manager with the Charleston County Public Library; cozy mystery author and former librarian Shari Randall; and Connie Davis with the wonderfully analog Timrod Library in Summerville, South Carolina. All truths are thanks to their wisdom. All mistakes are mine.

And, as always, I need to give a shout-out to my writing tribe—Nina, Signe, Nicole, Amanda, Ann, Catherine, Olivia, Judy, and Ellen. We stand on each other's shoulders in order to climb to new heights.

Finally, thank you to my husband and daughter for giving me space and time to write even when you didn't want to. I'm forever grateful.

Ready to find
your next great read?

Let us help.

Visit prh.com/nextread